JUMPIN' JIMMINY—
A WORLD WAR II BASEBALL SAGA

Jumpin' Jimminy—
A World War II Baseball Saga

American Flyboys and Japanese Submariners Battle it Out in a Swedish World Series

Robert Skole

iUniverse, Inc.
New York Lincoln Shanghai

Jumpin' Jimminy—A World War II Baseball Saga
American Flyboys and Japanese Submariners Battle it Out in a Swedish World Series

iUniverse, Inc.

For information address:
iUniverse, Inc.
2021 Pine Lake Road, Suite 100
Lincoln, NE 68512
www.iuniverse.com

American and British planes did make emergency landings in neutral Sweden in World War II. The *Jumpin' Jimminy*, its crew, the other characters and events in this book are fictitious. Any similarities or resemblances to real persons, living or dead, are purely coincidental.

ISBN: 0-595-31248-9

Printed in the United States of America

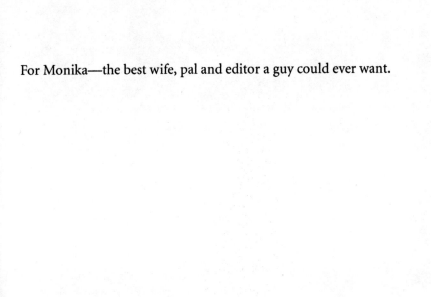

For Monika—the best wife, pal and editor a guy could ever want.

Acknowledgements

Jumpin' Jimminy is based on fact. American bombers did crash land in neutral Sweden in World War II, crews were interned, and many had fascinating adventures. Locations, companies, restaurants, hotels, streets, buildings, did exist and most still do exist. The many Allied and German offices described in the book did exist and their buildings still do exist, but their present tenants probably have no idea whatsoever of the amazing wartime episodes and intrigues that took place in their premises. There are no plaques commemorating the history made there.

However, like the *Jumpin' Jimminy* and its crew, and the Japanese submarine and its crew, all events and action and people at such places as recounted here are entirely fictitious. Stockholms Enskilda Bank did exist and still does, under a different name. The Wallenberg banking family did exist, of course, and descendants still do. The great bank "robbery" by "Kilroy" is pure fabrication. But if the bank did indeed have such records as described, well, truth then would be stranger than my fiction.

Jumpin' Jimminy was originally conceived during one of many wonderful creative sessions spent in Stockholm with William Aldridge, a talented British film-writer. William envisioned how heroic American airmen would have been most eager to devise ways to contribute to the Allies' war efforts, despite having the very bad luck of being interned in a neutral paradise. William's boundless imagination created most of the characters in the *Jumpin' Jimminy* crew.

Since the Swedish Government believes World War II documents that were once designated "Secret" and "Classified" must long remain "Secret" and "Classified"—obviously because they can be somewhat embarrassing—I will not divulge the identify of the magician who made those designations vanish with the stroke of a pen when William and I were digging through military archives. A tip of the hat to this delightful historian. (Yes, there was a real Romeo who served as model for Pvt. B.J. Jones!)

Kurt and Gittan Karlsson provided insights and memories of Stockholm during the war years of the 1940s. Paul Dickson offered his tremendous baseball knowledge, encouragement and know-how. Bill Meade's books of wartime baseball were most valuable. Ferris Maloof is always generous in sharing his expertise and total recall of baseball in general and Boston baseball in particular. Harold Flagg, a delightful challenger in Le Mans style creative writing competitions, got the book moving to publication. Kjell Holm advised on diplomatic matters. Ray and Carol Nelson provided memories of Chicago Swedes and of Chicago schools and baseball. The helpful curators at the Swedish TeleMuseum efficiently provided 1944 and 1945 Stockholm phone books, an excellent resource. And I would have surely struck out without Monika's editing, proofreading, language skills and sound advice.

Hits and runs are by these great folks. Any errors are mine and mine alone.

Jumpin' Jimminy—Prologue

In the air war over Europe in World War II, when American or British bombers could not make it back to England, the lucky ones turned north, to neutral Sweden.

In 1944, a total of 119 American bombers, mainly B-17 Flying Fortresses, made it to Sweden. Of these, 104 made emergency landings, officially caused by fuel shortages, navigational error, mechanical problems, or damage from enemy ground or air fire. Three planes were shot down, by mistake, by Swedish anti-aircraft fire. Twelve crashed on landing.

The crews were housed by Swedish military authorities, in *"interner-ingsläger"*, internment camps, until such time as they could be flown back to England. In no way did the interment camps resemble traditional prisoner of war camps. Fliers were lodged in hotels, inns, boarding houses and sometimes even in private homes.

They were given virtually total freedom to mix with the population of the community in which they lived. They received civilian clothing allowances, since wearing uniforms outside the camps was forbidden. They received the same rations and allowances given to the general Swedish civilian population.

They could work locally, and were allowed to travel in Sweden, after receiving travel permits. They could visit the American Legation in Stockholm, maintain their aircraft, visit friends at different camps, and enjoy outdoor life, theaters, restaurants, and night clubs. Fliers of Swedish descent made sure to look up relatives.

Although enjoying good living in a neutral haven of peace, the bomber crews, courageous men in their late teens and early 20s, eagerly wanted to return to England, to rejoin their units and fly again in the heroic war against the evil Nazis.

The crew of the *Jumpin' Jimminy* had a somewhat different mission.

CHAPTER 1

Jumpin' Jimminy's two starboard engines were coughing badly and starting to smoke as the plane crossed over the south Swedish mainland.

"Peaceful Sweden," said Capt. Jeff Cabot, the pilot.

"You are violating Swedish air space," the voice said over the radio. It came in loud and clear, which proved the radio wasn't shot up like much of the rest of the B-17. "Repeat. You are violating Swedish air space."

"We know," replied Lt. Ed Kowalski, the co-pilot.

Several puffs of smoke appeared, ahead and below of the plane.

"I thought you said the Swedes are neutral," said Ed Kowalski. Then, into the mike, "You're shooting too low."

"We know," the voice replied. "Kindly, follow our instructions and we'll guide you to the appropriate airfield."

Jumpin' Jimminy had completed its 23rd mission, this time on what was supposed to be another milk run over Frankfurt. Ed Kowalski had a rule, however, that said all milk runs turn sour, and this one did when a couple of Messerschmitts popped out of the sun and made one nice pass over the formation. *Jumpin' Jimminy* got it almost before the crew knew what was happening, and the Messerschmitts disappeared, back to where intelligence had said there were absolutely no German fighters operational.

It was the Autumn of 1944, and the crew of the *Jumpin' Jimminy* was thinking more of the World Series than the World War, which is probably why they got jumped so badly in the first place. Joe Bacciagalupo, one of the two waist gunners, was doing some mental math on the pool, which Capt. Jeff Cabot had started among the *Jimminy* crew, but quickly extended to every barracks and hangar and office on the base, and to three other American air bases in the area. Pools were even started at some village pubs. The local patrons were willing to bet a few bob on the outcome, even though they had no idea what baseball was all about, no less the World Series.

"I gotta do all the work around here," Joe Bacciagalupo would say, his pockets stuffed with betting slips and bets, as he unloaded the day's receipts on the table in Jeff Cabot's room. "You guys sit back and rake it in. The same old story."

Joe Bacciagalupo and Jeff Cabot were both from Boston. Almost from the same neighborhood. Almost. Jeff Cabot, yes, he was one of those Cabots, lived on one side of Beacon Hill, and Joe Bacciagalupo, yeah, one of those Bacciagalupos, lived just a few blocks away on the other side, the side known as the West End. Normally, they would never have spoken to one another. Those two sides of Beacon Hill were two very distinct worlds.

But they knew each other quite well, having met as kids playing ball on the nearby Boston Common. Jeff Cabot was the real outsider at first. But there were no other kids his age who played ball and who were from his social set on the "right" side of the Hill. Tennis, of course, and sailing on the Charles. But baseball, well, it was rather working class, even though they had a team at Harvard, in which "that man" Roosevelt had played. Jeff Cabot managed to play in pick-up games with his West End pals for years without his parents finding out. They thought he was studying at the Boston Athenaeum, the private library on Beacon Street. The library was so exclusive you had to be a member, voted in, to enjoy its collection, which included George Washington's own personal library.

Joe Bacciagalupo was a regular player in those games, too. His parents didn't find out either. They thought he was studying at the West End Public Library.

Jeff Cabot went away to private boarding school, and then to Harvard, where he was pitching for the varsity team when the war broke out. Joe Bacciagalupo finished Christopher Columbus High in the North End, and was working days at a meat wholesaler in Quincy Market and studying nights at Suffolk Law School, and catching for a semi-pro ball club when the war broke out. A few years later they were in the Air Corps, and, as was not uncommon in the war, they met up again. This time at an air base in England.

In the Spring of 1944, Jeff Cabot had taken command of the *Jumpin' Jimminy*, whose former crew was rotated back to the states after completing the required number of missions, which kept getting increased as the war continued and losses mounted.

The plane was named by its original pilot, a Minnesota Swede, who, in civilian life, had been a bush pilot. On his first landing of the plane, he must have forgotten what he was handling, and he set it down hard, like he used to do on short, grass runways up in the north woods. The Fortress bounced all over the place before settling down.

The comedian in the control tower congratulated the pilot with what became a local classic: "Swede, that's one Yumpin' Fuckin' Yimminy great landing."

The Swede, unamused, solemnly christened the plane *Jumpin' Jimminy*. "And without the fuckin'," he told the base artist. "And spell Yumpin' Yimminy with a 'J'!" He pronounced it "yea". Swedes have trouble with their J's.

The Fortress carried the same name with several different crews. Some crews, those who had owned boats, felt it was very bad luck to change the name of a plane. And the *Jumpin' Jimminy* had avoided bad luck. Until now.

At the air base in England, the ball players quickly learned who was who, and with a little help from a rabid Dodgers fan who worked in personnel, the crew of the *Jumpin' Jimminy* was made up of an All Star Team. At least it was All Star as far as the Eighth Air Force was concerned. This way, the team would always be together to play other air bases and Army teams.

Putting all your best players in one basket, so to speak, would not be considered wise if you were running a money-making professional team, but the base commander figured that the White Sox riding taxis in Chicago were in more danger than a crew of a Flying Fortress. Beside, he was a silent partner of Jeff Cabot, and that guarantied the integrity of the World Series pool in case something untoward might occur, which would be very unlikely, because the *Jumpin' Jimminy* always seemed to get milk runs.

Yeah, sure. Like today.

Jeff Cabot, following the Swedish controller's precise instructions, could see an airfield ahead, surrounded by miles of flat fields, many bright green, others dark green. He wondered what they were growing. His mother would like to know. She had a garden in the back of their town-house on Louisburg Square. Nice garden except it was too small to throw a ball in. Well, you can't have everything, Jeff Cabot used to say to his friends.

The airfield runways were more than sufficiently long. On one side, near some hangars, a couple dozen B-17s were neatly parked. For many months, American and British bombers that couldn't make it home from missions over north Germany would turn north to neutral Sweden. Pilots seemed to have an automatic radio direction-finder built into their brains, and it would be beamed directly to Sweden from wherever they were over enemy territory.

Some planes landed in Sweden in surprisingly fine condition. It was amazing how serious engine trouble cleared up the instant the planes were on the ground and the Swedish military took formal possession. Those Swedish mechanics were geniuses. But considering that a Swede invented the monkey-wrench and another invented the adjustable ball bearing, it was not surprising.

Such was not the case with *Jumpin' Jimminy*. Its starboard engines were smoking badly by now, and Jeff Cabot was sweating as he brought her down. His father would not approve. Cabots never sweat. Miraculously, none of the crew had been hit. The hydraulics were shot, but the landing gear could be hand-cranked down.

Sgt. Joshua Bennett, the radioman doing the cranking, shouted, "Hallelujah, God is on our side."

Considering everything, the landing wasn't half bad. Ed Kowalski had done far worse when Jeff Cabot let him set her down, with the plane in perfect shape and in perfect weather. But nobody ever said Ed Kowalski was much of a pilot. He was a damn fine second baseman, however, and as long as they had Jeff Cabot flying the thing, they were in good hands. They were in good hands too, when Jeff Cabot was pitching.

The plane bumped and screeched and groaned to a halt and a Swedish fire-truck was right alongside, foaming down the engines even before the hatches were opened and the 10-man crew started to scramble out.

"Get the sight," ordered Jeff Cabot, "and then get the hell out."

"I know, I know," said Lt. Carl Jacobson, the bombardier, as he frantically flipped the pages of an Air Corps manual, to find out how to destroy the very latest, very secret, version of the Norden bombsight. "The Swedes probably got better sights than we do, anyhow. So they'd sell this to the Krauts."

He finally found a page, fiddled with the sight, set a fuse, and rushed to the hatch and squeezed out. The rest of the crew was long gone. There was a slight bang as the sight went, and some smoke filled the plane.

"Get back, please," a Swedish officer said, as a half-dozen soldiers, rifles in their hands, stood by, more curious than threatening. "And welcome to Sweden."

He removed a paper from his pocket and read very carefully, "Under the Rules of War of the Hague Convention of 1907, amendments signed and ratified by the Kingdom of Sweden in the year 1920, I officially declare you, as members of a belligerent army, having entered this neutral nation for refuge, to be automatically interned according to terms of said Hague Convention."

He carefully folded the paper and put it in his pocket.

"You wouldn't have any Lucky Strikes with you, would you?" he asked.

As Jeff Cabot was fishing into a pocket, Joe Bacciagalupo shouted, "Hey, where the hell is Nappy?"

The crew looked at each other, puzzled, and then started to move toward the plane.

"Halt," the Swedish officer shouted.

"One of our guys is missing, squarehead," Joe Bacciagalupo said. "The tail gunner."

The officer shouted an order in Swedish. Three men tried to climb into the plane, but their rifles got in the way in a classic Three Stooges scene. The officer rolled his eyes and shouted again. The three handed their rifles to two other soldiers. Two of the Stooges squeezed in, through the tail-gunner's hatch on the belly. Seconds later they were out and shouted something. The officer shouted to an ambulance driver and two medics who were watching nearby. The medics ran to the plane, climbed in, and in a few minutes were pulling out Corporal Napoleon Anderson, completely wrapped up in blankets. They quickly put him into the ambulance, and not paying the slightest attention to the protests the nine crewmen, whom they couldn't understand anyhow, the ambulance screeched off, siren blasting.

"I am sorry to report," the officer said solemnly, "But my men said your comrade was badly burned. Third degree. Very bad. His skin was black."

The crewmen looked at each other and burst into a roaring fit of laughter.

The Swedes looked on, blue eyes wide, mouths wide open.

"Crazy Americans," they thought.

CHAPTER 2

The crewmen of the *Jumpin' Jimminy*—nine of them without Napoleon Anderson, the tail gunner—sat in a room that could be the orderly room of any army in the world. Beat up desks, two old typewriters, filing cabinets, a bulletin board, and a curious poster showing a blue and yellow striped tiger, with the words *"En Svensk Tiger"*, which Joe Bacciagalupo, a student of languages, learned in the polyglot West End, translated as "A Swedish tiger".

"No kiddin'! I didn't know there are tigers in Sweden," said R.B. Jones, a gunner, and formerly third-baseman for a minor league team in Alabama.

"Yeah, like they got tigers in Detroit," replied Ed Kowalski.

"Well, I'd like a Camel right now, I left a carton on the plane," said Carl Jacobson.

"Will you guys knock it off, so we can get this over with," said Jeff Cabot. "Joe, you're up."

Joe Bacciagalupo took a seat next to the desk, where a clerk sat at a typewriter. The clerk could have been a company clerk in any army of the world, at least in any army that had run out of recruits who knew how to type. He solemnly and carefully placed a printed form in the typewriter and rolled it into position. Then he took a minute to make a precise adjustment of the paper. In a waste basket on the floor next to him was a pile of crumbled discarded forms.

"Name?" he asked.

"Guiseppe Antonio Bacciagalupo."

The clerk looked at his keyboard and was about to start typing, two fingers ready to go. Instead he looked up at Joe Bacciagalupo.

"*Va?*"

There was no mistaking. Even a non-linguist would know by the puzzled look on the clerk's face and the inflection that "*Va?*" meant "what?" This would be the first Swedish word that the *Jumpin' Jimminy* crew, like every other Allied crew, would learn.

"Va fan goo, to you too," said Joe Bacciagalupo, smiling.

The clerk's expression changed from puzzled to extremely puzzled.

"Name?"

"I already told you once, Guiseppe Antonio Bacciagalupo."

The clerk looked even more puzzled. "Spell."

"Sure. Bacciagalupo," Joe Bacciagalupo said, and rattled off, "Baker-Able-Charlie-Charlie-Item-Able-George-Able-Love-Uncle-Peter-Oboe." All in one breath. It was a favorite performance.

"*Va?*" the clerk asked.

"Oh, hell, I'll write it for you," Joe Bacciagalupo said.

The clerk sighed in relief as Joe Bacciagalupo reached for a pencil and took a scrap of paper from the wastebasket. He printed his name, rank and serial number on the paper, very neatly, as the sisters had taught him at St. Joseph's school. Actually, Joe Bacciagalupo's crewmates had difficulty with the name, too. They just called him Joe Batch.

"Why don't these squareheads save time and let us fill in the forms ourselves," asked Carl Jacobson, to no one. "Like applying for a job."

"Or like registering at a hotel," B.J. Jones said.

"Because guys like you always register under a fake name, like Smith," Ed Kowalski said.

"Why don't we just show them our dog tags?" Joe Bacciagalupo suggested.

"Too easy, too logical," Carl Jacobson said. "We're dealing with the military here."

"Skipper, why don't you just give him the lineup?" asked B.J. Jones.

"Probably the Hague Convention prohibits it," said Jeff Cabot, taking a neatly-folded paper from an inside pocket of his flying jacket. It was the team's roster that he always kept available for reporters from local base papers and sportswriters from *Stars and Stripes*. The guys were delighted to see their names in print when the games got written up. It was something they could send home to prove to their families their heroic contributions to the war effort.

The roster, in order of rank and not the batting order, read as follows:

Jeff Cabot, Capt., Pitcher

Ed Kowalski, First Lt., Second Base

Carl Jacobson, Second Lt., First Base

Pete Fielding, Second Lt., Right Field

Joe Bacciagalupo, Sgt., Catcher

Joshua Bennett, Sgt., Third Base

Napoleon Anderson, Cpl., Shortstop

Gus Sanchez, Cpl., Pitcher, Utility

Mickey O'Mallery, Pvt., Center Field

B.J. Jones, Pvt., Left Field

Looking over the roster, Jeff Cabot thought that perhaps he should hand it over to the Swedes. It would probably end up straight in the hands of the Krauts, and would keep a couple dozen code-breakers in Berlin busy for months trying to figure out some secret meaning.

Although American bomber crews were delighted that Sweden existed, as a neutral haven to land in an emergency, they were well aware of the huge amounts of war material the Swedes were selling to the Germans. The crews had no illusions about Swedish neutrality, which was based on the firm and courageous principle of resolutely acting for what was most profitable and advantageous for Sweden.

"The Swedes don't seem to be in any rush," said Carl Jacobson, who had figured that the clerk-typist could punch ten letters per minute maximum.

"Are you in a rush?" asked Jeff Cabot.

"I'm not, but you should be, with that World Series pool you're running. By time we get back it will be time for Spring Training."

"The General can handle it."

"The bum better make sure I get my cut," said Joe Bacciagalupo. "I don't want to have the war end and I gotta chase all over the States trying to sue him. Hell, he might be in the Pacific ordering some guys to organize a pool on when Hirohito commits *hara-kiri*."

The clerk had mistyped three forms, which ended up in the wastebasket, before he got one right.

"Next, please," he said.

"You sound like my barber," said Carl Jacobson as he took the chair.

"Name?"

"Carl Jacobson." He showed his dog tags to the clerk, to make it easy.

"Jacobson?" asked the clerk, pronouncing it "Yakobson", in Swedish.

"No, Jacobson," Carl Jacobson answered, emphasizing the J.

"*Svensk?* You Swede?"

It was a forgivable mistake. Carl Jacobson was tall, six-foot, blonde, blue eyes, and with very fair skin. He could easily be mistaken for any one of the tens of thousands of Swedes named Jacobson, which was also spelled Jacobsson or Jakobsson or variations thereof.

"Not unless my grandmother stopped by here on her way from Minsk."

That was too much for the clerk, so he typed in "Karl Jakobsson". Jacobson corrected him. The clerk was in a much better mood now, having met what he was sure was a real Swedish American. He wondered if he was related to his wife's cousin's family who had a Jakobsson who emigrated to Minnesota.

He was readying the English words for that question in his mind when the Swedish officer who had greeted them walked in. He looked at the forms, saw they were almost all finished. Looked at the waste basket, rolled his eyes, and said to the crew, "As soon as these formalities are completed, you will be escorted to a train for a trip to an internment camp for Americans. It is a rather long ride, but it should be comfortable. The camp is in a very picturesque part of Sweden, called Dalarna. In the mountains, lakes, forests."

"You got tigers there?" asked B.J. Jones.

"*Va?*"

B.J. Jones pointed to the poster showing *"En Svensk Tiger"*.

The officer smiled. It was the first time they had seen a Swede smile.

"No, that is a very clever word play. It can mean a Swedish tiger, like the animal, ready to fight, or it can mean a Swede does not talk. Tiger also means not talking. Quite smart message, for these war times."

"Hilarious," said Carl Jacobson. "But what would you guys know about war?"

"It's hell," the officer said, fishing in his pocket and coming up with a pack of Camels. Now, one pack of Camels looks like any other pack of Camels, so Carl Jacobson couldn't prove those were his that he left on the plane. Except that Jeff Cabot had given the officer a pack of Luckies.

"Yeah, war in Sweden is hell," said Carl Jacobson. "You didn't happen to find my carton of Camels on the plane, did you?"

"Camels? What Camels?" the officer said, his face that of pure innocence. He quickly pocketed the pack.

"*Non te hagas el Sueco*," muttered Gus Sanchez.

That old Spanish expression was to be used plenty by the crew in the months ahead. It means, more or less literally, "Don't play the Swede." Why Swede and not Dutch or Belgian or Norwegian is unknown. Swedes say the expression originated in some war in the 1600s, when Swedish prisoners bravely refused to talk when interrogated by Spanish captors. Spaniards say that it was from Swedish sailors playing dumb and guiltless when caught red-handed, cheating, stealing or when a husband, peeking under his wife's bed, discovered a Swede. "Who me? I'm only fixing the bed-springs!"

The crew accepted the Spanish explanation. They quickly learned that nobody in the world could be as heart-wrenchingly innocent as a blue-eyed Swede explaining that it wasn't his hand you see in the cookie-jar, or someplace worse. Or better.

After all, who could "play the Swede" more authentically than a real Swede?

CHAPTER 3

The ambulance, siren hee-hawing, roared into the emergency room driveway of the regional hospital, and skidded to stop. The driver ran out, opened the back doors, and helped the two medics who were sitting inside, unload the stretcher. A nurse held open the emergency room door, and they carried it into the reception area, down a hall, and into a treatment room. They placed the stretcher on a table as two doctors and three nurses rushed in.

Napoleon Anderson, swathed in blankets, was almost completely knocked out from a pain-killer injection the medic had pumped into his arm. He opened his eyes and was convinced he had died and gone to heaven. All he could see were three, then six, then nine, absolutely beautiful blue-eyed blondes hovering over him. The blondes were pulling down the blanket, and quickly undressing him. Somehow, it never occurred to them, nor to the doctors, that if he were badly burned, why wasn't his uniform burned?

One nurse pulled down his trousers, and then his skivvies. Then there was complete silence.

Napoleon Anderson could hear a shriek, or was it a shout? Then a loud babble. The room had quickly become crowded with nurses, clerks, orderlies and doctors, as word went out that they were treating an injured American airman who was a Negro. They had never seen one before.

Napoleon Anderson was very slowly coming around, when he heard one of the doctors say, "*Fan, han är en neger.*"

Napoleon Anderson caught that last word, and it brought him to life.

"Watch how you pronounce that, squarehead, or I'll wrap you one," and then he said, in Swedish, "*Vad i helvete gör ni? Djävla, dumma svenskar.*"

A dozen mouths fell wide open.

"*Negern talar svenska*," the doctor said. "*Till och med småländska.*"

"You fuckin' A right. I do, you dumb squarehead, and probably better than you. *Vem fan har tagit mina byxor?*"

A nurse, who could not get her eyes off Napoleon Anderson's beautiful, compact, muscular body, just stood there, holding his pants. Another, equally mesmerized, held his shorts. Napoleon Anderson reached out to grab them and nearly fell off the stretcher. Several hands caught him. He was groggier than he thought. Well, what the hell, he said to himself, advertising pays, doesn't it? That's what Mr. Wrigley used to say back in Chicago, and look where it got him. Of course, I have nothing to advertise. If it were my big brother, these squareheads would go wild.

Napoleon Anderson lay back, relaxed, and closed his eyes, and let the crowd around him babble as they would. It sounded like Saturday morning shopping day back at his neighborhood. Napoleon Anderson grew up in the Black Belt of Chicago, the famous strip along the lake that the sociologists made famous in the 1930s.

Sandwiched between the Belt and the largest Negro section of Chicago was a Swedish-German neighborhood. When he was still a kid, Napoleon Anderson got a job in Swanson's Fish Market, on 59th just west of Halsted. He had a musical ear and a talent for mimicry, and it didn't take him long to learn Swedish, just like his boss, with a pronounced accent of the province of Småland.

Napoleon Anderson was a great attraction at Swanson's. New customers were dumbfounded that a "*neger*" could speak Swedish. After they closed their mouths and regained their speech, which took 15 minutes or so, they would ask where he learned Swedish.

If Napoleon Anderson were busy, he'd simply say, "*morsan och farsan.*" From Mom and Dad. This would stop the questioning for quite some time. But most often, he'd simply say, with a Norwegian lilt, "*Jag är faktisk norrman.*" I am actually Norwegian.

It would take a few minutes, but the Swedes would eventually get the joke. Swanson wept when he lost his star attraction to the draft.

Napoleon Anderson had played baseball with big Swedish kids at Washington Park. He learned one thing about Swedes in those years: they could make good hitters if they only learned to get out of the way of bean balls. Too many of the Swedes stubbornly stood their ground. They figured that the ball should get out of their way: they were at the plate first. If the pitcher wanted to bean them and walk them, well, "It was yoost as good as a base hit," they would say, staggering off to first.

Napoleon Anderson's reveries were interrupted by the entry of the head nurse, who took one look at the patient and the crowd of giggling nurses and the jealous doctors, and clapped her hands. It was not applause for what the guys used to call Napoleon Anderson's brother's Anderson Attraction. The chattering stopped immediately.

"*Vad har vi här?*" she asked sharply, to no one in particular and to the room in general.

"This is actually a welcoming committee for a long-lost relative from Chicago," replied Napoleon Anderson in Swedish, reaching to retrieve his skivvies from a nurse, and swinging his legs over the side of the table. The nurses took last admiring glances as Napoleon Anderson pulled up his skivvies, found his pants, and put them on, too. He straightened out his uniform, pulled himself to his full five feet six, smiled that big smile of his, and said, "I guess I'll be in Sweden for some time, so there's plenty of me for all of you girls."

How Napoleon Anderson got to be the first and only Negro American to be interned in Sweden is a story in itself.

His baseball enthusiasm was inspired by watching East-West All Star Games of the Negro Leagues played at Komiskey Park. He played for the Tilden Technical High Blue Devils, graduated to semi-pro teams, and finally made a team in the Negro Leagues, where he was an outstanding short-stop. Off-Season he worked at Swanson's.

After getting drafted, he ended up with a Negro service battalion at an air base in England. Naturally, Napoleon Anderson played ball with a Negro team at the base, and was spotted one day by Jeff Cabot, who never could drive past a game, no matter who was playing, without stopping to watch. Jeff Cabot talked with Napoleon Anderson when his team came up to bat, and was mighty impressed that he had actually played pro ball, even though it was in the Negro Leagues.

Jeff Cabot immediately informed the base commander, who immediately ordered Napoleon Anderson transferred to the crew of the *Jumpin' Jimminy*. It didn't matter too much that Napoleon Anderson had never been in an airplane, no less been trained as a gunner. Anyone who was as good a shortstop as Jeff Cabot said he was could learn to be a tail gunner in 15 minutes or less, especially anyone who was a decent hitter as well.

Assigning Napoleon Anderson, a Negro, to a flying crew, would be a violation of the military's policy of segregation. All flying crews were white, except for the all-Negro fighter squadron, the famous Tuskegee Airmen of the 332nd Fighter Group, flying out of Italy. A lot of B-17 crews based in England wished those black pilots were based in England and escorting them. The Tuskegee Airmen scored an amazing record of having never lost a bomber to enemy fighters. And they destroyed 251 enemy aircraft.

The General pondered the problem for half a minute and simply said that Napoleon Anderson was not a Negro, but Mexican. Besides, he would be flying as tail-gunner, and that's like sitting in the back of the bus. Just in case some redneck army bureaucrat wondered.

Napoleon Anderson was not all that pleased with the situation, since it might disrupt his regular evenings out with the English girls at the pub where the Negro troops were welcome, and which the white troops avoided. But being able to play ball with what was the best team in England, hell, in all Europe, made up for this inconvenience. The more worrying thing was flying.

Jeff Cabot assured him that flying was no more dangerous than driving a car, especially one in Chicago, where gangsters rode up and down the streets firing tommy guns.

"Beside, we only go on milk runs," Jeff Cabot assured him.

Napoleon Anderson said the only gangster he ever saw in Chicago was an old guy who claimed he was in on the White Sox fix, but nobody believed him because if he were so smart, he'd be rich, which he definitely was not.

"And how am I supposed to learn to be a gunner?" he asked as Jeff Cabot showed him the plane and his tail-gunner position. "Back of the bus," Napoleon Anderson thought to himself.

"Easy," said Jeff Cabot. "Joe Bacciagalupo can teach you in 15 minutes. I watched you handling short—you're a natural."

Napoleon Anderson couldn't figure the connection, nor could he figure why you need gunners at all if you're only flying milk runs. Joe Bacciagalupo did, however, manage to teach Napoleon Anderson the basic principles of loading, aiming, leading the target, clearing jammed guns and the other odds and ends of managing the rear turret. Napoleon Anderson was perfectly sized for the position, which seemed to be specifically designed for short, wiry guys who could squeeze into the tail-gunner space and get as comfortable as possible on what was little better than a bike seat.

On the first flight out, Napoleon Anderson kept his eyes shut until they were airborne, opening them only after they had climbed for five minutes or so. He then looked out and saw what was the most thrilling sight he had ever seen. Below, the green fields of England, puffy clouds above, other Fortresses of the flight all around.

"Hot dawg, if Mamma and Daddy could see me now," he said.

"Didn't I tell you you'd love it," Jeff Cabot's voice came back in the intercom.

"Welcome to the team. One day, we'll be flying into New York to play the Yankees in the World Series. So get used to it."

"Yeah, sure," replied Napoleon Anderson. "That'll be the day. You check what color I am?"

On the way home on that first flight, after an uneventful raid over a German factory town, Jeff Cabot radioed to his group leader that he was developing some engine trouble and had to fall back. This gave him the opportunity to fly low and let Napoleon Anderson do some practice shooting. There were always tempting ground targets to strafe.

"Nappy, we're going down so you can have some batting practice," he said. "You can start swinging whenever."

The plane dropped behind the formation, dropped fast, and leveled off at a few thousand feet. This is the kind of juicy situation German fighters loved, and the *Jumpin' Jimminy* was jumped pretty fast by three Messerschmitts.

"Are those ours or theirs?" Napoleon Anderson yelled, as the Germans swept past, bullets clunking into the plane and the side guns opening up. He figured out fast, they were theirs.

On the next pass, they came confidently in from the rear, figuring the tail gunner was knocked out or sleeping or the turret couldn't work since they had not seen it move or a shot fired. Napoleon Anderson figured they named the run wrong. It shouldn't be called a milk run. The Germans were not as dumb as Schultz the milkman, who never could figure out why milk was always missing from his wagon. After all, he never saw anyone steal it.

The Messerschmitts came straight in and Napoleon Anderson did the only thing he remembered to do, which was to fire the damn guns. He could swear he saw the surprised look on the lead pilot's face just before his plane blew up, throwing debris into the one next to it. The debris broke off part of the second fighter's wing and smashed the rudder. Napoleon Anderson was so surprised at what was happening, not to mention being more scared than he had ever been in his life—and as a little Negro kid in Chicago, he had plenty of experience in being scared—that he kept his hand locked on the grip and kept firing. The third plane swung directly into his line as the pilot turned fast to avoid the out-of-control second plane. Napoleon Anderson thought there was a resemblance to Schultz the milkman as the plane flashed past, smoke pouring out of it.

"A triple, at your first time at bat," shouted Jeff Cabot over the intercom.

"Yahoo!" someone else shouted. "What shooting!"

"Hey, Napppy, did you do what I saw you do?" asked another.

"Any gunner who can shoot like that, he's OK—and I don't care if he is a Mexican," said B.J. Jones, who didn't give a damn that Napoleon Anderson was a Negro, either, having played ball with plenty of black kids back in his small home town in Alabama.

"It's all in the coachin," said Joe Batch. "Didn't I always tell you to listen to me."

By now, Napoleon Anderson had stopped firing. The plane was climbing fast. Jeff Cabot wanted to catch up with the flight. As usual, intelligence had said there would be no Kraut fighters whatsoever.

"Napoleon, you okay?" Jeff Cabot asked.

"Sure. Nothing to it. Milk run. Safer than the streets of Chicago."

CHAPTER 4

After several hours, the piles of paperwork involved in getting the names, rank and serial numbers of the crew of *Jumpin' Jimminy* were finally completed. The crew had passed the time by shooting baskets, using a wastepaper basket and wadded up balls of the pile of forms spoiled by the ham-fisted typist. Joe Batch had a pool going, using strips of torn paper for markers.

The officer who had first met the crew on landing had been popping in and out of the office, watching the registration process, muttering for the clerk to hurry. This only resulted in the clerk's making a new error, and having to start a new form all over again.

"Officers, they're all alike," said Mickey O'Mallery, a New Yorker with the map of Dublin all over his face. "They never let a man do his job."

"If you're so smart, why are you here?" asked Pete Fielding.

"No choice, riding around with you pointing the way. Think you can find London when we get back?"

Pete Fielding was an excellent navigator, when he was airborne. But he had the uncanny ability to get lost on the ground. He never could live down how he wasted most of one day of a three day leave when he couldn't find London.

"Could I help it? I had no road map," he said. The three crewmen with him in the jeep were hardly convinced.

"You're supposed to be a goddamn navigator," said Ed Kowalski. "How the hell do you find the infield all the way from right field?"

"I listen to you swearing because the ball got through you."

The argument never ceased. But in reality, the two played superbly well together. They had both played on the Philadelphia Athletics' triple-A farm team in Scranton before being drafted, and before that had played together on the Temple University team. Because of their university education, they both got accepted for pilot training. Ed Kowalski made it easy, but Pete Fielding washed out when it was discovered that he was near-sighted and had only passed the eye test because he memorized the charts.

But the Army Air Corps was very short of navigators at that particular time, so Pete Fielding became the first navigator in Air Corps history to be allowed to wear glasses. Pete Fielding had also been one of the first pro-ball players who wore glasses.

The first time he came to bat, playing for a double-A farm team, the catcher made the mistake of saying, "Hey, Four Eyes, you gonna hit a double?"

Fielding looked at the catcher, and replied, "No, I'm going to get to first on two balls."

How Pete Fielding managed to do it, remains a mystery, or it may have been purely accidental, but on the very first pitch, a low fast-ball, he swung, and tipped the ball only slightly on the top. The ball spun backward and downward fast. Before the catcher could grab it, it bounced off the plate and back, some-how catching the catcher right in the nuts. The catcher went down and the ball rolled away. Fielding made it to first long before the pitcher came in to retrieve the ball and throw to second.

As they helped the groaning catcher to the dugout, he actually whimpered, "All I did was call him Four-Eyes."

Word got around. That was the last time anyone called him Four-Eyes. But they called him a lot other things, which he didn't mind at all. In the Air Corps, most referred to his ability to get lost on the ground.

"Hey, stop your bellyachin'," Pete Fielding said. "I got you here to Sweden, didn't I?"

"Yeah, you were probably aiming at Switzerland," Ed Kowalski replied.

As the two continued their never-ending bantering, the Swedish officer returned, gathered up the forms, completed at last, and nodded to a proudly-smiling clerk.

"Gentlemen, we will now proceed to the railway station," he said. "The train will take you to the internment camp for American fliers. We have cars to take you to the station."

"Hey, let Fielding drive," Kowalski said.

"I am sorry, but the rules are that we must use our drivers."

"For once the rules make sense," said Mickey O'Mallery.

The Swedish officer could not understand why the crew was laughing. But then, he rarely understood American jokes.

CHAPTER 5

The crew squeezed into three of the strangest-looking army cars they had ever seen. They looked as if the designer had simply expanded what might have been a nicely-rounded sedan.

"Where did you get these things?" Joe Bacciagalupo asked the Swedish army sergeant riding shotgun.

The sergeant looked puzzled. Joe pointed to the symbol on the horn in the center of the steering wheel.

"Volvo," said the sergeant. "*Svensktillverkad.* Made in Sweden." He pronounced the English as if he had practiced it often. He glowed with pride.

"You'll never sell them elsewhere," Joe Batch said. "Too heavy. They look like they drive like trucks. You could use them as tanks."

"Made in Sweden," the sergeant repeated, even more proudly, and patting the dashboard fondly.

"You'll never sell them with that name either, Volvo," B.J. Jones said. "Sounds dirty."

"Everything sounds dirty to you," Joe Batch said.

"It's a lady's very intimate body part," B.J. Jones said. He actually sounded refined, delicate, respectful.

"You dope, you're thinking of something else, as usual," Joe Batch said. "That's spelled with an A. This is Volvo. It's Latin. It means 'I run'. Didn't they teach you nothin' in school out there in Missouri, wherever the hell that is?"

"We were taught the American language, the salt of the earth American," B.J. Jones said, haughty. "Not foreign stuff people haven't spoken in three thousand years."

"Oh, yeah?" Joe Batch countered. "Latin is the basis for all kinds of languages. *Volvo, volvas, volvat, volvamus, volvatis, volvant.* That's the conjugation for the verb, but you wouldn't know conjugation from constipation, you ignoramus. The guys in my class always said *volvomit* for *volvamus* and the Sister would rap them on the knuckles with that stick of hers. They may not have learned Latin, but they learned not to be wiseguys. Well, some of them learned."

"I still say these cars would never sell in America, not with that name," B.J. Jones said.

"Well, I gotta agree with you there, you salt of the earth Americans always thinking of dirty stuff," Joe Batch said. "Nah, they'd never sell these Swede cars in America, even though they got good steel. Swedish tanks, maybe they could sell them to America, if they ever stop shipping them to Germany."

"And talking of made in Sweden, where are all the blondes?" B.J. Jones asked the driver. "I haven't seen a one. Did you ship them all to Minnesota?"

B.J. Jones would have seen a blonde if she were anywhere within half a mile. He would have seen a brunette, too. B.J. Jones had a special attraction to women. He once played first base, but got distracted too often by the girls in the nearby bleachers. He never lasted long at first, especially after one of his former girl-friends threw a baseball at him from the stands, ruining a beautiful double play. The manager figured he'd be safer in the field. B.J. Jones was hitting .350 and was going to be advanced to the majors from a Wisconsin farm team, when the draft caught up with him.

"*Ja,* Minnesota," replied the sergeant, still very proud. "*Många svenskar.*"

"See, what did I tell you," said B.J. Jones. "They shipped them all out as soon as they heard I was here. Did I ever tell you about the Swedish blonde I met after the play-offs in Minneapolis?"

The others in the car groaned. The sergeant smiled proudly. The driver grimly battled the wheel.

The three-car caravan drove into a small town. The *Jumpin' Jimminy* crew had been in England for almost a year, and was quite accustomed to seeing the very tough wartime day-to-day life that the British put up with, with good humor, indeed, quite cheerfully. The crew had expected to see neutral Sweden as a joyful island of peace in a grim world at war. Instead, they saw grim Swedes. Oh, they were well dressed and obviously well fed, compared with the British. But as the cars drove down the street, people looked without expression at the passing caravan.

"Where's the brass band?" asked Joe Batch.

"Where are the blondes?" asked B.J. Jones, again.

"Where's the Welcome Wagon?" asked Mickey O'Mallery.

The cars turned off into a side street and pulled to a stop in front of what was obviously the railway station. A staff car was waiting. A soldier opened the rear door, and out stepped Napoleon Anderson, smoking a cigar.

"Where you all been?" he said, flashing a bright smile. "I've been checking out the local talent."

The crew piled out of the cars and there was cheering and back-slapping, much to the dismay of the Swedish officer, who thought that this was hardly serious military behavior, especially considering there were four commissioned officers among them.

"What the hell happened?" asked B.J. Jones.

"These squareheads ain't never seen a black hero, so they took me to the hospital to see if it's true what their kin wrote back from Chicago. They gave me a complete physical and I passed with flying colors."

"They probably wondered what an MP was doing in a B-17, when they saw that Anderson billy club," said Mickey O'Mallery.

A train pulled into the station, and the crew was escorted aboard. They were given two separate compartments. A Swedish officer, a captain, was with the commissioned officers. Jeff Cabot, Ed Kowalski, Carl Jacobson and Pete Fielding in one compartment and a sergeant in the other compartment with the rest of the crew. After all, military protocol must be maintained. Officers should get special treatment.

The train eventually pulled away from the station, and the crew of the *Jumpin' Jimminy* settled down for what was to be a long ride northward, to an internment camp for American airmen, located in the province of Dalarna, famous for its lakes, rolling mountains and picturesque villages, northwest of Stockholm. It was only about 400 miles as the crow flies, but Swedish trains aren't crows. They like long winding. scenic routes.

"Not a bad way to spend the war," said Lieutenant Ed Kowalski, settling back in a comfortable seat in a First Class compartment.

Which were the exact words of Private Mickey O'Mallery, in a Second Class compartment.

CHAPTER 6

It was the most relaxing ride the crew of the *Jumpin' Jimminy* had in years. They were at peace, heading toward a peaceful haven. They looked out at the passing scenery, which at first consisted of broad, rich fields, ready for harvest. Gradually, the fields changed to forests, seemingly endless. Now and then, they would stop at a town, and several times in cities.

The men craned their necks eagerly looking at the sights, and more eagerly looking for girls. Every so often, the Swedish escorts would pull down the window shades. The crew understood it must be some security measure.

"Probably some good-looking dames out there," B.J. Jones said.

"Naw, he says it's a military secret," Napoleon Anderson replied.

Napoleon Anderson had astounded his fellow crewmembers with the fact that he could speak and understand Swedish.

"But that's nothing," he said. "My older brother speaks German. He learned it working at Schultz's sausage plant at the stockyards. All Germans there. He got himself a cushy assignment running a mess hall at a POW camp in Texas. He said the Kraut prisoners working for him refused to take orders because he was a *shvartze*. So he told them he came from their colony in Africa—the one that prints those triangle stamps with the kid climbing the tree for coconuts. After that, and after kicking the nastiest Kraut POW in the balls, he was made an honorary Kraut. Nobody fucks with my big Kraut brother."

The Swedish escorts were even more astounded—flabbergasted. thunderstruck, dumbfounded, and completely amazed—that Napoleon Anderson could speak Swedish. They had no colonies where a black could learn the language.

The sergeant in the compartment got into a long conversation with Napoleon Anderson. Like anyone listening to a conversation in a foreign language and not understanding it, it seemed endless. But eventually, Napoleon Anderson reported, in brief, what they were saying.

"I told him I was from Chicago and lived with the squareheads. He said that he had a great uncle who had moved to Chicago years ago and who had taken up with a girl he said was an Indian, but the family later learned she was colored. He was sort of a wild guy, if you can imagine a squarehead being wild, except when they get boozed up. Anyhow, the family knew he had some kids with this girl, but had eventually lost track of him and never knew his kids. The only thing they knew was that his name was Anderson, but then half of Chicago is named Anderson. Well, to make a long story short, I did not want to disappoint our friend here, so I simply said, well we must be related, because that sounds like my wild great-granddaddy and my name is Anderson."

"And so is Jack Benny's Rochester, he's an Anderson and he ain't no Swede," said Joshua Bennett.

"Now why go spoil a good family reunion?" said Joe Bacciagalupo. "If we landed in Italy, I'd look up my cousins, too. So when's the big get-together?"

"The sergeant says most of the family lives on an island way outside Stockholm. They're fishermen. He'd see about getting me out there, but thinks it might be off-limits or something. He says the family often told stories about my great-granddaddy."

"Wait a minute, you know damn well he wasn't your granddaddy," said Joshua Bennett.

"He might have been. What's the difference?"

"Well, it just wouldn't be true."

Joshua Bennett was known as "The Preacher." He came from a long line of Baptist preachers famous in tent meetings throughout Missouri. Bennett knew the Bible, Old and New Testaments, backwards and forwards, upside down and downside up. But somewhere during one of his daddy's Summer tours, he discovered that ball-playing was a greater gift to human joy and salvation than convincing the already convinced that they were sinners and should do something about it.

After high school, he told his folks he was off to the Bible College of Missouri, in Columbia, but instead, entered the University of Missouri there, studying engineering, and easily making the baseball team. He took rooms on the all-male top floor of the Bible College, the most central part of campus.

His folks never knew. Joshua Bennett's major claim to fame was that he was the only student ever living at the Bible College who succeeded in sneaking a co-ed up to his room, and spending the week-end with her there.

His folks still thought he was studying the Bible when he got drafted. His engineering studies got him assigned to radioman school. He was quickly spotted for his baseball talents at the air base in England, and joined the *Jumpin' Jimminy* crew. They figured his pull with God would not hurt, even though his contacts with Upstairs had become rusty once he discovered girls and beer, in that order. He was a regular customer and part-time bartender at The Shack, the most popular drinking place at Mizzou.

"You know it's a sin to lie," Joshua Bennett continued. He could be serious as hell once he got going. He loved to bring out those old preachin' skills of his boyhood. He heard himself talking, but he knew it was the voice and words of his old man.

"Hey, it could be true," argued Napoleon Anderson. "I bet you don't know who your granddaddy was either."

"I sure do," said Joshua Bennett, a hurt tone in his voice. "He was one of finest preachers west of the Mississippi. At least that's what folks always claimed."

"You see, you see! You ain't sure either. I wonder if being part-Swedish will entitle me to join their army. I like their army. They never fight. I'll see what my kin-folk say when I go visit them."

Napoleon Anderson fished into one of his pockets and came up with a deck of cards.

"You play poker?" he asked the Swedish sergeant, who shook his head.

"No? I'll teach you. Since you're my cousin, I'll teach you so you never get taken by sharks like Joshua Bennett."

"Aw, c'mon, Nappy, you know it's a sin to cheat at cards."

"That's why I'm teaching him right."

CHAPTER 7

In the next compartment, Carl Jacobson had finally gotten the Swedish captain to speak. It had not been easy. Jeff Cabot had first tried to start a conversation in English.

"How long will this train ride take?"

"*Ja*. Long."

The "*Ja*" was unmistakably "Yes," especially the way the captain dragged it out, and nodded his head. It sounded more like "*Ummmyaaaa*."

"How many Americans are there in the camp?"

"*Ja*. Americans."

"You do speak English, don't you?"

"*Nej*."

There was no doubt about that meaning "No".

"The nays have it," said Jeff Cabot, giving up.

"*Sprechen Sei Deutsch?*" asked Carl Jacobson.

The captain's face lit up.

"Certainly," he said, in German. "Learned it in school. I used to holiday in Germany. Wonderful wine. Wonderful beer. Wonderful women. A nation of culture."

The captain and Carl Jacobson continued their conversation in German.

This was the crew's introduction to the Swedish ketchup bottle personality. It's hard to get started, but once you manage to get it moving, by shaking, pounding, sticking a spoon in it, it comes gushing out. The trick with the Swede is to find the right shake, or pounding, or spoon to break the vacuum and get the person talking. In the captain's case the right way to open the ketchup bottle was the subject of was Germany. In many Swedish army officers' cases, it was Germany.

"I normally escort German officer internees," he said. "Real gentlemen. Very brave. Always wanted to be repatriated as soon as possible so as to continue the war. Against the Russians, of course. We used to get a lot of German planes making emergency landings in Sweden. But not too many now."

"I guess Marshal Finkelstein doesn't have that many left," said Carl Jacobson.

"Who?"

"Your pal Göring. Don't you remember? He boasted that if the British ever bombed Berlin, you could call him Finkelstein."

"I met Göring when he lived in Sweden after the first war," the captain said. "He married a beautiful Swedish noble-woman. He named his great home in Germany after her, after she died. Karinhall. A beautiful place. Full of wonderful art treasures."

"And he stole every goddamn piece. The *momzer goniff*."

"You speak a curious German," the captain said. "Are you of Swiss descent? It sounds like *Schwyzer-dütsch*."

"It's actually a very old low German, called Yiddish," Carl Jacobson said.

The captain looked dumbfounded. That is, he simply looked. The crew had seen the same look when Joe Bacciagalupo gave the clerk-typist his name. They would see this look often in the future.

The captain slowly took out his papers from an inner pocket, and scanned the names of the American crew.

"I first thought your name was Jacobsson, and that you were Swedish descent. There are a lot of Jacobssons in Sweden. You're not Swedish?"

"Actually not, unless one of my grandmothers took a side trip up this way on their way to America from Russia."

"But you look Swedish."

Carl Jacobson had heard it before, but it usually was, "That's funny, you don't look Jewish."

Which was easy to understand. Carl Jacobson, as the clerk-typist had immediately noticed, looked like a perfect Swede: tall, blonde, blue-eyed, straight nosed, square-faced. His mother's side of the family were blonde and blue-eyed. His father's side was all big guys, and big women. His father was the only Jewish longshoreman in Brooklyn. Or so he used to boast, as if that was something to boast about.

Carl Jacobson went to CCNY, the City College of New York, where he made the varsity basketball team. At that time, it was one of the best college teams in America. Carl Jacobson wished he could play for the Harlem Globetrotters, but was the wrong color. Instead, he would have to settle for the House of David, if he ever were to play pro. One problem he would have to overcome was that the House of David team all had black beards. Jacobson, with his blonde beard, would stick out as noticeably as if he played with the Globetrotters.

But the draft saved him from having to solve this problem. His college training got him to the Air Corps and bombardier training. Like everyone in Brooklyn, Jacobson was a baseball nut, and at his first pick-up game at the air base in England, he caught Jeff Cabot's eye. His size and reach were just what they needed for first base. And for a basketball player, the guy could hit.

"The captain says I could pass for a Swede," Carl Jacobson told his crew.

"I wish I could, I'd join their army. They never fight," said Ed Kowalski.

"My pal here says he'd like to join the Swedish army," Carl Jacobson said to the captain in what was pretty good German, since he had taken three years of German in high school and a few semesters in college. "Any chance?"

"Is he Swedish?" the captain asked.

"Of course, everyone named Kowalski is Swedish."

The captain looked very serious. "No, I don't think so. Kowalski is Polish. We have a camp for Polish internees, too. We actually have three Polish submarines, and their crews. They preferred Sweden to being captured."

"You seem to have everyone here."

"Yes, we have Italians, they give us much trouble with the girls. And Yugoslavians. They give us trouble with the girls. And French. They give us trouble with the girls. Everyone gives us trouble with the girls except the Japanese."

"You have Japs here?"

"Yes, indeed. They're the crew of a submarine that was built for them in Germany. They were taking it home, but had compass problems and ended up on rocks on our coast."

"Where do you keep them?"

"The rocks? A secret. Part of our defense."

"No, The Japs."

The captain smiled knowingly. "I cannot tell you that, either. It's secret. But I feel sorry for them. They don't get out and socialize like the others. They only stay in their compound and do exercises and practice *ju-jitsu* and make strange noises and eat raw fish and play baseball."

The crew had been ignoring the conversation, but looked up when the heard that last word.

"Play baseball?" asked Carl Jacobson.

"Yes. I understand it is their national sport."

"Holy Keeerist, guys," Carl Jacobson said to his guys. "There's a Jap baseball team here. Sonuvagun!"

CHAPTER 8

The train rolled on. And on. The crew slept. Played cards. Ate bread and cheese and tasteless sausage sandwiches provided by their escorts.

"You can eat this sausage on Fridays—there's no meat in it," said Joe Bacciagalupo.

"Brother, if you saw the meat they put in sausage in the plants in Chicago, you'd be just as happy," said Napoleon Anderson.

Turning to the sergeant, he said in Swedish, "This *Falukorv* is not half bad. Almost as good as we used to make in Chicago."

The sergeant smiled proudly. He was most impressed with Napoleon Anderson's knowledge of Swedish ways. Any foreigner who could not only recognize *Falukorv* but could make taste comparisons must be, well, a Swede.

"And that's where we're going," said the sergeant conspiratorially. "Falun. Although I'm not supposed to tell you. But since we'll be there in two hours, you'll know by then anyhow."

"Hey, fellas, we're going to be in a camp in the sausage capital of Sweden," Napoleon Anderson announced.

"If we're going to live on this sausage, that's a violation of the Geneva Convention," Joe Bacciagalupo said. "Maybe I can teach them to make decent Italian sausage."

Right on the button, in two hours as the sergeant said, the train pulled into Falun station. The town was actually quite picturesque. You could call it sleepy. Heck, fast asleep. The main street was lined with shops in wooden buildings, none over a few stories high. All were painted red, like barns back home. The corner strips and trimming was white. It was all very well kept up, very neat. A few cars were on the streets. Several had big boiler-like devices attached to the trunk. They belched smoke. One was parked, and the driver was putting char-coal into a firebox at the base of the boiler.

"They run on steam?" Carl Jacobson asked the captain, in German.

"No, they make gas, coal gas, from the coal, and the gas is used in the motors instead of gasoline," said the captain, a note of pride in his voice. "It's a Swedish technology."

"Well," said Jacobson in English, "Swedes who invented the monkey wrench can't be all dumb."

The crew was escorted into a waiting bus. It was quite comfortable. The captain pointed out it was made in Sweden.

"Scania-Vabis. They make trucks and tanks, too," he said.

"And you probably do a great businesses selling them to the Krauts," Carl Jacobson replied, again in English.

The captain did not understand. He only smiled proudly.

The bus drove through the town, and out onto a country road, up and down hills, through forests and finally pulled up a long drive, bordered with pines and poplar trees. At the end of the drive was a huge building that obvi-ously was a Summer tourist hotel. It was built of wood, of typical Swedish gin-gerbread style popular at the turn of the century. There were smaller buildings, a barn, and garages nearby.

In a field adjacent to the main building a dozen young men, in an odd mix-ture of American uniform and civilian clothes, were playing touch football. They stopped the game and watched the bus pulling up.

As the crew piled out, an American colonel stepped out the front door onto a small porch. He was in his late 40s, a very advanced age in the Army Air Corps, at least for a flying officer. He had red cheeks, a sandy-colored mous-tache, and puffed a pipe. He wore no wings on his uniform. Just behind him was a Swedish officer.

"Welcome to Internment Camp Four," he said, returning the crew's very sloppy salutes. His was just as sloppy. "I'm Buford van Dyke, Special Services, and, sorry to say, senior officer here. And this is Major Karl Karlsson, camp commander. Let me tell you that we'll do all in our power to make your stay as comfortable as possible."

"And as long as possible," said Jeff Cabot.

Col. Van Dyke laughed. "You know, every crew says that. But the Eighth Air Force says just the opposite—make it as short as possible. But forget it for now. Come in and we'll get you squared away."

"Hey, Joe Batch, you steal the pool money?" one of the football players shouted. They had run up from the field to greet the crew. "How the hell did the General let you guys get away?"

"Skill, personality and charm," said Jeff Cabot.

"And expert navigation," added Pete Fielding.

"You couldn't find your dick with a string attached," said one of the football players. "What the hell happened?"

Jeff Cabot explained briefly. The Colonel and the Swedish major waited patiently. They had evidently been through this kind of reunion many times before. Several of the football players had been at the same air base as the *Jumpin' Jimminy*. Their plane was last seen over Hamburg, trailing smoke and turning north to Sweden.

The hotel, and adjacent buildings, could quarter up to 200 airmen. There were a number of hotels and inns elsewhere in central Sweden where other American and British air crews were interned. Being strictly neutral, as they insisted they were, the Swedes provided German internees with very similar, pleasant quarters, but kept hundreds of miles from the Allies for obvious reason. Unfortunately, other internees from other nations did not fare quite as well, but were kept mainly in military-like camps.

"Ever since Stalingrad, the Swedes have been much more accommodating to the Allies," Colonel Van Dyke explained as the crew gathered for coffee in the pleasant dining room. "But let's not get political."

The colonel explained his presence in Sweden by the simple fact that he was at an air base in England as advance man for a USO show featuring some Hollywood stars, and the base commander asked if he'd like to go on a mission, "just to get a feel of the war."

"He promised it would be a milk run," he said. "I should have known. Maybe he didn't like one of the films I produced. Anyhow, that milk run ended up here. I don't want to bore you with war stories. Major Karlsson can give you the low-down and routines of this quaint situation."

"We operate very informally," Major Karlsson said. His English was excellent. He had an American accent. "There are no real guards. You may go into town as often as you wish, as long as you don't wear your uniforms. We will provide ration coupons so you may purchase civilian clothes. You will get ration coupons for food and special coupons needed to buy at the state liquor store, but since you are all fliers, I don't expect you drink."

Major Karlsson knew he would always get a laugh with that line.

"Your Legation in Stockholm provides your pay. You have no restrictions on fraternizing, but we are certain you will treat our local girls with all respect of real gentlemen."

He knew that line would get an even bigger laugh.

"And now, you have just been in England and seen the latest papers and heard latest radio news. Who is going to win the World Series? I am betting on the Cardinals, if anyone of you is willing to put money on the Browns. The Browns! How in the world did they ever win a pennant?"

CHAPTER 9

The crew couldn't believe it. Here was this squarehead in the uniform of a Major in the Royal Swedish Army or whatever it was called, and he was a total, 100%, complete American, hot dogs, peanuts and Cracker Jack baseball nut.

Major Karlsson explained why, and in great detail. He was a lad living in Stockholm during the 1912 Olympics. His father, a policeman assigned to the newly-built Olympic Stadium, could sneak the boy into all the events. The most famous athlete at the Games was the great Jim Thorpe, the American Indian who won Gold Medals in the pentathlon and decathlon.

"I had squeezed my way up front that day when the King presented the second Gold Medal to Jim Thorpe," explained Major Karlsson. "The King said, 'You are the world's greatest athlete,' and Jim Thorpe said, 'Thanks, King'. The King actually smiled."

But Major Karlsson went on to tell that the biggest thrill was to go out to a field near the stadium to watch an exhibition baseball game.

"They had a team made up of American Olympic athletes, and a Swedish team brought down from the town of Västerås. That's where the Olympic Games president came from. He was head of a large company there. As a young engineer, he worked in the United States, and that was where he learned baseball. He was a famous track star when he was young. He organized some baseball teams in Västerås.

"Of course, the Swedish team was outmatched. So the Americans lent them a few players, to try to even up the game. Jim Thorpe pitched in that exhibition game. He was absolutely magnificent."

Karlsson explained how he continued to follow baseball, as best he could in Sweden when he went to school. "We played a game similar, called 'bränn-

boll'—burnball—but it's hardly baseball. The first chance I had after I got out of school was to take a ship to America. I worked in Chicago and Minneapolis for 10 years. I loved to play ball, with real Americans. Strictly amateur. I wasn't that good. You have to be born with the game. I came home to Sweden after the 1929 crash. No baseball in Sweden, but there were jobs."

When Major Karlsson learned that the crew of the *Jumpin' Jimminy* was actually composed of some of the best American baseball players in the European theater, tears welled in his eyes. Then he jumped up and shouted and hooted and laughed and shook a fist at an imaginary foe. Most extraordinary behavior for an emotionless Swede.

"We'll beat them. We'll have a real World Series and beat them," he shouted. "We'll beat them good."

Eventually, he calmed down and explained.

"We have a Japanese submarine crew interned in Sweden," he said.

"Yeah, we heard about it," said B.J. Jones. "They'd rather play baseball than play with dames."

"Yes, well, sort of. When I heard they play baseball, I felt it would be good for Swedish relations with Japan to organize a game," Major Karlsson went on. "The Japanese agreed. So I rounded up, best I could, all the Swedish boys who had played ball. It wasn't easy. Most were scattered all around, in the army or navy. But we got what we thought was a pretty fair team, and we had the game. Those little Yaps slaughtered us."

Despite his years in America, and his fluent English, Karlsson still had a bit of trouble with the letter J, especially when he was excited.

"What did you lose by?"

"Well, the first game was called on account of darkness. The Yaps kept careful score. We stopped counting after a few innings. When the Yaps were at bat, the innings would never end. We got one run. Four of our batters in a row walked when they got hit with pitched balls. The Yaps just laughed when our boys didn't duck fast enough."

Major Karlsson's team played a half-dozen more games.

"We did get better with practice," he said. "Our boys finally learned to get out of the way of bean balls. And they were starting to hit and field good. But we were still out of their league. The Yaps got tired. They said my players were meatballs. They called my team the Swedish Meatballs. But they pronounced it, 'Swedish *Meatbarus*'."

The Jumpin' Jimminy crew roared laughing. Like all Americans, after Pearl Harbor, the crew knew that Japanese couldn't pronounce the letter "L". Nothing in their phonetics had the sound. When they tried, it came out as the "R" sound. And for Chinese it was just vice-versa.

Every American kid knew that the best password when fighting the Japs was "Lollapalooza". And the best counter-sign would be "Lincoln Logs." Or "Louisville Slugger." If it came out "Rorraparooza" or "Rincorun Rawgs" or "Rooisviru Srugger", you could feel pretty sure a Jap was trying to sneak through the lines.

"Oh, yes, they thought Swedish *Meatbarus* was very funny, too," Major Karlsson said. "And when they stopped laughing, they told me, smiling and bowing, that when I could get up a good team they would like to play."

Major Karlsson explained that all Spring and Summer of that year, 1944, he had tried to get American crewmen organized into a team and get a Series going with the Japanese. But as soon as he had a team set up and willing to play, the guys on the team were flown back to England. By this time in the war, Sweden was allowing the Allies to ship back their airmen, even if an equal number of Germans were not going home, as they should do under the Convention rules. The Americans were running almost a regular airline shuttle service between Scotland and Sweden.

Major Karlsson had one Series all ready go. But when the American Legation in Stockholm heard about it, they put an immediately and complete halt to it.

Karlsson said, "And do you know why they stopped it? 'Suppose the goddamn Yaps win,' they said."

"Well, that's a good point," said Jeff Cabot. "Especially if the Yaps are any good."

"It's not that they are so especially good, although they do play good. They've had nothing else to do but practice while sitting in their camp. But my boys were pretty bad, no match at all. If I can get a good team, if I could get you boys to play, and if you're as good as you say, we could beat the pants off those Yaps."

"If you can keep us here in Sweden 'til the Season opens next Spring, we'll be overjoyed to help you out," said B.J. Jones, eyeing an amazingly buxom blonde kitchen worker setting up a fresh pot of coffee. "And we guarantee we'll beat the pants off those Yaps."

"And to show our confidence, I'll make book on it," said Joe Batch.

"The question is how to keep them from ferrying us back," said Jeff Cabot. "When does Spring come around here? April? That's six months away."

"I'll organize it," Major Karlsson said. "You leave that to me. From now on, I'm the Yumpin' Yimminy team General Manager."

"Hey, C'mon," said Jeff Cabot. "You can't call a ball team after a Flying Fortress. You name them after cities."

"OK, we name the team after Falun," said Major Karlsson. "The Falun...the Falun...the Falun..."

"The Falun Angels!" shouted Joshua Bennett, giving Falun an American pronounciation. "We're Falling Angels, all right. The Falun Angels! Hallelujah!"

"And let the Yaps try to pronounce that!" said Karlsson. "We'll show those Yaps who the real *Meatbarus* are!"

CHAPTER 10

Major Karlsson was not a regular army officer. He had received his wartime officer's rank, starting as a lieutenant but climbing rather quickly to major, because of his civilian skill at running hotels. He had learned the business in Chicago and Minneapolis, which was hardly Paris or Geneva or London, but it was exotic enough.

When working in the United States, he saved his money carefully, sending it home to Stockholms Enskilda Bank, the Wallenberg bank, the country's most prestigious. He returned from America after the 1929 crash quite well off, especially for a young man who had worked his way up. He was rightfully regarded as a rather sharp businessman.

Karlsson first met Marcus Wallenberg, one of the banking family sons, in Minneapolis. Wallenberg had been in the U.S. trying to sell a Swedish electrical equipment company the family controlled to General Electric Co. Luckily for the Wallenbergs and the company and Sweden, the 1929 crash gave the GE brass something more important to worry about. The Swedish company did very nicely on its own in the succeeding years. Its original trade mark used a swastika, an ancient Nordic symbol. After Stalingrad, the trade-mark was gradually withdrawn.

When Karlsson returned to Stockholm, he called on Wallenberg, as a polite, friendly gesture. Karlsson had learned many things in America beside baseball. One was to be polite and friendly. He had read Dale Carnegie's *How to Win Friends and Influence People*, and memorized most of the important advice. The Wallenbergs owned the Grand, Stockholm's finest hotel. Karlsson was immediately offered an executive job there.

When the war in Europe broke out, Sweden mobilized, to demonstrate its neutrality. The military desperately needed people with administrative and organizational skills, and especially people fluent in English. They had no problem getting German-speakers. It was the primary foreign language taught in schools—at least up until the time when there was no doubt that the Germans would lose the war.

Karlsson, with his wide contacts with leading businessmen and government officials, through his hotel position, received an army commission and assignment to head an emergency quartering group. Initially, he worked with refugees and military who escaped from Norway and Denmark. As the war continued, more and more refugees arrived.

And then came more and more fighting men, from just about every European army, it seemed. Germans mainly arrived by ship. Their compasses were invariably 180 degrees off. Some sailed into Swedish waters to escape pursuing Allied planes. Some Germans deserted from their units in Norway and Finland.

Although the Swedish Government in the early years of the war were very accommodating to the Germans—allowing German troop trains to cross their "neutral" nation between Denmark and Norway and from Norway to Finland—their attitude changed a bit after Stalingrad, and when it was quite sure Hitler would not waste manpower attacking Sweden. German deserters were no longer returned to Germany, and refugees from Norway were not turned back at the border as a number had been by pro-Nazi police chiefs in the early years.

A large number of Estonians, Latvians and Lithuanians, who had volunteered into German service, claimed they were forced to join the Nazis. They deserted when it was quite obvious they were on the losing side. Three Polish submarines took refuge in Sweden, rather than scuttling the vessels or allowing them to be captured by the Germans. Several crews of Italian ships were interned. They were the happiest of all, it seemed. A large number of Yugoslavs, whom the Germans used for slave labor in Norway, escaped to cross over into Sweden. Norwegians and Danes had their own camps, where the Swedes finally started to train them for "police" duties after the war.

And, of course, there were the crews of the British and American bombers and of the Japanese submarine.

It took all of Major Karlsson's diplomatic skills to keep the combatants apart. But even with his Dale Carnegie training, and with his superb patience and diplomacy, he simply could not calm the protests of the German Legation, which insisted that German military internees be given finer quarters and rations than the Allies. How the Germans knew how the Allies were treated was a mystery, but the Germans always protested about everything out of sheer habit and old tradition. Karlsson knew quite a few of the German diplomats: their Legation was just a few doors from the Grand Hotel.

Karlsson wanted a rest, to get away from the "bellyaching Krauts" as he privately called the pompous, overbearing German Legation staff, most of them card-carrying Nazis. They were as obnoxious as the German businessmen and tourists he had to serve at his hotels in peacetime. The German military internees were happy enough, just being safe from the Eastern Front, although their stay in Sweden was generally short-lived, being repatriated home as fast as transport could be organized and as fast as an equal number of Allied internees could be returned.

Major Karlsson asked to be "demoted", to the assignment of running only one facility, the Falun hotel for American fliers. It was Springtime 1944, and he figured he could organize some ball games, and get some Americans to help coach his team of locals. It would be a good Summer.

And it was a good Summer, except for the devastating beatings his boys received at the skilled hands of the Japanese ball players. What was even more embarrassing was the Japanese scornful rejection of playing more games "until your *meatbarus* learn to play *besubaru*", as their General Manager, who was the senior officer, said in his surprisingly fluent English, even though he usually pronounced "baseball" the Japanese way.

CHAPTER 11

One can easily understand Major Karlsson's euphoria at having as his guests the best baseball team in the Eighth Air Force, possibly the best in the entire European theater. But he had to insure that the *Jumpin' Jimminy* crew remained in Sweden until he could open the Spring baseball Season.

The Americans and British were flying interned crews back to England as fast as they could. And now it was only October, which meant at least six months before he could have his new team play the Japanese. He was less concerned with problems of getting approval to organizing a ball game between internees of two nations at war. That was a problem he would take care of later.

"A game?" he thought. "Hell, I'll make it a Series, a real World Series. The first Swedish World Series."

He gathered the crew of the *Jumpin' Jimminy* in a private session in his office. The crew had already been to town, bought civilian clothes, and scouted out girls, restaurants, the coffee shops—known as *konditori*—and the very sad excuses for saloons, in that order.

The crew gained immediate notoriety because of Napoleon Anderson. Not only was he the first black American soldier they had seen in Falun, but miracle of all miracles, he spoke Swedish fluently.

"*Titta, en neger!*" a big Swedish youth said to his pals as Napoleon Anderson and the crew had a beer on their first day in town.

"Watch your mouth, squarehead," said Joe Bacciagalupo, getting up. Joshua Bennett and Mickey O'Mallery did the same.

"Hey, wait, you guys," said Napoleon Anderson, dragging Joe Batch back to his chair. "He didn't say what you think he did. That only means Negro. I've heard worse. In Swedish. And in English."

Napoleon Anderson walked over to the Swedish lads and introduced himself. In Swedish: "We just arrived. Hope to stay a while. Nice town you got here. Good-looking girls."

The lads assumed the Swedish look. The crew had named it "The Vah Dough Look". Mouth open, face totally puzzled, the wearer would utter, *"Va då?"* which is literally translated as "What then?" but which is best translated as a good old hick's "Huh?" In this case, the lads were so shocked to hear a *"neger"* speaking Swedish, they couldn't even say *"Va då?"* They just looked. Mouths open. The Swedish look.

Napoleon Anderson became a local celebrity very fast. At least as fast as the people in the cafe could recover their wits and spread the story around town that a newly-arrived American crew not only included a *"neger"* but that the *"neger"* spoke Swedish.

Everyone in town started to think of relatives who had emigrated to America and what they may have done there that they never wrote home about.

But here in his office at the hotel, Major Karlsson served coffee, passed around cigarettes, and got down to business.

"Look, if I can keep you all here in Sweden until next Spring, we can play a Series against that Japanese team."

"You keep us here and we'll play Hirohito and Hitler, too" said Jeff Cabot.

"Hell, we'd play the Phillies, and they're hardly worth the effort," Ed Kowalski added.

"When does the season start around here?" asked Pete Fielding. "If it's like Wisconsin where all the other Swedes are, the snow won't melt until next July and the war'll better be over by then."

"With luck, if we don't have a bad Winter, we can start playing in early April," Karlsson said. "Before that, we can do some practicing in the big barn if it's not too cold. Spring Training. Or maybe we could go south, to Skåne, where you landed. Spring comes a month earlier there. We could set up a Spring Training camp. Like in Florida. But no palm trees. Maybe organize some exhibition games."

"But how can you keep us in Sweden?" Ed Kowalski asked. "They're shipping crews back as fast as they can."

"Ah, that's the big question and it will require some work," Karlsson said. He had thought it out. "What I will need is to talk to each of you, so that I can find special reasons for your Government to allow you to stay in Sweden."

"You don't think whippin' the ass off a Jap team would be good enough reason?" Joe Bacciagalupo asked. "Hell, it would be the only time we get to beat the Japs in Europe."

"Yeah, we'd make World War II military history," said Carl Jacobson.

"We'd pay 'em back for Pearl Harbor," said Pete Fielding.

"That's all very admirable," said Karlsson. "But I know it is not enough. We have to find convincing reasons that by staying in Sweden, you contribute greatly to solidify Swedish-American relations, or that it's good for Sweden, and obviously for the good of the Americans and Allies. Or, just the opposite, bad for the Germans and the Japs."

The crew of the *Jumpin' Jimminy* had earlier and privately tried to figure out Major Karlsson. How did they know he was legit, and not working for the Krauts, getting military secrets, or personal information that could be used for propaganda? Hadn't they been warned about it in lectures about being captured or interned—lectures that they only vaguely recalled. The anti-VD films were far more memorable.

After long discussion, they came to unanimous conclusion: anyone who could talk baseball as passionately and knowledgeably as Karlsson, had to be all right. He had discussed the World Series for hours on the day of their arrival, and had listened to the games broadcast shortwave by Armed Forces Radio. He was enthusiastically rooting for the Cardinals, although the team he normally backed was the White Sox. If he were a Kraut spy, he deserved an Academy Award. Or induction into the Baseball Hall of Fame.

The crew had nothing to lose by staying in Sweden, and, come to think of it, everything to gain. Despite the decimation of Göring's Luftwaffe, the Krauts were still putting up a helluva fight, and plenty of bombers were still being lost. Like the *Jumpin' Jimminy* damn near was.

"Okay," said Jeff Cabot to Major Karlsson, ending the discussion. "You find something to keep us all here, and we stay. And in exchange, we'll whip that Jap team in your World Series next Spring."

CHAPTER 12

Major Karlsson set to work immediately. It wasn't all that much different from hiring a new staff for a hotel. It was just a matter of looking at a man's background, training, and special qualifications, and then fitting him into the right position.

Karlsson's task was greatly simplified by the fact that because of his Grand Hotel career, he had an amazing web of contacts in finance, politics, business, theater, press, diplomacy, you name it. Countless people in very high positions owed Karlsson many favors. The Grand was the finest hotel in Sweden and only the most important ladies and gentlemen stayed there. Although he was thoroughly trusted for his discretion, these people knew that he knew much. He knew that not all ladies and gentlemen were always ladies and gentlemen.

Not that rank meant all that much, but Karlsson first took care of Jeff Cabot. It was the easiest. Jeff Cabot came from a Boston banking family and Karlsson got him a job at Stockholms Enskilda Bank. The bank had been founded in the 1850s by a smart young fellow named Wallenberg who started out as a Swedish Navy officer. He jumped ship in Boston, worked as a stevedore. But being a bright young man, saw there was more money to be made financing cargo than hauling it on your back. Easier, too.

Sweden, at the time was rather primitive when it came to banking. Boston was the American financial and trade center. Wallenberg learned as much as he could about banking, and then returned to Sweden to open Stockholms Enskilda Bank, literally, the Stockholm Private Bank. It was Sweden's first modern commercial bank.

Sweden prospered in the latter part of the century. Industries expanded. Exports increased: timber, wood pulp and paper, steel, and iron and copper ore. The nation's valuable natural resources, plus a large number of companies based on brilliant inventions and technical improvements, turned Sweden into one of the industrial giants of Europe. There were early multinationals like Alfred Nobel's dynamite, Winqvist's adjustable ball bearing, the deLaval cream separator, J.P. Johansson's adjustable wrench, L.M. Ericsson's telephones, Gustaf Dalén's automatic lighthouse, Ivar Kreuger's worldwide match empire, and C.E. Johansson's measuring blocks that Henry Ford credited with making possible his assembly line production. And these were expanded through super-salesmanship and international marketing genius, if you could believe the silent Swedes could be hot-shot salesman.

As Swedish trade and industry grew rich, so did Stockholms Enskilda Bank and its owners, the Wallenberg family. The Wallenbergs expanded their interests into manufacturing industries. By time of World War II, the Wallenbergs were one of Europe's most powerful families, combining banking with heavy industry and international trade.

Sweden's position as a neutral couldn't have been better for business. Actually, Sweden had long ago learned the value of staying neutral. It had not been at war since 1815, after choosing to join the winning side, England and Russia, against Napoleon. As a reward, Sweden got Norway from Denmark, and then figured it would quit war as long as it was way ahead.

Wars came and wars went, and Sweden sold to all sides. It built up an efficient and prosperous armaments industry. Best-known was Bofors, the cannon-maker, owned for several years before his death by Alfred Nobel himself, the famous founder of the Nobel Prizes, including, of course, the Peace Prize.

In the 1920s and 1930s, Sweden, like many nations, had figured that World War I had been so horrible that it was indeed the war to end all wars. Sweden cut its defense spending to the bare bones. Officers were expected to support themselves. The air force was a joke. Mechanized forces were almost non-existent. Troops not only wore uniforms designed in the 1890s, but carried rifles of the same vintage. The only really unique weapon was the Bofors 40 mm. automatic anti-aircraft gun, which its manufacturer gladly sold to anyone who would pay, and just about every nation did.

At the outbreak of World War II, Sweden suddenly realized how weak it really was. It bought what it could from abroad, including a small fleet of Caprioni bombers from Italy. The Swedish Government contracted with an American company to build planes in Sweden, and a team of American engineers and production specialists got the aircraft industry going. Pearl Harbor put a stop to American help, with all Yank experts needed at home. But by that time,

Svenska Aeroplan Aktiebolaget, SAAB, was in operation, building planes of its own designs. The latest model SAAB plane was one of the fastest fighters in the air. The *Jumpin' Jimminy* crew had seen one escorting their Fortress as it coughed and spluttered to the airfield, but they had other things to think about at the time.

SAAB, by coincidence, went public on D-Day. Stock analysts strongly recommended the stock, figuring that even if the invasion were successful, and the war was shortened, Sweden would still need military planes. If the invasion failed, it wouldn't hurt, either. More worrisome for business was how the invasion would curtail shipping between Sweden and Germany.

Indeed, war is hell.

The Wallenbergs and Stockholms Enskilda Bank were playing a key role in SAAB and much of the Swedish armaments industry, as well as in heavy industry in general. The Wallenberg empire was run by brothers Marcus and Jacob Wallenberg. Each represented the family and bank interests on a large number of boards of directors. What was particularly sweet about their operation was that Marcus concentrated his attention to England and the U.S., while Jacob was close to Germany. They could do business neatly with both sides.

It was into the center of this spider-web that Major Karlsson placed Jeff Cabot. Actually, Marcus knew the Cabots quite well. It was at the family's old Boston bank that his great grandfather had apprenticed and learned the trade. Marcus welcomed the chance of having a young Jeff Cabot at his bank. It would certainly be of value to business in the post-war years.

Wallenberg's request for having Jeff Cabot on special assignment at the bank could not have been more welcome by American authorities. Top OSS officers in Stockholm cracked open a bottle of champagne. They had been trying for years to get a high-level source into the bank. Oh, they had a few bank clerks on the payroll and some secretaries, but what they needed was someone who could check things at "the Wallenberg level", as they put it. Certainly Marcus was extremely friendly and cooperative, but they knew that he had to play his cards very carefully so as not to endanger present—and more important, post-war—relations between the bank and its German banker friends and industrialists.

The OSS officers put Jeff Cabot through a crash course, not in banking and finance, which he had plenty of at Harvard, but in good old-fashioned spying. His job was to get as much information as he could about Swedish business with Germany. He should be able to get plenty of help from executives at the bank, now that it was obvious that Germany would be defeated.

Swedes who had openly admired Hitler and the Nazis were now burning their copies of *Mein Kampf*. On streetcars, they would be seen reading the pro-Ally newspaper, *Göteborgs Handels-och Sjöfartstidning*, one of the few Swedish papers with guts, instead of being seen, as they had been for years, with their beloved pro-Hitler *Aftonbladet*.

When Jeff Cabot took up his "job" at the bank, he was introduced at a luncheon, hosted by Marcus Wallenberg himself, in one of the bank's formal executive dining rooms. Cocktails, excellent food, fine wine, very polite conversation. Jeff Cabot would enjoy this assignment. And he certainly did until time for Spring Training.

CHAPTER 13

❀

Napoleon Anderson had no problem either. The American officers in charge of internee matters at the United States Legation in Stockholm were greatly amused at the idea of a Chicago Negro visiting his relatives in Sweden.

"I'd love to see their faces when they open the door, and there he stands and says, 'Hi, y'all, ah'm yo' flesh an' blood kin,'" chuckled a major, who came from Mississippi.

"Well, if you'd like to see it, why don't you go with him?" asked a colonel.

"I'm not all that curious."

"He'll be in civilian clothes, so nobody would know you're associating with an enlisted man," the colonel said, seriously.

"Very funny," the major muttered, as he stamped Napoleon Anderson's official passes and identification papers, put them in an envelope and called the mail room to have them sent to the Falun camp.

Napoleon Anderson got the papers in a few days. He was delighted to see that there was no expiration date given.

"Major Karlsson, you're a genius," he said.

"It is in the best interest of Swedish-American relations," Karlsson replied, a modest note in his voice. "We do all we can to bring families of both nations closer together."

Karlsson arranged for leave for the sergeant who had escorted the crew, and who was convinced that he was related to Napoleon Anderson. The sergeant would accompany Napoleon on a visit to his family's home village. There was only one slight problem. The village was on Möja, an island in the Stockholm archipelago that was strictly off-limits to foreigners, especially foreigners who happened to be soldiers of an army at war.

Major Karlsson laughed when the Swedish military indignantly refused to issue a pass for Napoleon Anderson. He simply made a call to the Navy commodore-captain who was in charge of archipelago security.

"Totally and absolutely off limits to foreigners," the commodore-captain said. "I am surprised that you, a major, would not know this."

"Off limits to the German Navy, too?" asked Karlsson.

"Strictly and absolutely," the commodore-captain said.

"Well, how come your Swedish Navy ships have been escorting German warships through the archipelago on their way to Finland?"

The Germans obviously preferred Swedish territorial waters than risking Russian submarines patrolling the Baltic.

"We have never done such a thing," the commodore-captain protested. "And beside, it's top secret."

"Well, if I know, and I'm not in the Navy, it's no big secret, is it?" Major Karlsson said. "Maybe the Brits and Yanks would like to know about it. Maybe the Ruskies, too. Those islands aren't virgins."

Causally, he also mentioned the German troop trains through Sweden, to and from Norway, and the entire Engelbrecht Division, that crossed Sweden to attack the Russians from Finland.

"And then there's that German depot up in Luleå," major Karlsson added. "Been supplying German troops in Finland. Supposed to be secret. Yeah, only everybody Norrland knows about it."

"That's the Army," the commodore-captain said. "And we had no choice in those years. You know that as well as I. It's different today. We are enforcing strict neutrality."

"Bullshit," said Major Karlsson, who didn't hesitate to speak his mind to superior officers when necessary. He could get away with it because of his well-known connections in high places. "The German troop-trains are an old story. But how would it look if it came out that the Swedish Navy was actively helping the German Navy? And the German Army supplying its troops in Finland from a secret base in Sweden? Churchill will love it. By the way, I met an old American friend of mine the other day at the Grand Bar. He's a correspondent for the Minneapolis Star. He'll be reporting from Sweden for a while."

The commodore-captain was silent. Karlsson patiently gave him time to weigh the threat, most subtle by Swedish standards.

"You say this American airman is of Swedish descent?"

"As Swedish as you can get. Anderson, from Chicago. He speaks fluent Swedish."

"Well, in that case it's different. He's obviously Swedish. He'll get the pass."

Major Karlsson shook hands with the Naval officer, thanked him for his cooperation, and left the office, thinking: "First rule of dealing with a Swede or Yap: let them save face."

Napoleon Anderson and the sergeant, also named Andersson, but with two s's and with the obvious first name, Anders, took the train to Stockholm. The trip was most pleasant. Fellow passengers speculated who the two were. It wasn't every day that you'd see a Negro Swede. Maybe he was from the old Swedish colony of Saint Barthélemy, in the West Indies. Maybe he had been adopted by Swedish missionaries in Ethiopia. Finally, one huge man, highly fortified with *brännvin*, as Swedish vodka was known, got up enough courage to ask.

"*Vem fan är du?*" he asked. This means "Who the hell are you?" It was the most polite way he could express himself.

Napoleon Anderson stood up. He was at least one foot shorter and 100 pounds lighter than his questioner. He looked up to the red-faced giant and answered in Swedish.

"I am Napoleon Anderson from Chicago, enjoying Swedish hospitality as I visit my long-lost cousins. I like peace and quiet, but I should tell you that in Chicago I worked for Al Capone."

"*Al Capone! Fy fan!*" The giant, mouth open, backed away and disappeared from the compartment.

"It works every time," Napoleon Anderson said.

"You really worked for Al Capone?" the amazed sergeant asked.

"Of course—everyone in Chicago worked for Al Capone."

Napoleon Anderson spent the rest of the train trip telling of adventures with the Capone mob. What true Chicagoan couldn't recite the same stories?

They took a taxi from Stockholm Central Station to the quay in front of the Grand Hotel where the ferries sailed to the islands. The whole dockside was filled long, high rows of stacked firewood.

"Fuel," said the sergeant.

"For what?"

"Everything. Even *brännvin*."

Naturally, Napoleon Anderson knew what *brännvin* was. Swedish hard liquor. And he knew that it was either unflavored, like vodka, or flavored, which was generally called *akvavit*. And it was damn good, especially in those Chicago Winters. But making it out of wood? He had heard of wood alcohol, but the stuff was dangerous. Could kill you. Swedes must be able to tame it, he thought.

He didn't have time to question the sergeant about it. Nor did they didn't have time to stop at the Grand Bar, either, as recommended by Major Karlsson. Their ferry to Möja was leaving in a few minutes.

They got tickets, showed their papers to a dumfounded policeman at the gangway, and went aboard. Napoleon Anderson wondered if they'd ever get going, no less make it to the island: the captain and crew simply stood open-mouthed and looked at him and the sergeant. But after a while, and without a word, they got moving.

It was a fine, crisp Autumn afternoon. The birch and maples on the islands of the archipelago were at the peak of color.

"You know, I'm going to enjoy this visit to the kin-folk," Napoleon Anderson said.

"They will be happy to see you, Sven's boy," the sergeant said. "It's amazing that of all the millions of Americans in the war, you end up in Sweden, and I meet you. Unbelievable."

"Well, as Bob Ripley says, 'Believe it or not.'"

The sergeant pondered that for a long while. Napoleon Anderson had become well accustomed to Swedes' fondness for pondering. When the customers in Swanson's didn't catch one of his jokes, which was quite often, they would "Turn dumb Swede," as Napoleon Anderson phrased it.

He explained to his pals that Swedes were as dumb as foxes.

"It's just that they don't talk like most people, especially us guys. They gotta think about it first. And they like to think slow."

And although Napoleon Anderson had come up against unbelieving new customers in Swanson's Market, Swedes who thought it was some kind of Seventh Wonder of the World that a Negro could speak Swedish, he had never met such total dumbfoundedness as he was meeting now in Sweden.

The ferry captain had turned the wheel over to his mate, and sat down with Napoleon Anderson and the sergeant.

"I knew a black oiler on a Swedish tramp in the West Indies, and he could speak some Swedish," the Captain said. "I knew a Chinese cook, too, who knew enough to get along. But I've never met a foreigner who could speak it like you."

"I'm not a foreigner. I'm Napoleon Anderson, from Chicago."

"Chicago? I have a cousin in Chicago. Lundström. He married a girl from Norway, but she's nice anyhow. They visited here before the war. They told us all about Al Capone."

"Here we go again," Naopoleon groaned.

"You know Al Capone?"

"He worked for him," the sergeant said proudly.

The other passengers, who had been listening most attentively above the noise of the engine, now leaned in even more attentively. Napoleon Anderson heard one tough-looking man, obviously a seaman, mutter a local curse that Napoleon Anderson had never heard, but he did understand the following: "Al Capone is moving in."

Napoleon Anderson figured it was a good time to change the subject. He asked the sergeant about the islands they were passing and the villages they stopped at. The sergeant said it was very top secret, the archipelago was strictly off-limits to foreigners, and foreigners not supposed to see anything here or take pictures or draw maps or know anything. The archipelago was on the main approach to Stockholm from the east, and you know what country was to the east, and he didn't mean Finland. He then proceeded to answer Napoleon Anderson's questions in detail.

After three hours of very pleasant sailing, stopping often at small docks, the ferry reached Möja. As at the other stops on the way, several dozen men and women were at the dock to meet passengers and help unload freight.

The sergeant was warmly greeted. Well, warmly for Swedes. Napoleon Anderson got the usual open-mouthed stares.

"And this is Sven Andersson's boy!" the sergeant said proudly.

"*Fy fan,*" muttered one old-timer. The rest simply "turned dumb Swede".

"Delighted to be here," smiled Napoleon Anderson. "I've heard so much about the family."

"*Fy fan, negern talar svenska!*" the old-timer said. "*Till och med småländska.*" Goddamn, the Negro speaks Swedish. And even the Småland dialect!

The crowd on the dock grew larger.

"No secrets in this place," thought Napoleon Anderson.

After a long series of introductions to most of the people on the dock, almost all of whom were named Andersson or Johansson, Napoleon and the sergeant headed up the street to an inn, where Major Karlsson had booked a room for the visiting Swedish-American relative for the next few months, until Spring Training started.

Napoleon Anderson was introduced to his long-lost cousins. He had a bit of trouble with their local dialect, and they had a bit of trouble with his Småland accent. They asked him about it.

"That's what most of us speak in Chicago," he said. It was as "yust as good" an explanation as any.

By this time, he had pretty much convinced himself that he was actually related to the Anderssons from Möja. And he had almost convinced himself he had worked for Al Capone, and not Swanson's Fish Market. His new-found relatives became extremely friendly that first night, as Napoleon Anderson passed around Luckies and handed over bottles of Scotch whisky.

He was surprised that the cigarettes were appreciated more than the booze.

The next day, he found out why.

Wandering around the village, Napoleon Anderson caught a whiff of a scent that he remembered as a very little kid. Moonshine cooking. Even after Prohibition was repealed, some of the hillbillies who had moved up to Chicago from Kentucky insisted on making their own. They said it was better than store-bought booze, and it was, at least it was much better than the stuff they could afford.

Napoleon Anderson smiled to himself, thinking of the hillbillies in Chicago. Maybe Swedish hillbillies settled here on Möja.

Naturally, he was asked about Al Capone.

"Are you still working for him? Here?"

"No, I retired."

The good people of Möja said, "Yes, of course," but they didn't believe him, even though he was an Anderson.

"Who can believe a *Smålänning*?" they said. "He's here to take over."

It was a logical conclusion. The islanders had a very nice little, profitable business going. They made quality moonshine, some of which they consumed locally and were generous enough to ship most of it to the mainland. It was in the spirit of the times, when people had to pull together, help each other, and do what they could for the nation's welfare, even though it was slightly illegal.

Thus the islanders had no objection whatsoever when Napoleon Anderson took up with Ingrid Svensson, the local beauty queen. If anyone could get at the truth behind Napoleon Anderson's visit, she could. But the only truth she found out was that Napoleon Anderson lived up to the reputation of old Sven Andersson.

"What he says about *brännvin* is that we should filter it a few more times through charcoal," she reported. "And he says we definitely must find much better water. Deep well water. The secret is in the water."

"*Fy fan, negern är en hembränningsexpert!*" Goddamn! The Negro is a moonshine expert!

Well, he wasn't really a moonshine expert, but he had learned something from those Kentuckians in Chicago. Besides, he had worked for Al Capone, hadn't he? Anyone who worked for Al Capone must be an expert.

Napoleon Anderson was slowly taken into the clan's confidence. He said they accepted him despite his being a *Smålänning*. Everyone knew how those people were: tight-fisted, clever with money, independent, and—what was most suspect of all for rustic Swedes—willing and able to start profitable businesses.

Napoleon Anderson worked in the stills, constantly insisting on improving quality of the product. And helped with boat engines. His training at Tilden Tech paid off here. He had warm quarters at the inn, plenty of pocket money supplied by the Legation, pretty fair food (although most of it was fish), and Ingrid.

It was a lovely way to fight the war, and to rest up for Spring Training.

CHAPTER 14

Carl Jacobson was quietly enjoying a cup of real coffee in Anna's *Konditori*, on the main street of Falun. The boys at the inn would slip Anna coffee from their mess, and she would reserve it for them and for other special customers. Like the girls who always hung out there, not so much interested in coffee but in the American fliers.

It was a lovely October day, bright sun, and the girls, with hair matching the gold of the Autumn trees, would soon arrive after their shift in the mill. It hadn't taken the *Jumpin' Jimminy* crew long to meet the girls. Just about every unattached girl in town, and a few who were attached. It was always a mystery how Swedish guys were so cold and Swedish girls so warm.

As Carl Jacobson was pondering this monumental question, two middle-aged men, in civilian clothes, walked in and sat at a nearby table. Until then, Carl had been alone in the place. Carl Jacobson could immediately see they were not Swedes. The cut of their suits and topcoats were distinctly different. English maybe. Their manner was different, too. They ordered coffee. Anna served them the local stuff, which meant they were not regulars.

Carl Jacobson paid little attention to them. He found an old copy of Life magazine on the rack, and was idly flipping the pages when he heard the men start to speak, in German.

"Damn Jews, it's all their fault," one said.

Carl Jacobson turned and looked.

"They are all Communists and international bankers," the man continued.

Carl slowly put down the magazine.

"Hitler's right," the man added.

Carl Jacobson stood up, calmly walked to the two men, and without saying a word punched the man in the face. The man toppled backward and sprawled on the floor. His nose bled profusely. Carl Jacobson turned to the other man, grabbed him by the front of his suit and yanked him to his feet.

"I didn't say a word, it was him," the man said quickly. He spoke perfect English. American, actually, with some kind of Midwest twang. He actually laughed as he looked at his pal trying to stop the nose-bleed.

"Who the hell are you, anyway?" Carl Jacobson asked, slowly releasing his grip.

"Just take it easy," the man on the floor said, also in perfect American, as he got to his feet, righted the chair and sat down with his head back and a napkin at his nose. "Christ, my nose will never stop bleeding. Hope to hell you didn't break it."

"No, I was saving that for later," Carl Jacobson said.

Anna was not unaccustomed to bloody noses, although she saw most of them outside the Folk Park dances on week-ends. She got a cold damp cloth for the guy. And a mop for the floor.

"Put it on their bill," Carl Jacobson said.

"You betcha," Anna said. She loved that American Swede expression.

"Now what the hell are you jerks up to?" Carl Jacobson asked, still mad as hell.

The man without the bloody nose ordered more coffee, and Carl Jacobson now noted that the man had spoken Swedish to Anna. The man pulled out his wallet and showed Carl Jacobson an American military intelligence identity card, made out to a major. As far as Carl Jacobson could see, it was legit.

"He got one, too," the man said, pointing at his friend. "But don't make him show it, it'll get all bloody." He laughed. His friend, still trying to stop the bleeding, didn't.

"We think we've found our man," the major said. His friend nodded.

"Look," he said to Carl Jacobson, "forget the ranks. Just call me Hank. My pal is Joe."

He then explained in detail. For a long time, the American OSS in Sweden had been trying to plant someone in the German internment camp. They figured they could learn plenty if they had someone who could talk to the German internees, mostly from the Luftwaffe. The internees had much better communications with Germany than prisoners of war held by the Allies. And the internees also were in constant touch with the officials of the German Legation in Stockholm.

But Washington had much higher priorities for its available German spies, so the Stockholm OSS branch was left on its own, and was trying to recruit someone locally. Their best chances were from B-17 crews interned right in Sweden. But whenever they had a candidate, something would turn out wrong. They had a model officer some months back, a guy with a German name and ancestry. He even had what could pass as a dueling scar, although it was from an ice hockey game in St. Paul. One slight problem. He didn't know a word of German.

"And then there was the guy from Pennsylvania," Hank said. "Perfect type. Spoke German fluently. One more slight problem. He told us to go to hell. He joined up to fight Germans, not to live with them. He had enough of them back home."

"Tell him about Kansas," Joe said. His nosebleed was slowing.

"Yeah, Kansas. Also perfect. Grew up in a German-speaking town in Kansas. Christ I never knew we had so many Krauts in America. Anyhow, he was delighted with the assignment. Figured his chances of survival were far better than going back to flying. He said he was actually afraid of flying back to England. How did you become a pilot, we asked. 'I'm not afraid when I'm at the controls,' he said. We should have suspected something right there. Anyhow, we get him briefed, outfitted, and he's brought to the camp as a Luftwaffe Colonel. He liked the promotion. He was driven in in a German staff car. Don't ask how we arranged it, but we did. He got settled, and as highest-ranking officer, he called assembly to introduce himself.

"There he stood, on the porch of his cottage in the compound, facing a couple hundred Germans. He raised his arm, shouted '*Heil Hitler*' and then ripped off the greatest fart you ever heard. The Krauts couldn't believe it. The whole camp just stood and stared. Kansas lowered his arm. 'And a message to Marshal Göring,' he said, and ripped off another great fart. He saluted, clicked his heels, made a snappy about-face, and walked back into his cottage. We got him out of there pretty fast. 'Now what the hell did you do that for?' we asked. 'You blew the whole damn thing. We could have you court-martialed.'"

"And he said, 'Court-martialed? Aw shucks. Who ever got court-martialed for farting at Hitler and Göring? It's something I always dreamed about doing. Right in the Luftwaffe's face!'

"We found out later that Kansas was famous in his squadron for his farting talents."

"Which shows how bright the OSS is," Carl Jacobson said. "Maybe you haven't found out either that as a German Aryan, I'd be the worst candidate."

"Oh, we know you're Jewish," the man with the nose-bleed said. "That was just our test of how well you understood German."

"You should have discussed Kant," Carl Jacobson said.

"Knowing you flyboys, I'm sure you'd misunderstand." The nose had stopped bleeding. "We also wanted to see if you could handle yourself. You passed on both counts."

"How did you find out about me?"

"We have our sources."

"Bullshit. Major Karlsson tipped you off."

"Well, no matter. How about it? What do you say? You'll be promoted to full colonel."

"Great, in the Luftwaffe. I bet I make more now as a lieutenant. And what do I tell my girl-friends in Falun?"

"The Germans have girl-friends, too."

"I wouldn't touch those Kraut-fuckers with a ten-foot pole."

"You'd better not. They could squeal. Unless, of course, you'd want to have a minor operation. We could arrange it. Give you an extra inch."

The OSS duo laughed a huge "Har, har har."

"You guys got a weird sense of humor," Carl Jacobson said. "But, what the hell. As long as I'm the top-ranking Kraut in the compound, I give the orders. I'd like that: I'll have those Krauts wishing they were on the Russian front. But one big problem, other than my tipped-off pecker, which I expect I can keep private. How do we explain my goofy Kraut accent?"

"Easy, first you rarely speak. After all, you're in command, and nobody dares talk to you unless you talk first. We'll let it be known that you were orphaned and raised by aunts in Switzerland. Ever hear of *Schwyzer-dütsch*? Sounds just like Yiddish. Funny as hell actually. And you can't hear an accent when you shout orders. Krauts are always shouting orders. Why they always shout is a mystery. You'd think the whole Kraut military is deaf."

"And nobody would dare laugh at your accent," Joe, the nose-bleeder, added.

"After all, you are the colonel in charge. And you can speak English with your bat-man. What the Brits call an officer's aide. He's also your clerk. He's a Luftwaffe sergeant. The guy speaks English, used to work in a hotel in London. Tell him you want to practice for the victory."

"One more thing. Who will I be? If I'm in the Luftwaffe, someone in the camp would know me. Or know about me."

"Oh, you wouldn't be in the Luftwaffe. We blew our Luftwaffe colonel identity with Kansas. Yeah, he blew it all right. No, you'll be a colonel in the SS. The Luftwaffe guys are scared shitless of the SS."

"So am I," said Carl Jacobson. "So how the hell did I get interned in Sweden?"

"Simple. Your transport plane from the northern Russian front to your new posting in Denmark got way off course and ran into engine trouble."

"You guys think of everything," Carl Jacobson said.

"Actually, between us, it was Major Karlsson," Hank said.

CHAPTER 15

Major Karlsson was on a winning streak. He had wangled essential assignments for half the crew. Jeff Cabot was already busy at the bank. Carl Jacobson was getting set to take command of the German internment camp. Napoleon Anderson was off cementing Swedish-American relations.

Joe Bacciagalupo was teaching English to high school kids in Falun and nearby towns. An entire generation of Swedes in the Province of Dalarna would insist that proper English pronunciation means dropping the "r" at the end of words, as in Bacciagalupo's classic example, "Pahk the cah in Havahd Yahd," and adding an "r" when a word ends in a vowel, as in the island nation of Cubar.

Joshua Bennett was on a revival tour. American officials at the Legation were getting amazing letters of praise, particularly from Småland, a hot-bed of Swedish Bible-thumping. Bennett was the most inspiring preacher they had heard in years. And it didn't make his message one bit less powerful because it had to be translated into Swedish by an assistant preacher, Maria, of all names, a young lady whom Bennett met in Falun.

It hadn't take him long to make her see the wonders of the Lord's message. Bennett figured that a couple hell-fire sermons a week were well worth the nice life he and Maria were living. When they were not preaching, Bennett tried to teach Maria the basics of baseball. After all, she would accompany him to Spring Training, just like the wives and girlfriends accompany players to Florida.

Ed Kowalski got an obvious assignment. He was made liaison officer with a camp at which Polish military were interned. His biggest job was keeping the

Poles supplied with Polish exile newspapers printed in London, and with Swedish moonshine and American cigarettes and polka records.

He was able to afford all this by convincing a Falun sausage company to let his guys rent the facilities to make *kielbasa*. The Swedes shook their heads, wondering how anyone could eat that spicy Polish sausage, containing garlic of all damn things! The Swedes couldn't imagine anyone not loving *Falukorv*, the local delicacy. The Poles insisted boiled wood pulp had more flavor.

To each his own, Ed Kowalski philosophized, as he and his Poles made a nice bit of money selling *kielbasa* to the specialty shops in Stockholm catering to central European refugees and foreign diplomats.

Pete Fielding was given a highly important assignment that would be of tremendous value to the American Air Corps. Since he was an experienced navigator, he was put in charge of preparing new maps to guide American aircraft making emergency landings in Sweden. He would have to visit each of the airfields to which American planes were directed.

Nobody told the air attaché at the American Legation that Pete Fielding couldn't find his way home when he was on the ground. And he wasn't going to be allowed to fly over Sweden taking aerial mapping photos. Bad enough he was violating Swedish secrecy laws driving all over the place, off-limits or not. When Pete Fielding took off on his first assignment, the *Jumpin' Jimminy* crew wondered if the right fielder would find his way back in time for Spring Training.

Mickey O'Mallery was a problem for Major Karlsson. The New Yorker had no real schooling after high school and he had no trade nor specialty.

"I'm a hustler," he told the Major. "When I'm not playing ball, I do a little of this, a little of that. Don't worry. I'll think of something."

Karlsson hoped it would be half-way legal.

It was.

O'Mallery came up with Sweden's first Welcome Wagon. He convinced a dozen Falun merchants to provide samples of their wares that he would present to the crews of every newly-arriving American plane. After all, a large number would be coming up to Falun, and what better way to weld their future loyalty as customers. And you know how good customers those Yankee fliers can be, with pockets full of kronor.

Major Karlsson said he couldn't have done better, which was his ultimate compliment. Using his connections, he came up with a small Volvo van that was converted into a show room for the merchants' wares. Mickey O'Mallery had no trouble recruiting two buxom Falun blondes to serve as Welcome

Wagon Hostesses. Major Karlsson asked why he needed two. Wouldn't one hostess be enough?

"Hey, take a gander. Four is better than two, no?"

Major Karlsson couldn't argue that point. And soon, Mickey O'Mallery, the well-stacked hostesses and the well-filled van, carrying the bright sign "Official Falun Welcome Wagon" and flying Swedish and American flags, were off to take up their post in south Sweden, near the most-used emergency air bases. Armed with an impressive letter from Major Karlsson, and carrying official seals and stamps that no one had ever seen before, Mickey O'Mallery could speed through air-field sentry posts and, with latest Tommy Dorsey and Glen Miller records playing over a built-in loud speaker, he would roar up to the arriving crews. The hostesses would start handing out samples. The crews figured they definitely had landed in heaven.

B.J. Jones knew he had landed in heaven. Karlsson got him an essential job in the town of Malung, not too far from Falun. Malung was famous as a leather garment center. Karlsson had served several company owners very well when they would make business trips to Stockholm, and he asked for favors returned.

B.J. Jones was one of those Americans who could do anything with his hands. A lot of young ladies would confirm this. He was assigned to get production going making baseball gloves. He simply brought sample gloves from the camp to the Malung factories, and got a few girls there to cut leather and sew them up. The American Legation paid for them, even though the picky accountants never knew it. Invoices for the baseball gloves truthfully listed the item as "gloves" and everyone knew that interned crewmen were prohibited from wearing uniforms and thus couldn't wear their flight gloves. They needed civilian gloves.

B.J. Jones was also credited with producing the first Swedish-made baseball bats. He found a ski factory that had a fine supply of ash, enough to put the entire Swedish army on skis. Jones simply showed a Louisville slugger to an old Swedish woodworker, Johan Johansson.

"I can make much better," Johansson said.

Swedes always insisted they could make anything better than anyone else. Funny thing is, they usually could. Johansson was soon spinning perfect copies of Louisville Sluggers on his lathe.

Jones got him to make variations to accommodate different hitters' tastes. The bats were branded as "Dalarna Slugger" and carried the company name "Jones and Johansson".

Johan Johansson even came up with a model that had notches carved into the handle. He said it would provide better finger grip. Jones promised he'd have it tested and if the batters liked it, they would patent the design.

But what definitely got B.J. Jones his long-term reprise from being shipped back to Britain was the fact that a number of young ladies in Falun insisted that a Private Jones was the father of their children. Several others insisted the father's name was Corporal Smith. No matter what, the local court wanted the matter cleared up, and paternity payments guaranteed. Using Swedish logic, the courts ruled that because B.J. Jones was an American flier, and was in the Province of Dalarna, he was obviously the Jones in question. He would have to remain.

The leather-goods plants employed hundreds of local girls, and since young men were scarce and B.J. Jones's pockets were overflowing with cash and ration coupons, well, as he put it: "It's not a half bad way to spend the war."

One crewman was left: Gus Sanchez, who was the quietest guy of the crew, and for good reason. His English wasn't all that good. He was fluent only in English in baseball lingo.

Joe Bacciagalupo had been doing his best to teach him proper Bostonian, which the rest of the crew said was no favor whatsoever. Gus Sanchez was Mexican. He had been playing on a Mexican pro team when spotted by a scout for the Cardinals. He was brought to a Card farm team in Texas, and played a season before being drafted. Drafted into the United States Army, that is.

He didn't need to speak much English to work in the kitchen, where he ended up and where he made the best damn chili anyone ever tasted. An Air Corps general from Texas heard about him, and had him transferred to his unit, and Gus eventually ended up working in the officers' mess at the *Jumpin Jimminy's* air base in England. Joe Bacciagalupo spotted him playing ball, caught for him, and in a few days, Gus Sanchez was a member of the *Jumpin' Jimminy* team and air crew.

Like Napoleon Anderson, he wasn't all that enthusiastic about flying, but he figured playing ball was better than working in the kitchen and if he had to fly to play ball, so be it. Joe Batch taught him all he ever needed to know about manning a waist gun. But he didn't have to teach him anything about playing ball. Gus could pitch, field, or play the infield. He said that the village he grew up in was so small that three guys would make up a full team.

He was a perfect addition to the *Jumpin' Jimminy* team. He wasn't a half-bad gunner either. As a matter of fact, he was a natural. He was officially credited with downing at least six Jerry fighters.

"My oncle, he teach me to shoot, but with pistol," he said. "My oncle, he ride with Pancho Villa."

"If every Mexican who said he rode with Pancho Villa actually did ride with Pancho Villa, he could have conquered the United States—and Canada, too," said Joshua Bennett, always a seeker of truth.

Gus Sanchez only smiled. Pancho Villa would never want Canada. It's too damn cold.

Major Karlsson's problem was not whether Uncle Sanchez did nor did not ride with the Mexican hero. He had to do something with Gus. He checked it out with his old friend, the Mexican Consul General.

"I have a Mexican-American young man who needs a job," Major Karlsson said.

"I wish I could give him one," the Consul replied. "But I have more Mexicans on my payroll than Mexicans who rode with Pancho Villa. What can your man do?"

"He can play baseball. He can cook." Karlsson diplomatically forgot to mention Gus's shooting skills.

"If he can cook chili, he got a job," the Consul said. "My present cook is the only Latino in the world who makes lousy chili. I can't understand it. I think he's really a Spanish fascist spy."

Major Karlsson, like most everyone else, knew that the Consul's cook was actually on the Soviet Embassy's payroll. There were even rumors he was a lover of Madame Kolontay, the Soviet Ambassador. But everyone in wartime Stockholm was supposed to be Madame Kolontay's lover. Everyone was also supposed to be a spy for one side or another.

"Can you cook chili?" Major Karlsson asked Gus Sanchez.

"Can I cook chili? The Pope, can he talk Italiano? Can Joe DiMaggio hit? You loco? Of course, I cook chili."

"And it's the best damn chili you'll ever eat, that's the God's honest truth," said Joshua Bennett.

Gus Sanchez got the job. "Assignment: to cement Swedish-Mexican-American relations," the official transfer said.

Major Karlsson didn't tell his friend the Consul that the assignment was only temporary, until Spring Training started. But the Consul loved baseball as much as he loved chili. He'd understand.

CHAPTER 16

❀

The pleasant Swedish Autumn quickly turned to unpleasant Swedish Winter. Cold. Dark. Snow. And as time passed it got colder, darker and snowier.

Lucia Festival, December 13, and the Americans were treated to wake-up by beautiful blondes, candles burning in crowns on their heads, attended by a chorus of more blondes, all dressed in white gowns, carrying lit candles, and singing *"Santa Lucia"*, just like the angels, or so it seemed.

"Hey, that song's Italian," Joe Bacciagalupo said. "I can sing it." And he did.

"How come the Swedes sing a song to a Sicilian Saint?" he asked.

The blonde girls with the crowns of candles didn't really know. Something to do with the Saint of Light, or something, they said. The matter was forgotten as they served the guys the traditional coffee and ginger-snaps and hot *glögg*, and the guys figured that maybe one could survive Swedish Winters.

At least if they put enough *brännvin* into the *glögg*.

It wasn't a half-bad way to spend the war. At peace. Maybe the Swedes had something after all.

Christmas was even more pleasant. The American airmen had a plentiful supply of Christmas food, thanks to the Legation services. They managed to round up plenty of liquid Christmas cheer themselves. They were most popular with the families of the friendly young ladies of Falun. B.J. Jones was often mentioned, and mostly in warm terms.

New Year. 1945. How much more could Hitler take? The number of air raids on Germany continually increased.

Mickey O'Mallery's Welcome Wagon was kept very busy. He had branched out, establishing a British subsidiary to serve the crews of British bombers that landed in Sweden.

The others of the *Jumpin' Jimminy* crew also kept busy at their essential tasks. But they dreamed of late March, when Karlsson had promised they could start Spring Training.

By this time, Carl Jacobson had become well-established as senior officer of the German internee camp. He was well-liked by the men. He was the first officer they had ever served under who didn't continually shout and scream and threaten. As a matter of fact, he rarely spoke. And when he did, he usually spoke English, which he said he had to practice for the time when they invaded England. None of the men laughed when he said this. At least not to his face.

Carl Jacobson had gained immediate respect the first day at the camp. It was at a meeting of officers. Each introduced himself and gave a brief description of their jobs. One smarmy-faced SS lieutenant, who everyone knew full well was a spy for the German Legation in Stockholm, said his assignment was to maintain surveillance over Swedish Jews, Communists, and anti-Nazis.

"In this camp?" asked Carl Jacobson.

"No, in all Sweden."

"Why?"

"When we take over, their days are numbered," he smiled.

Carl Jacobson stood up and walked to the lieutenant, who was smirking confidently. Without saying a word, Carl Jacobson gave him a short left to the gut and followed with a right to the jaw. The lieutenant went down, out cold.

"We are guests of the Swedes and you will please remember that," Carl Jacobson said calmly. "Take that trash out of here."

The other officers quickly obeyed. The lieutenant, whose broken jaw never did set straight, did not return to the camp. Nobody in the camp missed him. He had become a real embarrassment. By this time in the war, all the Germans were busily practicing to be anti-Nazis. By time the war ended, they would have convinced themselves that they were actually peace-loving Swiss.

Carl Jacobson never had any problems after that introduction. Word got around very quickly. He may not have had any dueling scars, but he was not a man to mess with. He was always polite, listened carefully to what officers and men had to say about their units, the war, home. He spent a lot of time by himself, reading. He had a few girl-friends in the nearby town, and would often be driven to Stockholm by Swedish escorts on "official business".

Exactly how his OSS handlers managed to bluff the German Legation about Carl Jacobson remains classified to this day. After all, the senior officer of a camp for internees had the right and duty to contact his diplomatic mission. Carl Jacobson obviously never did contact the German Legation.

On his alleged trips to the Legation, he met for debriefing with Hank and Joe, who remained his OSS contacts, in elegant safe houses, way out in the suburbs.

They had cocktails, a fine lunch, real coffee, cognac, and Carl Jacobson couldn't report a damn thing that the OSS didn't know full well already. The Germans were worried about their relatives in the air raids, worried about the Russian army's advances, worried that Hitler's promised mystery super-weapon would not destroy London but would probably destroy all Germany instead, worried that nobody would believe them when they said they had really opposed the Nazis. Nobody could worry like a German losing a war.

Carl Jacobson suggested that perhaps he could learn something useful at the Japanese camp.

"By God! We never thought of that!" said Hank.

"That's why they call you Office of Special Services and not Office of Intelligence," Carl Jacobson said. He could get away with just about anything by now.

Carl Jacobson sent his compliments to the senior officer of the Japanese camp, a Navy Commander. He was promptly invited to visit. The date turned out to be a rare warm day, only ten below freezing. Jacobson brought gifts of cigarettes, a case of French brandy, and a signed portrait of Hitler. Jacobson was proud of the signature and dedication. He had written them himself.

The Japanese officers thanked him profusely for the cigarettes and brandy. Except for the Commander, they did not speak much English, and they had the customary trouble pronouncing the letter "L".

"Ahhh, Adorf Hitrer," they said, making admiring noises but silently wondering where they could hide the damn thing. They didn't know that the great German leader signed his name: *"Adolf Hitler, Shmuck".*

"That is the honored title he uses for special occasions," Carl Jacobson explained.

The Commander and several officers showed Jacobson around the camp, which consisted of a number of large buildings and cottages that had formerly been a holiday resort. It was similar to the resort the Americans were in. But much smaller.

The Commander explained they had taken command of the submarine, the very latest design in the German fleet, at the Baltic Sea shipyard at Rostock. They were to sail it to Japan, where it would be faithfully copied for a new class of Japanese subs.

"Much easier to copy from original model than from blueprints," the Commander said. "We also correct all German mistakes."

And one mistake, a big one, was the navigational system. The submarine had been somehow fitted out with totally cockeyed compasses. Running submerged, its first night at sea, the sub wound up on rocks just outside the Swedish navy base of Karlskrona. The crew was prepared to commit *hara-kiri*, but was ordered by Tokyo to await the outcome of negotiations between the Swedish and Japanese foreign ministries. The Commander was promised he would get his submarine back and go to sea and rejoin the war.

"That was two years ago," the Commander said. "We keep waiting. Very difficult to negotiate with Swedes. Hard headed."

"Where did you learn English so well?" asked Jacobson.

"Cal Tech. I studied engineering. I wish I studied navigation."

The Japanese hosted lunch. They explained that the best thing about being interned in Sweden was that they could get very fresh fish.

The waiter brought in a huge dish containing what looked to Carl Jacobson like rice balls and fish. He had heard Japanese lived on fish-heads and rice, and by God, now he would have to eat the damn stuff.

"Ahhhh, *sushi*. Very good," said the Commander. He explained in detail how it was prepared, and with what great difficulty they had in getting proper Japanese rice, and if not the real stuff, at least rice that was similar to it.

"War is hell," Jacobson said.

His ability to use chop-sticks won admiring comments. He didn't explain that every Jewish kid growing up in New York loved Chinese food.

"I learned at Chinese restaurants in Paris," he said, figuring there had to be Chinese restaurants in Paris and that a German officer would be eating there.

He copied his hosts. They watched him closely as he deftly picked up a piece of *sushi*, dipped it in the sauce, and took a bite. He couldn't believe it. Absolutely, positively, delicious. He sampled the complete variety. One was better than the next. His hosts were delighted. The waiter came in with a new tray.

"Ahhhh, *kujira*," said the Commander. "Whale. Fresh from Norway."

It took a bit of time for Jacobson to fathom the fact that he was actually eating raw whale meat. His hosts were wildly enthusiastic. They explained it was a rare treat in Japan these days, since their Pacific whaling fleet's operations were all but eliminated. But it was readily available to the Japanese internees via the Japanese Legation in Oslo. Jacobson could easily understand their delight. He thought it would go great, thinly sliced, on bagels, with cream cheese and maybe sliced onion.

The Commander explained with great regret that they could not offer *sake*.

"Traditional rice alcohol drink with *sushi*," he said. "In Winter, it's served warm. We've tried to make it, but impossible without proper rice and fermenting. Instead, we drink *brännvin* That, we make ourselves. Our brand name is *Tokyo Torpedo Juice*."

That got a big laugh from the officers, and they all raised their glasses, again, toasting, "*Kampai!*"

"*Prosit!*" toasted Carl Jacobson, and then added, "*Skål!*"

"*Skoru!*" the Japanese responded, proud of their Swedish.

During brandy, Jacobson finally got down to business.

"I understand you have a baseball team here," he said.

"Best baseball team in Sweden," the Commander said proudly. "Best baseball team in Europe. I am the general manager."

"I saw some exhibition games in Berlin, but I was told they were not very good," Jacobson said.

"I saw Babe Ruth and Lou Gehrig, best baseball players in America, play in Tokyo in 1936," the Commander said proudly. "But you want to see good baseball? We show you."

The Commander barked some orders. His officers jumped to their feet, bowed quickly amid a chorus of "*Hai, Hai*" and cleared out.

"My officers will organize an exhibition game. You will see best ball players. We have another drink meantime."

Jacobson noted that the Commander's English deteriorated in direct proportion to the amount of *brännvin* and brandy consumed. A few more drinks and Jacobson would have to learn Japanese if he wanted to communicate.

It seemed only a few minutes before one of the officers returned to report the team was ready. They set off for a large barn at the edge of the camp.

"It too much snow to pray outside. We pray in indoor stadium." The commander laughed hilariously. His officers joined in.

Inside the barn, something that could best be described as half a diamond had been set up. There was a pitcher's mound, home plate, first base, and second base near the far wall of the barn. A shortstop was positioned at about a 30 degree angle from the plate, to the pitcher's right.

"This indoor stadium designed special for Swedish Winter practice," the Commander said. "We move horses out, we move Sharks in." He found this hilarious. His officers did too.

Jacobson sniffed the air and guessed, correctly, that it had been, or perhaps still was, used as an arena for horseback exercising or dressage.

"Sharks?" he asked.

"We first name our team Horse Hitters, but Swedes cannot say it right," the Commander laughed. "So we name it after our home navy base, Yokosuka, and our new secret class submarine, Shark. We are the Yokosuka Sharks. Swedes not say that better than Horse Hitters, but we can."

The Commander roared with laughter. So did his officers.

At least I'll have something to tell those OSS clowns, thought Jacobson, and the way the Japs like the brandy, I'll be very welcome back. Say what you will about the Japs, that *sushi* is damn good—better than Mama's *gefilte* fish, although he'd never dare tell her that.

"Play ball!" the Commander ordered. Evidently the brandy had worn off a bit. He could pronounce the Ls.

The team and all spectators responded with *"Banzai! Banzai! Banzai!"*

Carl Jacobson knew what that meant. He'd seen enough war movies. He was happy his hosts weren't waving samurai swords.

The pitcher wound up in a beautiful copy of Bob Feller. A fastball. The batter hit it high against the far wall and took off for first. The shortstop caught the ball as it bounced back off the wall and threw to first. The runner slammed into the first baseman, who went down fast but stuck up a leg, tripping the runner, who slid head first toward the wall.

The players waiting to bat and field roared approval. The runner staggered to his feet, smiling broadly and wiping his sleeve on his bloody nose. Next batter was a short, broad shouldered, muscular youth.

"He lift torpedoes," the Commander explained.

The first pitch hit him square on the upper left arm. He didn't move an inch to get out of the way.

"He always say, let ball get out my way," the Commander laughed. "He always gets on first."

The next batter was as thin as the previous batter was fat.

"If we have no more torpedoes, we use him," the Commander laughed. "He fits in torpedo tube."

The batter swung and missed the first two pitches, then grounded to the shortstop, who tossed to second to set up an easy double, but the torpedoman came charging down the base line, head down. The second baseman put up a knee to nail the man, but was a second too late. The runner rammed him head-first in the gut. The second baseman dropped the ball as he released a mighty "Oooooofff" and slammed onto his back about ten feet beyond the base. The runner stood proudly on base and shouted "Safu".

Meanwhile, the thin guy slid, actually slid, into first, with spikes high, ripping the first-baseman's pants but failing to draw blood.

"This doesn't look like the kind of baseball I saw in Berlin," Jacobson said.

"Ahhh, our manager, he played pro baseball in Tokyo and had hobby in *ju-jitsu*," the Commander smiled. "He join both sports together." The Commander laughed. His men laughed. Jacobson laughed. It wouldn't be polite not to.

But the more he watched the game, the worse he felt. Those players were killing each other. And they loved it. Anything was allowed. The manager shouted orders continuously, demonstrating swings one moment and *ju-jitsu* tricks the next.

Biggest cheers went to those who did something particularly sneaky, like a runner on first standing in the way of the ball being thrown from the shortstop and jumping out of the way at the last minute. The ball would invariably slam into the first baseman's head. The other players keeled over laughing. The first baseman would shake his head to clear it, smile and bow. The runner would advance to second, and slide in, spikes high of course, even though the ball had bounced far away off the first baseman's head.

Jacobson watched inning after inning of mayhem, bloody noses, spectacular body-throws, bean-balls, tripping, elbowing, rabbit punches, spikings, and even one instance of the catcher untying the laces of a batter's shoes, causing him to trip and slide on his face into first. Of course, batters tried to swing wide so as to slam the catcher's hands. But he was fast and got hit only once. He shouted something to the manager.

"He say it nothing, only one finger broken," the Commander translated.

The pitcher alternated with sidearm pitches. He was the only pitcher Carl Jacobson had ever seen who could pitch overhand and sidearm, maintaining both speed and control. He even had one amazing sidearm pitch that started almost from the ground, almost underhand, and with startling accuracy and with so much stuff on the ball it was almost impossible to hit.

"We call that our submarine pitch," the Commander said proudly. "Specialty of the Sharks."

Jacobson realized that the Sharks had given baseball a whole new dimension. Hell, they had invented a whole new game.

He thought of the *Jumpin' Jimminy* team.

"Boy, have I got news for them," he said to himself. "*Banzai*, all right."

CHAPTER 17

❦

Jeff Cabot was strolling down Hamngatan, looking into the show windows of Nordiska Kompaniet, Stockholm's largest and most elegant department store, known simply as NK. The elaborate Christmas displays had been removed—put in storage until next year, when they would once again bedazzle and thrill kiddies as well as grown-ups.

He was on his way to a long, leisurely lunch. He carried a copy of a quite recent *Life* magazine, and he looked forward to reading it to make sure the war was still progressing despite *Jumpin' Jimminy's* being temporarily out of the fight. Jeff Cabot was usually invited to have lunch with some of the bankers in the executive dining room. Nothing as boring as dining with extremely sincere Swedish bankers, telling him over and over how much they admire America and Britain. Jeff Cabot knew very well that as recently as two years before, these same bankers were telling the same things to Germans about Germany. Today, he wanted to relax. It was late January. A very short Spring thaw in an otherwise cold as hell month.

He stopped to admire a nicely cut suit on display in a window. Two men joined him, one on either side.

"Not much of a necktie," one said.

"Shirt isn't much either," the other said.

"Am I supposed to give you gentlemen a password?" Jeff Cabot asked. "If so, I don't know it."

"That's OK, Captain, we'll excuse you. We're not formal," the first man said. "We just thought we'd buy you lunch."

Jeff Cabot knew the gentlemen. Hank and Joe. OSS. He didn't know their last names. And he wouldn't believe them if they told him. They had met with him soon after Captain Karlsson had arranged for him to work at the bank, killing time while waiting for Spring Training. They had thoroughly briefed him on documents they needed him to copy, using the tiny Minox camera they gave him. Jeff Cabot made excellent use of the camera, taking pictures of lovely Ulla almost as much as he photographed documents. Ulla dreamed of going to Hollywood. Or to Boston with Jeff Cabot. They made a handsome couple, she always said. And they did.

The three Americans walked to Riche, an elegant restaurant a few blocks down from Stureplan, in the heart of the downtown. They checked their hats and coats. The headwaiter escorted the three Americans to a quiet table in the rear. The head waiter had a half-dozen quiet tables in discrete locations set aside for the various and sundry diplomats, businessmen, politicians and spies from who knows how many different countries. They were excellent tippers, especially the Americans.

A thin, balding Swede, wearing rimless glasses, sat at a nearby table, reading *Dagens Nyheter*. Hank looked at the man and said they would move to a table near the front windows. The Swedish secret police had the waiters well trained. Every foreigner knew that certain tables were bugged. When they were directed to a certain table, especially quiet, it was bugged. And every foreigner could spot a secret police agent a mile away.

"Swedish secret police." What a misnomer. An oxymoron if ever there was one. A secret policeman could spend half an hour staring at one page of a newspaper. Now they read *Dagens Nyheter*, which had finally gotten some spine and was sharply critical of the Nazis. Or they would now be demonstrative pro-Allies and read *Göteborgs Handels-och Sjöfartstidning*, the most courageously anti-Nazi paper in Sweden. Actuallly, there only two truly courageous papers, that Göteborg paper and *Västmanlands Läns Tidning* in Västerås, about 75 miles north of Stockholm, home of the electrical power equipment giant Asea. Göteborg, the port city on the west coast was always strongly pro-British—proud to be known as "Little London" and proud that it was the only city in Sweden with an "official" English version of its name, Gothenburg.

Until recently, the secret police watchers would always be reading *Aftonbladet*, a devoted supporter of Hitler and his Nazis. The paper was owned by Torsten Kreuger, brother of Ivan Kreuger, the world-famous "Match King" of the 1920s, who killed himself when his fake bonds and international financial swindle was exposed. If the police watchers had a sense of humor, they would think that reading *Aftonbladet* would annoy the British and Americans whom they were watching. But they never thought of it. Imagination, sarcasm and satire were rare Swedish characteristics. Among Swedish police, those things were totally unknown.

The watchers neither ate nor drank. They were not the tallest trees in the Swedish forest, which was clearly evident from their close ties with the Germans during the first four years of the war. But now, at the start of 1945, most Swedes—even the dim secret police—realized the Allies would win the war soon. Only die-hard Nazis would still be convinced that Hitler had a secret weapon up his sleeve that would bring victory.

The Swedish secret sleuths had little heart in keeping an eye on Allied agents. No gain in being on the losing side. It was time to play a new role. They would start practicing the classic Spanish "playing the Swede" line: "Who us? Pro-German? We were always secretly working for the Allies."

Yeah, so totally secret nobody knew about it.

The three Americans moved to a table Hank picked out near the front of the restaurant. Four Germans had just settled down at the adjoining table. They got up and moved to a table in the rear. The thin Swede folded his newspaper and walked out. He was replaced at the table by an even thinner Swede with even less hair.

"Changing of the guard," Hank said. "This genius is a switch-hitter, a watcher in both English and German."

The headwaiter escorted two new guests to the table the Americans had left. They smiled at the skinny Swede with the newspaper, looked around the room, spotted Hank and Joe, waved, and got up and moved to the table the Germans had vacated. They shook hands with Hank and Joe, passed a few pleasantries about nothing. They were from the British Legation.

Four squat bulky men in bulky suits entered the room, looked around and took the table that the Brits had first taken. They didn't smile until they saw the Swede with the newspaper. They nodded a polite hello to him. The Swede did not look amused.

The headwaiter sighed at the musical chairs. He was used to it. He knew the Swedish secret policeman would move to a table near the Americans and Brits. He did, and folded his newspaper.

"Slim got a big problem," Hank laughed. "Don't know whether to listen to us or fetch a watcher for the our Russian Allies." He nodded across the room at the four newcomers.

"NKVD or GRU or something. Who knows?" Joe said. "Nice guys as long as you stick to drinking and saying nothing. They spend their days translating stuff from the German papers—just like some of our guys."

"Shouldn't your pal Slim be listening to the Germans?" Jeff Cabot asked.

"Don't have to," Hank said. "The Krauts don't say a word. If they want the Swedes to know something, they call their contacts to a meeting. The Swedish Navy brass are their biggest supporters. Army and Air Force are OK, mainly with us—especially the Air Force. As you know."

Joe ordered SOS to start, for all three.

"SOS—Save Our Sweden," he said, when the waiter left. "I love it."

Jeff Cabot didn't think it was particularly brilliant. He heard it every time they had lunch.

SOS did not stand for "Save Our Sweden" nor for "Shit on a Shingle", the chipped corned beef on toast breakfast classic of the American army. In Sweden, it was "Smör, Ost och Sill"—butter, cheese and pickled herring, to go with and a shot of *akvavit*. Why it was not called bread, butter, cheese and herring, since it was served with bread, was a good question, except that SOS sounded much better than BSOS. But then, *smörgåsbord* meant, literally, "butter goose table." Go figure.

Restaurants could only sell booze with food, so the food was the abundant pickled herring. So SOS was truly a rescue call. Tales were told of dishes of herring being served, left untouched, returned to the kitchen when the guest left, and served again and again, day after day, never eaten. The *akvavit* was never left untouched. With Sweden's rationing system and complicated liquor laws, no drop of booze was ever wasted.

The three Americans, within earshot of the Swedish secret policeman, avoided talk of anything important.

"You know why people tell so many ghost stories in this restaurant," said Hank asked.

"No, why?" Jess Jeff Cabot answered dutifully.

"Because there are so many spooks around."

He and Joe looked at the secret policeman who pretended not to have heard a word. He had heard the joke before. Hundreds of times.

"And you know why everyone here discusses booze so much?" Joe asked.

"No, why," Jeff Cabot answered dutifully, again.

"Because there are so many boozer spooks around."

Hank and Joe burst into a har, har, har. The secret policeman reddened slightly and was not amused. He had not touched his obligatory plate of SOS and a shot of *akvavit*.

Indeed. Booze was a popular topic of conversation. Almost as popular as girls.

The Americans in Sweden during the war, of course, had no problems getting as much liquor as they could drink. It was brought in by the courier planes from England, along with other highly essential goods for the diplomatic staff and for interned fliers. There was almost scheduled air traffic between Stockholm and airfields in northern Scotland, the closest point. The Americans mainly flew DC3s, the workhorses of the Air Corps. The Brits also flew DC3s, which they called Dakotas, as well as Mosquitoes, the DeHavilland wood-framed bombers that were much smaller, but had the advantage of being among the fastest planes in the war.

"You know," Jeff Cabot said, as he sipped his shot of O.P. Anderson, his favorite brand of *akvavit*, flavored with caraway, anise and fennel. "I've been looking at payments at the bank for trucking our stuff from Bromma airport to the warehouse. I got an idea. You guys can tell Washington to save a lot of money, a lot of aircraft, a lot of fuel, a lot of bother, by just sending over a planeload of cash every few months. We can buy anything we need in Sweden as long as we got the dollars."

"We'll tell them," said Hank.

"I'm sure they'll seriously consider it," said Joe.

"And although nobody is interested—except guys in the planes—there'd be less risk if you had fewer planes making the run between England and here," Jeff Cabot added. Some planes had been shot down over Norway, the riskiest part of the flight, but there had been less enemy action in recent months. Herr Finkelstein needed all the planes and pilots he could get to defend the Fatherland.

"I'm sure the brass never thought of that," said Hank.

"Yeah, but I know one thing they thought of," said Joe. "If you had fewer trips, you wouldn't be able to bring as many fliers home to England. You guys would be forced to stay here for the duration."

"That would be tragic," said Hank.

"Aw, c'mon. There are a lot of young replacements itching to get some of the action. We can share the glory," replied Jeff Cabot. "Here's to the heroes."

They lifted their glasses and toasted in the Swedish fashion. "*Skål!*"

Funny how fast the Yanks learned three things when they got to Sweden.

First were the two most popular Swedish curse words: *djävla* and *fan*, which weren't all that shocking, since they both mean "devil."

Second were the Swedish versions of "Hi, Gorgeous."

And third was the proper way of toasting. In Sweden, it involved a complex ritual. The American fliers insisted it was because the stuff was rationed that the drinkers had to make the most of it. Like Americans celebrating Thanksgiving.

Swedes lifted a glass to a level of two buttons down on the jacket. This was especially important for men in uniform. They would look directly into the eye of the person with whom they were toasting, and say in a very clear and formal tone, "*Skål.*" None of the glass-clinking stuff, that was for fairy Frenchmen. Holding that eye contact they would down the drink. Then the glass was returned to the second-button position. A nod, and the glass was returned to the table.

That's the short version. There was a long formal rigmarole of who toasts first, by rank or age, or who was sitting at your right or left, toasting all around the table, unless it was too large, toasting the hostess and not toasting the hostess. Amazing that anyone ever could get to eat with the never-ending "*Skål!*"

The Americans finished their SOS and ordered steak. With a fine Bordeaux wine. Here was Sweden, across the Baltic from the front in Poland and the Baltic states, a couple of miles from occupied Denmark, a neighbor to occupied Norway, the Finns had been fighting the Russians but had quit and now the Germans were fighting in Finland—and the Swedes are importing wine from France.

"Long live brave neutrality!" Joe toasted.

"I'll drink to that," said Hank.

Jeff Cabot had heard their toast many times. So did the secret police watcher. He had been on watching duty for several years and never could understand how the Allies were winning the war. The police would often discuss this.

"The Yanks, all they do is make jokes, and the Brits, all they do is talk about cricket," they would say. Indeed, although the Swedes had very early broken the German military and diplomatic codes—and probably all the Allies' codes—they had wrestled with Brits' cricket talk for a year, figuring it was a secret language. Then, they found a Swede who grew up in England. He confirmed it was indeed a secret language, understood only by Brits and native gentlemen in the British colonies.

Hank, Joe and Jeff Cabot finished their meal. Jeff had the boiled cod, said it reminded him of a dish at a favorite Boston restaurant, Durgin-Park. Jeff explained that it was often called scrod in Boston, referring to a smaller, more delicate cod.

"Hear about the California lady who visited Boston?" he asked Hank and Joe. "She got home and was asked what she did in Boston. She said, 'I got scrod.' 'Oh, so that's the past tense,' they said."

More har, har, har all around. It was the oldest joke in Boston. The secret policeman wasn't amused. He tuned in to the Brits at the other table and their talk of cricket. Oh, no, now they were on the weather. Always the weather.

"Hear about the two Swedish secret police who got caught red-handed bugging the British Naval Attaché's apartment?" Hank asked. "True story. The Naval Attaché, a good guy, got suspicious when some stuff he told a contact was used against a Swedish guy arrested for spying for the Allies. That was in late '43. They brought in a guy from England to check the apartment for bugs. Found nothing. Great expert. Then the attaché was told how the Swedish police had been caught a few years earlier using a microphone lowered down the chimney from the attic into a Brit's fireplace. Except they lowered it a few inches too far and the Brit spotted it dangling above the kindling. So the Naval Attaché used the old trick of pasting a couple almost invisible hairs across the attic door leading to his chimney flue—hairs donated by a blonde in his office—lucky the door was made of light pine."

"If it was made of curly maple, he'd have to get a brunette secretary," Joe har, har, har'd. "A really patriotic brunette."

"Anyhow," Hank continued—and he knew the secret policeman was listening, even though he had heard it many times, since Allied diplomats and operators always told the story to newcomers to embarrass listening secret cops. "Anyhow, he later saw the door had been opened—the hairs were gone. The floorboards and the cover of the chimney-sweep flue were free of dust. Obviously used often. So a week later he invited in a bunch of guests for a party. They had a fine time, and for dessert, so to speak, he gave a signal, and they all quietly sneaked up to the attic, and there sat two genius goons with headsets and wire recording equipment. The Brits laughed like hell. The cops didn't say a word. Hell, what could they say?"

The secret policeman turned red, and stared into his newspaper. Nothing makes a dumb cop madder than being caught being a dumb cop.

"Then there was a top diplomat at the Brit Legation who got tired of the secret police watching his apartment from an apartment across the street," Hank added, to rub it in. "The squarehead dicks thought they were invisible behind the curtain. So the diplomat invited the Brit Minister, the Swede Foreign Minister, and the Swede Foreign Ministry's top guy, to lunch. During drinks, he brought them all to the window, pointed across the street at the watchers' apartment and said something like, 'Your police over there keep a close eye on me—nice to be cared for, but visitors are curious why.' The Foreign Minister and his guy were duly embarrassed and the dumb cops disappeared a few days later."

Hank and Joe picked up the bill, tipped the waiter very generously, discretely passed some notes also to the headwaiter, and strolled out and across the square to Berzelii Park. The park had been set up with air raid shelters, which looked like giant concrete pipes. People were supposed to crowd in them, in the event of a raid, like Londoners sheltering in subways.

Stockholm had no subway system. So a large number of underground facilities had been carved out of the Swedish granite around the city. One whole hospital was underground. And in Klara, the heart of newspaper row, a huge multi-level underground shelter had been carved out, as if newspapermen were the nation's most vital human resource to protect. Of course, the newspapermen would insist they were. They only complained there wasn't enough room in the shelter for Tennstopet, their favorite watering hole. But if there ever were an air raid, they would never leave the bar anyhow.

In the park, standing guard above the concrete tube shelters, was a large statue of Jöns Jakob Berzelius, the Swedish chemist who discovered all kinds of stuff, including tungsten, now a very important wartime mineral used in drill bits, drills and electric light bulb elements.

"Funny thing," Hank said. "Swedes call it wolfram—the German name—while we call it tungsten, which is Swedish and is the name Berzelius gave it, means literally, heavy stone. So you get something with a Swedish name used internationally while the Swedes prefer the Kraut name. Shows you something."

"Yeah, what?" asked Jeff Cabot.

I don't know. Something about Swedes preferring German, or something," Hank said.

The park also had a statue of John Ericsson, the Swedish inventor who patented a screw propeller and designed the famous Civil War warship Monitor.

"Another funny thing," Hank said. "Ericsson over there got so seasick on his voyage to America he said he'd never cross the ocean again. He had to be dead to do it. The President—whoever it was, I forget which one—ordered his body returned to Sweden for burial, just as Ericsson wanted, aboard a U.S. battleship."

"Harrison," Joe said. "Benjamin Harrison"

"Yeah, that's it," Hank said "President Benjamin Harrison shipped Ericsson home. Can't remember anything else he ever did."

And not wanting to be one-upped on trivia, Hank added, "He was grandson of the ninth president, William Henry Harrison."

"But talking of Germans," Joe said to Jeff Cabot, which they weren't, but he was sure now that they could not be overheard in the little park, surrounded by car and truck and trolley traffic, "there's a little favor we'd appreciate your doing."

"I'm surprised," said Jeff Cabot. "Thought you'd never ask."

"A small thing," Joe said. "Just some papers at the bank."

"Hey, I'm taking pictures of everything I can," Jeff Cabot protested. "Poor Ulla is working her pretty little fingers to the bone. You think it's easy. She got to figure out which invoices are the ones we want, sneak out the papers, help me take the pictures, and then she got to sneak the papers back in. She's a very sensitive young lady. She worries."

"About what?"

"Getting caught, losing some papers, misfiling them, all kinds of things," Jeff Cabot said. "Small things worry her. Like going to jail."

"Well, if you get these new papers, you can lay off the invoices. These can be your crowning achievement as a Swedish banker."

"What papers are these? Complete drawings of the Buzz Bomb launching sites? The bank doesn't have them. I checked. You want Hitler's bank account number in Switzerland? The bank doesn't have that either. I checked that, too. You want Hitler's bank account statement from Enskilda Bank. He doesn't have one. I asked."

"Very funny, but close," Hank said. "We would like to get the records of a bunch of Hitler's guys who do have accounts at the bank."

"OK, I'll ask Wallenberg for them. He'll be delighted to hand them over," Jeff Cabot said. "You must be kidding. They'd keep that kind of information so locked up, it would be tighter than Fort Knox."

"Actually, we know exactly where it is in the bank," Joe said. "A bank employee told us a while back."

"Well, get him to get the account documents," Jeff Cabot said.

"Slight problem. He doesn't work there any more."

"Get fired? Go to jail?"

"No, but if he had a pension, he won't collect it. Poor guy met with an accident. Got hit by a car. Hit and run. There was a rumor that someone recognized the driver as one of the Gestapo goons working at the German Legation. The police called it a tragic accident, and couldn't find the driver. Or the car."

"Count me out," Jeff Cabot said. "Bad enough trying to cross the street here with the crazy left-hand driving and the steering wheel on the wrong side. At least in England, the steering wheel is on the right side. Crazy Swedes are the world's worst drivers."

"Look, Jeff, it will be one last little favor, and then you can go off to Spring Training." Joe said.

"You wouldn't want to miss Spring Training and miss the Series, would you?" Hank asked. "The team really needs you. Be a shame you'd be ordered back to England. Hear the Eighth really needs experienced pilots to teach new guys the ropes."

"That's dirty pool," Jeff Cabot said, understanding the subtle hint. Yeah, subtle like a Kraut Tiger tank. He had other words that could describe his thoughts, but he rarely cursed. He kicked at a pebble in the path as they wandered around the park. "OK. What's the deal?"

"Ahh, glad you like our offer," said Joe. "It's a piece of cake."

"I've heard that before," Jeff Cabot said. "Next, I'm going to hear the good news and the bad news."

"Since you brought it up, here's the good news," Hank said. "Our former friend, our late friend, that is, described exactly which file in which vault the Kraut accounts are kept. So you can find it easy and fast. He even described the file name: Special Foreign Corporate Executive Accounts. The Swedish file name is *Särskilda Utländska Företagsdirektörskonton*. The file cabinet is locked with a cheap key. We already made a duplicate key. The vault is open during the day. See, a piece of cake."

"What's the bad news?"

"The bad news is that the Krauts informed the bank security boss that they suspect someone was trying to get those account files," Hank said, "The security boss was insulted that a foreigner—even if he were a Kraut—was implying that the bank was not 100 percent safe and secure. We heard he even compared it to Fort Knox. Which is why the Krauts took things into their own hands and why our friend no longer works at the bank."

"Or anyplace else," added Joe, unnecessarily.

"So they have not changed any security for the files?" Jeff Cabot asked.

"Not that we know of."

"And how do you expect me to get those files?" Jeff Cabot asked. "Just walk into the vault, find the right filing cabinet, unlock it, remove the entire files, put them in my briefcase and walk out, saying thank you very much to anybody who asks?"

"Something like that," Hank said. "Except you won't be able to fit them all into your briefcase. You'll need a suitcase. A rather large suitcase. Actually, probably two."

"And how exactly do I do all that? I get pretty much a free run of the bank, and so does Ulla, but never in a vault."

"We'll let you reconnoiter—that's the military word, no? Or do you say recon in the Air Corps? Whatever it is, you look it over, do some snooping, make like Dick Tracy, and figure something. We'll do all we can. We'll supply what you need."

"OK, how about a couple of Sherman tanks?"

"Sorry, Patton needs them," Joe said. "We can get you a Colt .45, army issue, however."

"Thanks a lot," Jeff Cabot said. "Only thing that pistol would be good for would be to hammer open the lock if your keys don't work."

"C'mon, trust us," said Hank. "We ever lead you wrong? You check it all out, and let us know. Lunch a week from today. How about Opera Restaurant?"

"Might as well dine at the best places," said Jeff Cabot. "But robbing banks isn't protected by the Geneva Convention, last I looked. Prison chow in Sweden probably isn't anything to write home about."

"It's a piece of cake, we tell you," Hank said. "Just walk in and get those files. Easy. We promise."

"I got one big question," Jeff Cabot said.

"Shoot," said Hank and Joe, in chorus.

"Are you out of your fuckin' minds?"

Hank and Joe keeled over laughing.

"Oh, shit," said Jeff Cabot, who rarely cursed.

CHAPTER 18

Carl Jacobson was enjoying the quiet January days following Sweden's Christmas and New Year parties. He was enjoying his rank as *SS-Standartenführer,* the equivalent of a Colonel, which he definitely was not, and his own assignment as scout of the Japanese ball team, which he definitely was. His duties as highest ranking officer at the German internment camp were limited to stamping documents of no consequence whatsoever, but they kept the Swedish bureaucrats in charge of papers of German internees happy and the German bureaucrats in the Stockholm Legation even happier, and his office clerk most delighted. There is nothing as happy as a military clerk with papers in order.

His clerk was very proud of his rank, *Unterfeldwebel,* a staff sergeant, and even more proud of his official regimental clerk's title, in one word that consisted of at least 56 letters with umlauts sprinkled here and there and which Jacobson never could remember. The clerk was a short, chubby, highly efficient fellow, and, of course, wore thick-lens eyeglasses. He wore a medal for having been the fastest typist in an entire Luftwaffe division.

Being a clerk, like clerks in all armies, he did most of the work that his superior officers were supposed to do. Thus, he was highly appreciated and favored by Carl Jacobson, just as he was by all offers he ever worked for. Among his fellow internees, of course, his nickname was "The Ass-Kisser." It was the same nickname he had carried through his entire Luftwaffe career.

Having worked in a hotel in London for some years before the war, he spoke English very well. This was quite handy when interrogating British and American airmen who happened to be captured by his Luftwaffe outfit after bailing out over Germany. It also helped when he had any English documents to translate.

How he got to be interned in Sweden was, for him, a matter of great fortune, like hitting the winning number in the Frankfurt lottery. He was enjoying life pushing papers at an air base in northern Germany in early 1943 when his commanding officer needed a trustworthy man to take inventory of and accompany a plane-load of beer, ham, bacon, cheese, butter—ahhh, Danish butter, worth its weight in gold on the German black market—Aalborg *akvavit* and other highly-prized Danish specialties back to the base. The goods were a gift from a fellow officer and business partner stationed in Denmark. Who better to trust with this valuable load than his ass-kissing clerk, even though the clerk was afraid of flying despite being in the Luftwaffe for five years?

The clerk never made it. The transport plane got lost on its way to Denmark, missed the country completely, ran low on fuel, and landed in Sweden. The crew, including the clerk, was interned. A heaven-sent miracle for the clerk.

"If I may, sir..." the clerk hesitatingly asked Carl Jacobson one evening when he felt his commander was especially relaxed, after a particularly fine dinner, topped off with two glasses of cognac. Jacobson normally did not drink more than a glass or two of beer or wine at dinner. He knew well the American wartime warning, "Loose lips sink ships," and in his case, lips loosened with booze would sink this nice Brooklyn boy.

"Sure, what's up, Finkelstein?"

The clerk wasn't named Finkelstein, but Jacobson called every German Luftwaffe man in the camp Finkelstein. Nobody protested. If the *SS-Standartenführer*, the camp commander, calls you Finkelstein, you're Finkelstein. They all knew why. Their great Luftwaffe commander-in-chief, the nation's air hero of World War One, brave, brilliant, one of the Nazi Party's first members and Hitler's staunchest supporter, highly decorated—his fat gut almost too small to display all his medals—none other than *Reichsmarschall* Hermann Göring himself had promised *Der Führer* that his mighty, invincible Luftwaffe had undisputed and complete control of the skies of all Europe, insuring that Germany remained impregnable.

"If the British bomb Berlin, you can call me Finkelstein," Göring boasted.

Nobody ever heard *Der Führer* address Göring as Finkelstein. But his men called him many other things, far, far less complimentary. And so did the people of Berlin once the British started to bomb the city. Naturally, they called him these things in total silence. Göring and his thugs had little sense of humor.

"Yes, if I may, sir," Jacobson's clerk continued, "I have an old family friend who I have heard was recently assigned to the Legation in Stockholm, and, well, since you do visit the Legation, I would respectfully like to request, if it is no trouble, to carry greetings, perhaps a letter…."

"I'd be happy to, Finkelstein. What's his name?"

"Thank you, sir. It's a she—she is a clerk typist. We are from the same town. She was much younger than I. Perhaps now 23. Very talented. We went to the same typing school. And very pretty, at least as I remember her as a child. Very patriotic, of course."

Jacobson had never stepped foot in the German Legation. And he wasn't planning to. When he would leave the internment camp, it was ostensibly to visit the Legation, as was most appropriate for the camp's highest-ranking officer. Instead, he'd be picked up by Hank and Joe, his OSS contacts, and he would be driven to various safe houses. He'd tell them what he had learned, if anything, from the newest German internees. More and more were arriving, as the war didn't quite seem to progress as well as *Der Führer* promised. And, of course, he would bring any and all papers and documents that passed through his desk, for copying, while they talked.

They talked mainly of what's happening back home, and most important things like next season's baseball. They would enjoy a long lunch, supplied at a very high price by the Opera Restaurant in Stockholm. Jacobson would describe in detail the raw fish he'd have at the Japanese camp. His OSS handlers thought he was nuts, but didn't dare say so. He was too good at his job.

The Swedish secret police—which was so secret everyone knew it existed and most people had at least one friend working as a secret policeman—were very well aware of Jacobson's meetings with the OSS handlers and his not going to the German Legation. They couldn't really care less. For it was 1945, and if anyone thought that Germany had the slightest chance of winning the war, well, that person was a total idiot. And the Swedish secret police were not total idiots. A little slow on the uptake, perhaps, but not entirely stupid. Like all other Swedes in high position, they knew which side their bread was buttered on, so to speak. And it was, as always, the winning side.

So the secret police took note of where the German camp commander went, noted whom he met and he spent time with, wrote their reports, which were filed away somewhere where they would be lost, and it was all wisely forgotten. Nobody was going to risk his ass by informing the Germans at this point in the war.

The German spies in Stockholm were also getting less attentive to their work. They stopped checking on German military internees and instead concentrated fully on Russians. They were all busy trying to demonstrate to the Americans and the Brits that their skills would be most valuable in the future when the time came for the free, democratic world had to conquer the Godless Communists. Naturally, the free, democratic world included their Germany, under *Der Führer*.

The next time Jacobson met with his handlers, he happened to mention his clerk's family friend at the Legation. And he immediately knew he made a mistake.

"Terrific, terrific," said Joe.

"Beautiful, excellent," said Hank.

"Oh, shit," said Jacobson.

He knew that when his contacts got excited it meant they would be putting his ass on the line. The visit to the Japanese camp and spying on the Jap team, that was OK. Hell, it was great fun. But it definitely was not fun that time when the OSS guys got him into a German plane, even if it were a civilian plane, to fly from Stockholm to Malmö. That was a bit risky. Yeah, just a bit risky, like 100% risky.

"What the hell do you want me to do in that plane? Hijack the damn thing?" he had asked.

"No, just listen. The Kraut passengers are all supposed to be civilians, but two are Luftwaffe Colonels and two are Generals. Find out what they're doing. Get them to talk. They'll talk, even though you're SS—or maybe because you're SS. They're more afraid of SS than of the Russians."

So Jacobson, in his long black leather coat and his black civilian suit—beautifully cut, by the way, and Jacobson knew a well-cut suit, since half his family were in the rag trade on Seventh Avenue—and his black hat and his blonde hair and blue eyes and his official SS unexpressive face—climbed into the Junkers tri-motor at the busy Stockholm Bromma airport for his flight to Malmö, at the far south coast of Sweden.

It was 500 kilometers distance, more or less, as the crow flies, although as far as Jacobson was concerned it was now as a scare-crow flies. The Luftwaffe officers, in civilian clothes, sat near him. His OSS handlers had pointed them out to him as they waited in the airport lounge. It wasn't hard to spot them. Arrogant Kraut Luftwaffe officers in civilian clothes stood out like, well, arrogant Kraut Luftwaffe officers in civilian clothes. There were a half-dozen other passengers also in the plane.

The goofy-looking plane, with one engine in the nose and one on each wing, looked like an old Ford Tri-motor. The engines sounded awful—like they had a lot of hours on them, which they undoubtedly had. The plane's fuselage looked like it was made of corrugated sheet metal, which it was. The seats were not much better than the bucket seats on US Army DC-3s. Jacobson could see the pilot and co-pilot at the controls, going over a check-list. He looked closely, and thought he was seeing things. The pilot had only one arm and wore an eye-patch.

Jacobson wished he were back in a B-17. He couldn't believe a one-armed, one-eye guy was flying this crate. He tried to check the co-pilot, to see if he had all or most of his original parts with him. He looked OK, but he also looked as if he were at least 80 years old. The papers in his hand shook visibly. The old man had a bad case of the tremors.

Jacobson didn't look so good either.

"Nervous about flying?" a Luftwaffe officer asked, smarmy.

"Isn't everyone, these days?" Jacobson replied.

The officer didn't answer. Just smiled. It was obvious he enjoyed seeing a frightened SS officer. He knew that the German civilian airline was scraping well below the bottom of the barrel to get pilots. The Luftwaffe itself wasn't in much better shape, although you couldn't convince the crew of the *Jumpin' Jimminy* or any other airmen in the Eighth Air Force, that the Luftwaffe was anywhere near total kaput.

It wasn't easy to talk above the noise of the engines. Just as well, Jacobson thought. Good excuse for keeping my mouth shut. Just listen. And wish the flight were over. After a short while in the air, he saw the officers were studying maps. The plane was flying at a seemingly low altitude. But who the hell knew what the flight regulations were for a civilian plane from a combatant country over Sweden?

Every now and then, the officers would make a mark on a map, after nodding in agreement about something they spotted on the ground. It was quite obvious they were identifying landing sites for planes or gliders or paratroops. Or for escaping Nazi bigwigs.

When the plane landed in Malmö, some three hours later, and the passengers were squeezing toward the door, Jacobson had the foolish idea of picking up one of the officer's briefcases, which was on an empty seat. It was such a stupid idea, he couldn't help himself. Like stealing candy in Lou's corner store in Brooklyn. Lou made it a game. If the kids got away, OK, it was only penny candy. If he caught them, he gave them a dope slap: dumb kids ain't got no respect and, worse, they ain't got no talent.

Before Jacobson even realized it himself, the briefcase was under his coat, and he was off the plane and walking to a waiting OSS car beside the terminal. He heard the officers screaming at each other in the plane as they searched for the briefcase.

His flight and theft became legendary in OSS circles. At least ten agents took full credit for it and were duly decorated and promoted, even one guy who was serving in Geneva and had never stepped foot in Sweden. Jacobson got, as he would later say, *bupkes*. And heartburn.

"Oh, no, not again," he said, when his handlers were exclaiming in wonder about his newfound close friend at the German Legation.

"She's no close friend of mine," Carl Jacobson protested. "I don't know her. I don't even know if Finkelstein really knows her."

"Look, it's beautiful," Hank said. "We'll set it up. You get into the Legation. You meet the dame. Get her to help you. All you gotta do is walk out with a few papers. Just like you did on the plane. We've been trying to get our hands on some certain documents ever since we heard about them."

"How did you hear about the papers?" Jacobson asked. "I'm just curious."

"Well, to tell the truth…" Joe hesitated. "OK, to tell the truth, we had a source inside."

"So get him to get the papers."

"As I said, we had a source."

"What happened to him?"

"Well, to tell the truth…" Joe hesitated again, "To tell the truth, we don't really know. We think he retired."

"Retired? Nobody retires in Germany. The co-pilot on my plane must have been at least 100 years old. He probably taught the Red Baron to fly. The Krauts retire people when they bury them."

The agents and Jacobson discussed the idea at great length. They would work out details later, but the basic plan was simple: Jacobson would finally pay an official visit to the Legation. The diplomats would want nothing better than to be someplace else when a high-ranking SS officer appeared, and they would do their utmost to make his visit, or visits, short and sweet. He would meet the old friend of Finkelstein. It would be easy for a good-looking, high-ranking fellow like Jacobson to get her cooperate, fully and completely. Expense funds would be unlimited.

Jacobson thawed. Walking into the German Legation—which undoubtedly was guarded by tough, skilled, brave, patriotic Gestapo thugs in civilian clothes and with diplomatic status—yeah, walking into the place would be like, well, walking into a fortress guarded by tough, skilled, brave, patriotic, Gestapo thugs. Brave? Of course. Why else would they go to such great lengths—make trouble getting close relatives in high Nazi Party places to pull strings—to be able to serve in the highly dangerous, risky assignment: guarding a Legation in peaceful, neutral Sweden.

"Nah, you don't have to be afraid of those guys," Hank insisted. "There are only two dozen assigned to guard duty."

"So it boils down to this," Jacobson said. "I stroll into the German Legation."

"That's right. But you don't stroll. An *SS-Standartenführer* marches."

"OK. I march into the Legation. Nobody stops me. What about all those Swedish police and Krauts that gotta be guarding the door. Probably shaped like beer barrels. I've seen them in the movies. They don't look like Tourist Office greeters."

"You have perfectly legal documents."

"And nobody asks me any questions?"

"Right. Everyone is scared shitless of an *SS-Standartenführer* they have never heard of other than you are top guy at the camp. You outrank them all. Even the Gestapo bunch. We checked."

"I pay compliments to the Ambassador."

"He'll be away. He wouldn't want to know you anyway."

"Yeah, so who do I talk to?"

"Some nervous dinky diplomat."

"What do I tell him?"

"We'll figure that out later. Some bullshit. You'll get him to complain to the Swedes about something. The Krauts are always complaining. But you'll be there primarily to bring regards to Finkelstein's girl-friend or whatever she is."

"And I invite her to dinner."

"Or lunch. Sure. She can't say no."

"And all the while I'm watched over by a couple dozen Kraut heavies—brave warriors who've been aching for years to kill at least one Jew. Height of their career."

"Will you get it through your Aryan skull? You're an *SS-Standartenführer!* Nobody asks you questions. Nobody screws with you. You ask the questions. You do the screwing."

"Yeah, but all this is in the Kraut Legation—off limits to Swedish police—official German territory—a bit of the Third Reich—where guys have been know to vanish, disappear."

"Aw, nobody we know vanished there recently."

"Recently. Thanks. How do I get those papers you want me to walk out with?"

"You get her to help you—after you talk to her alone. We'll figure a way. You're Prince Charming."

"By the way, what's in those papers?"

"You really want to know? Really?"

"I think I should say, no, I don't want to know. OK, what's in them?"

"The complete Kraut plans for getting a bunch of top Nazis to South America or someplace, through Sweden. It got names of contacts, companies, sources of new identities—and locations of copies of all the papers and stuff."

"Cripes! They'll be keeping that in an underground vault. You gonna supply me with dynamite?"

"Actually, it's in unlocked filing cabinets. They keep only good cognac and wine in the vaults."

"If you know all this, why didn't your old contact walk out with it?"

"Problem was, he never walked out."

"Wonderful. Yeah, I just thought. Suppose there's some secret SS password or handshake. You know, like the Masons."

"Only special thing is the SS tattoo. In the armpit. We can give you one."

"The hell with a tattoo," Jacobson said. "If they ask—and I don't know how the hell they would see, unless my shirt splits when I give the *Heil*—if they ask where it is, I'll just tell them tattoos are against my religion. And if they want proof, I can show them my beautiful circumcised dick."

The agents roared laughing. Jacobson wondered about the Finkelstein friend and if she might be curious about such a dick. He figured he should be so lucky.

"I got one last question."

"OK—shoot."

"Are you out of your fuckin' minds?"

Joe and Hank thought that was even funnier than the dick.

"What's so goddamn funny," asked Carl Jacobson.

"That's exactly what Jeff Cabot asked," they said.

Jacobson didn't catch the joke. But he did start to see the bright, warm side of the project.

Finkelstein's beautiful family friend became more beautiful the more he imagined her. A *Fräulein* who could not say no. Entertainment at Berns night club, the Opera Restaurant, and other high-class places in Stockholm. Ending up for a nightcap in his room at the Grand Hotel. He wasn't prejudiced.

He could spend some evenings with an Aryan Kraut beauty, convert her into a human being, it would be his American officer's duty—for God, King and Country, or something like that, as the Brits say. The King? Sure, for the King too, great guy, but he'd do it first for President Roosevelt.

The assurance that he outranked all the Gestapo toughs in the Legation was the decisive factor. From his experience at the German internment camp, rank was not only important in the German military and bureaucracy, it was all-important. And SS rank was higher than everything—*über alles*, to put it in their charming lingo. Being an *SS-Standartenführer* meant he was a top dog, not to be questioned.

The more Jacobson thought about this new scheme, the more he liked it. A Jew making an entire Kraut Legation shit its pants. Stealing important papers from under their Aryan noses.

And the gorgeous Finkelstein friend, converted into a human being, as an enthusiastic, loving, devoted helper.

CHAPTER 19

❀

Jeff Cabot was slightly puzzled. He could wander around the bank, talk to just about everyone, even the Wallenberg brothers on special occasions when he was invited to join them for lunch in their elegant private dining room at the bank. Although that was mainly when they wanted to impress visiting American or British bankers with their close connections with the Cabot bank in Boston, where their grandfather had learned the business.

They liked to tell the story over and over. Granddad was a young naval officer serving on a merchant vessel when he took a fancy to Boston and went ashore. Boston in the mid-1800s was booming and the young Swede figured there was something there for him, too. There was: banking. He studied the business closely. He returned home a couple years later and in 1856 opened Stockholms Enskilda Bank, literally Stockholm's Private Bank. It was the first "modern" bank in Sweden. And the rest was history—Swedish banking and industrial history.

Jeff Cabot was slightly puzzled because he could wander around the bank pretty much as he wanted, he couldn't think of any good reason to go down into the basement and to the vault containing the files of the top Krauts' secret accounts. He asked Ulla, in his customary innocent fashion, a fashion that the girls in the bank found irresistible, what the floors below the ground floor contained.

"Just storage, for safe keeping," she said. "Things people don't want left at home when they go to their Summer cottages. The family silver. Good porcelain. Paintings. Rare books. All the junk that won't fit in a bank box."

"Boy, oh, boy," Jeff Cabot said. "They must have a warehouse down there."

"Oh, yes, but they also have a lot of old records, from the start of the bank, they never throw anything away, and other papers and accounts from many years ago, and some new accounts that are not touched very often. Sort of sleeping accounts."

"Must be some great historic stuff there," Jeff Cabot said, putting on the enthusiasm that Ulla found especially boyish in the American. "I wonder if there is correspondence from my great grandfather."

"Probably," Ulla said. "Let's go look."

Jeff Cabot thought it was too easy—at least so far. But better being too easy than being too hard. They went to the basement and Ulla introduced him to an elderly clerk in charge, the only clerk there, who was delighted to meet the young American. He didn't get many visitors down in his domain. He was proud of it, nicely organized, even though it looked to Jeff Cabot like a warehouse or a pawn shop, although he had never been in a pawn shop. Aisle after aisle of shelves, on which were stored neatly wrapped paintings and neatly wrapped boxes and suitcases, with heavy twine around the kraft paper wrappings. The twine was sealed with wax seals.

"Everything we accept must be sealed, for safety, to show it has not been opened," he explained.

They went to a section of the basement with musty old boxes filled with musty old records.

"Earliest are over there at the end—everything in order," the clerk said, obviously proud of the library-like filing system. "The first records, year 1857. Let's see, the Cabot bank, under C…"

He pulled out a box and there was a string-bound collection of papers. He carefully untied the bundle. The paper was in excellent condition. Old rag paper did not deteriorate like modern paper made from wood pulp. There were letters to and from Jeff Cabot's great grandfather, some were just personal greetings and others business news and gossip. Transaction accounts. Financial deals. Loans. Letters of Credit.

Jeff Cabot was not much for family history, there was too much of it, but he was fascinated with the papers. It brought his bank more alive than he had ever imagined. Here was his great grandfather helping a young Swede get started.

"This is amazing," he said, and he wasn't faking his amazement. "Our bank has nothing like this. A lot got burned in a big Boston fire in 1872."

"You should make copies—for your bank history," the clerk said, who had been working on a history of Stockholms Enskilda Bank for the past 30 years.

"Think I could? No trouble? Would I get in your way?"

"Anytime. Anytime. Be happy to have you. Gets too quiet here. Sometimes we do get professors, economists, writers, doing research."

Jeff Cabot figured he was right on the beam. But exactly how to get from 1800 banking history to 1945 Nazi bank accounts, well, he could figured that out later.

He thanked the clerk, promised to take him up on the offer of research, and continued the tour of the basement. The clerk was delighted to show the large vault containing older safety deposit boxes which were used for "long term storage" and the vault containing new records that were "not very active," as the clerk described it. The vault contained rows of steel filing cabinets. Jeff Cabot stepped in, innocent as always, and easily spotted a drawer with a label "*Särskilda Utländska Företagsdirektörskonton*"—Special Foreign Corporate Executive Accounts.

Well, now he knew where the file was. He only had to steal it. Piece of cake.

While wandering around the basement, the clerk pointing out this and that, and finally came back to where they had started, at the storage area of the large wrapped, wax-sealed suitcases and boxes and paintings.

"This is where I call in the young fellows to help," the clerk said. "Some of these are damn heavy, pardon the language. They sometimes feel as if they contain gold bars. They probably do." He thought that was funny.

"The heavy pieces we try to keep on the bottom shelves," he said. "If one of those with a complete silver serving for 24 people fell on you from one of the top shelves, it would be your Last Supper." He thought that was hilarious. More Swedish humor.

Jeff Cabot suddenly knew how he would "liberate" the Nazi documents. Indeed, a piece of cake.

CHAPTER 20

Carl Jacobson had spent the night at the Grand Hotel, which was almost just around the corner from the German Legation.

The Grand Hotel was one of the most posh in northern Europe. It faced the Royal Palace, just across the waters of Strömmen, the Stockholm waterway flowing from Lake Mälaren to the Baltic. Guests in the front rooms had as good a view as the Royal Family had in their suite in the 600-room Palace built in the late 1700s.

The hotel's dining room, also facing the water, was one of the city's most popular meeting places for Sweden's top businessmen and their foreign guests. It wasn't particularly private, but it was convenient and the food was excellent. Jacobson has enjoyed the fabulous buffet breakfast there. It confirmed his determination to become wealthy after the war by importing Swedish smoked salmon to New York. For a topping on bagels, it made New York's "nova" salmon a joke.

Carl Jacobson had taken a room at the hotel, after his train trip to Stockholm from the German internee camp. His OSS handlers wanted him to be fresh, bright and alert for his entry into the German Legation. Or, as Jacobson put it, "walking into the jaws of the Kraut lion." His handlers, Hank and Joe, got a big laugh out that.

"Yeah, you can laugh," Carl Jacobson said. "It's not you who's walking in there."

"Don't worry. We're right behind you," said Hank.

"Thanks, so far behind you're out of sight," Carl Jacobson said.

Although he had passed through Stockholm several times, meeting with Hank and Joe and other OSS agents in various safe houses in the suburbs, this was Carl Jacobson's first real visit to the Swedish capital as a tourist. Well, almost a tourist.

Every time he had met someone on official business from the German Legation, he insisted they meet at the camp or at a nearby town. The diplomats did not argue, nor did the military attachés who came down. At this point in the war, official Germans wanted to become invisible. The fewer waves made, the better. Especially when confronting the most arrogant son-of-a-bitch *SS-Standartenführer* or any other kind of SS *führer* they ever met. He could mean trouble.

Jacobson had been shown detailed photos of the area around the hotel, including some beautiful aerial shots. As a bombardier, he could easily get himself oriented, feel right at home. He walked out the hotel's front door. He wore an overcoat with fur-trimmed collar, an elegantly cut suit and a fur hat of the type all Swedish gentleman wore in Winter. His civilian clothes—internees couldn't wear uniforms outside of camp—fooled no one. He was quickly recognized as a German officer. He did not return the salute of the doorman, who wore a smart, brass-buttoned Grand Hotel uniform, but only nodded curtly.

He stood for a moment in front of the hotel, looking across the waters at the Royal Palace, the Old Town, the Parliament building, and the Royal Opera. It was almost a tradition for guests leaving the hotel to pause and admire the view. And Jacobson did agree: it was indeed beautiful in this crisp, cold January morning. Even if the huge piles of split logs stored there disturbed the view over the docks for the archipelago ferries. Wood was a prime source of heating in the unusually cold Winters that Sweden and the rest of northern Europe were suffering through in the war years. Luckily, Sweden's endless forests provided virtually unlimited supplies of wood.

Carl Jacobson studied the Royal Palace closely, looking for the windows with the curtains drawn that indicated that it was the apartment or office of Prince Eugen, an outspoken anti-Nazi. It was said that he kept the curtains drawn so he would not see the Nazi flag flying at the German Legation, which was almost directly opposite the Palace.

The Royal family was very much on the Allies' side, especially the Crown Prince, Gustaf Adolf. His first wife, who died in 1920, was English, of the titled Connaught family, and his second wife, whom he married in 1923, was Louise Mountbatten, sister of Admiral Mountbatten. You couldn't get much closer to Britain and the British Royal Family than that.

"Hey, don't get us wrong," Hank told Carl Jacobson during one of their early sessions, in what they called "basic training" for the assignment as top banana at the German internment camp. "Most Swedes are on our side."

"It's just that they didn't have the *cajones* to say so out loud, at least until recently, even with Göring to protect them," Joe added.

"You mean Finkelstein, har, har, har," Hank said, adding, "And look, don't call the Luftwaffe guys Finkelstein. They're a bit touchy."

Naturally, Carl Jacobson ignored him as soon as he learned how much the German internees feared him as the big-shot *SS-Standartenführer*. Carl Jacobson wondered if he'd meet any Finkelsteins at the Legation today.

Jacobson turned left and walked one long block, down Blasieholmsgatan, toward the National Museum, past the Royal Automobile Club and past a stately building on the corner of Hovslagargatan. He had been told that means "Blacksmith Street", or perhaps more precisely, "Horseshoer's Street". He felt he needed a horseshoe in his pocket for luck. Or for emergency brass knuckles. He would actually have preferred a .45, or more appropriate, a Luger, but Hank and Joe advised against it. Too risky. His most formidable weapons were his brains and well-practiced SS arrogance.

Carl Jacobsson walked, in what he had learned was the perfect walk of a top SS officer—in other words, as an arrogant bastard top SS officer would walk. He turned left on Hovslagargatan. Number 2 was the huge building on the right, with a little park separating it from the National Museum. The sign on the door was unnecessary. The Kraut flag, with the ugly swastika in the middle, was flying from a pole sticking out from above the door.

Two Swedish policemen stood guard on the sidewalk. The sign on the door said the Legation was open from 10 to 12:30. They must be very busy in there, Carl Jacobson thought. It was exactly 10:01 when he turned the huge door handle and swung the heavy oak door open. He had been told the guard would be in the outer entrance hall, which he was.

The guard had Gestapo written all over his red, ugly face, which was plastered to a huge head, almost shaven bald. Call central casting for a Gestapo thug, Carl Jacobson thought. The guy was huge, although obviously more blubber than muscle. The fat didn't hide the bulge of a shoulder holster under his jacket, which was a size too small.

The guard gave Carl Jacobson a dirty look, reserved for anyone who has no influence whatsoever and who would be easily cowed, and asked gruffly what he wanted. Carl Jacobson returned the look, but his was much better, his blue eyes staring into the eyes of the thug and saying almost in a shout, "You sniveling swine, I'm the most ornery *SS-Standartenführer* ever created, and you're on the way to the Russian front in five minutes and in the clothes you're wearing if you dare use that tone to me."

The guard understood Carl Jacobson's look. He had managed to avoid the Russian front—actually, he avoided any front, and every fight in his entire cop career—by understanding a certain look. He bowed and asked, "*Bitte?*" in a civil tone.

Jacobson couldn't believe his play-acting arrogance worked so well. Conning a bunch of interned army and navy and air force officers, who were delighted to be sitting out the war in Sweden, knowing nothing and questioning nothing, was one thing. But here's a Gestapo goon, in German territory, and he's pissing in his pants.

Carl Jacobson said nothing, but continued his look. He slowly opened his obviously expensive briefcase, withdrew identification papers, and an official letter requesting, politely, to see the German Minister immediately. The request was prepared by the OSS wizards. The "official" authority that signed the request was an SS organization that was so secret nobody knew it existed, which it didn't. He handed the papers to the goon.

The guard's eye's widened. He bowed even lower, and broke out what was assuredly an often-used ass-kissing smile. Jacobson continued his perfect arrogant *SS-Standartenführer* stare. Talk of call central casting, he thought. He could envision himself in front of the cameras. But, Oy! What would his mother say? A nice Jewish boy playing a Nazi!!

The guard broke Jacobson's flash reverie, saying that the Minister, von somebody, was not at the Legation, but he would get the second secretary, another von somebody.

"Second? Get me the first secretary," Carl Jacobson ordered.

"Unfortunately, sir, he's with the Minister. The second secretary is in charge."

"Disgraceful," Carl Jacobson said. "Get him."

Carl Jacobson knew full well that the Minister and his first secretary had been called back to Berlin. His OSS handlers knew where every Kraut in Sweden was. The goon directed Carl Jacobson to a waiting room off the interior entrance hall, motioned to a couch and magazines on a table and walked quickly out of the room. He was happy to get as far as possible, and as fast as possible, from this SS son-of-a-bitch.

Carl Jacobson quickly gave the room the once-over. The window was barred. He wondered if that was to prevent people from breaking in or out. Or both. That killed any hope of a fast exit, if necessary. The room was comfortably furnished, with heavy upholstered chairs and couches. He had been warned they all held microphones.

The magazines on the table were German propaganda and Swedish editions of German propaganda, including the once highly popular *Der Stürmer*, Julius Streicher's vicious anti-Semitic rag. There also copies of German military magazines. Swedish Nazis couldn't get enough of those beautiful uniforms and the action photos of brave, blond soldiers victoriously wiping out Russians and Americans and Brits and anyone else getting in their way. But the popularity of the German magazines had declined in the past few months, surprise, surprise.

On one wall was the Nazi flag. The Krauts loved that ugly flag. And on another wall was a large photo of *Der Führer* himself. Jacobson thought it was very similar to the one he gave the Japanese Commander. But this one was not signed *"Shmuck"*. But then, *Der Führer's* face is *Der Führer's* face.

Jacobson couldn't help but sing to himself the classic Donald Duck song, made popular by Spike Jones:

> *When Der Führer says, "We ist der master race,"*
> *We HEIL! (phhht!) HEIL! (phhht!) Right in Der Führer's face.*
> *Not to love Der Führer is a great disgrace,*
> *So we HEIL! (phhht!) HEIL! (phhht!) Right in Der Führer's face.*

He was giving the raspberry when the second secretary walked in, and for a minute Carl Jacobson feared he was singing out loud.

"Second Secretary von Schneider," the tall, thin man in a black suit said, bowing slightly and extending his hand. Carl Jacobson clicked his heels and gave a half-assed *Heil* salute, and shook the man's hand. He handed over his identification papers and the letter to the Minister, and said that since the Minister was not there, nor the First Secretary, then the Second Secretary could possibly be of assistance.

Jacobson said that as highest-ranking officer at the camp for German internees, he was on "official business."

"I insist that the Minister protest to the Swedish authorities that favoritism is being shown to the enemy internees," Jacobson said. "I have prepared a list of unfavorable actions and denials of travel permits. It's scandalous! Outrageous!"

"*Schändlich!*" Carl Jacobsson repeated, louder. "*Schändlich! Unverschämt!*"

He loved those words. Always got action. Especially when shouted. Actually, they were always shouted. Probably some rule in German speech.

Carl Jacobson handed the secretary an official letter that he had signed the night before in the hotel. He admired what was supposed to be his own brilliant bureaucratic language. His German professor at NYU, a Jewish refugee from the University of Heidelberg, would have been proud of him. Little did he know that the professor was doing exactly such document work in an OSS office in Britain. Perhaps he had been the one who actually prepared the document.

"I will see that the Minister attends to this immediately on his return," the second secretary said, knowing full well the Minister was making plans to get transferred as fast as possible to Brazil.

"You or someone else attend to it immediately," Carl Jacobson ordered. "Outrageous to have any delay. *Schändlich! Unverschämt!*"

Ah, those magic words. There were a lot of them in German. Especially when shouted.

"Yes, sir, immediately. Immediately."

"And now, I have a more personal request," Carl Jacobson said, showing a hint of a smile. "I want to meet *Fräulein* Schultz. She is a secretary here, I understand. She is a close family friend of my clerk…" and he almost called him Finkelstein. "They are from the same home town, and he asked me bring her his regards."

The Second Secretary was clearly relieved. The less he had to do with the SS, the less he had to do with anyone from Germany, or from anywhere else, the better he felt. His one main, patriotic duty to the Fatherland during these days of trial and sacrifice was to save his own scrawny ass.

"Of course, of course, certainly" he almost fell over himself, assuring the *SS-Standartenführer* of his usefulness. "I'll call her immediately. Immediately. An excellent secretary, a model of a German patriotic woman, superb staff member. A moment, please."

And out he scampered almost as fast as the fat Gestapo hero. Carl Jacobson started to hum again:

> *When Der Führer says, "We ist der master race,"*
> *We HEIL! (phhht!) HEIL! (phhht!) Right in Der Führer's face….*

He wondered if he'd have time to scrawl, "Greetings from *Der Shmuck*" on the portrait of Hitler, as he had written on the portrait he presented to the Japanese commander. It would be his crowning achievement. But he figured it would be pressing his luck just a wee bit too far. Instead, he thumbed through a recent copy of the Swedish edition of *Der Stürmer* and could see that the Germans were far from giving up in their propaganda war. He expected that the subscription list would be part of the documents he intended to borrow from the Legation.

He was still humming *"Der Führer's Face,"* when he was interrupted by the Second Secretary accompanied by a young lady, 25 or so, blonde, of course, hair tied in a knot, prim in a black dress and white collar. Not half-bad looking, actually darn good looking, fine shape, terrific knockers and good legs. What a waste to be a Nazi, Jacobson thought.

He introduced himself and brought the official greetings from his clerk. The girl was delighted. She explained that the last she had heard, his plane had crashed, and she feared he was killed. She said that news from home was sporadic, and she had been recently transferred to several different postings.

Carl Jacobson said that he had promised his clerk—an excellent clerk and most loyal patriot, by the way—that he would invite *Fräulein* Schultz to lunch. He knew his clerk was so fond of her and her family, and he would like to bring back any news from the hometown. The girl turned to the Second Secretary.

"Of course, of course," he said. "You may take all the time necessary. Please accompany the *Standartenführer*. It's near lunchtime. I will get you proper funding. One moment."

Carl Jacobson liked that. He would enjoy dining directly on *Der Führer*. Better than using kronor supplied by the OSS. And he had been informed by Hank and Joe that most restaurants had closed their German Legation accounts. Up until last year, the best places gladly ran a tab and sent a monthly bill, which was paid promptly with German efficiency. But being very practical Swedes, the restaurateurs now figured that the way things were going for Hitler and his gang, there was a good chance that their good old friends and customers would stiff them—and probably do so gladly because they always suspected they were over-charged. Go sue the Third Reich when it no longer exists.

He discussed restaurants with *Fräulein* Schultz. She had no favorite. She was quite new to Stockholm and dined at the Legation or in her apartment she shared with two other Legation typists.

Carl Jacobson had been advised to invite the young lady to Gondolen, the restaurant at the top of Katarinahissen, the elevator connecting two levels of Söder at the busy Slussen traffic roundabout. The restaurant offered the finest view of heart of Stockholm. It overlooked the Old Town, the city center, the docks, and the waterways that gave Stockholm the nickname "Venice of the North." To the east, one could view the beginning of the Stockholm archipelago.

Gondolen—the Gondola—was popular with tourists, mostly Swedish these days, and with resident foreigners. This meant Carl Jacobson and his luncheon date would fit in nicely.

The Second Secretary returned and handed a fat envelope to Carl Jacobson, who put into his briefcase without checking the contents. Probably counterfeit kronor, he thought. *Fräulein* Schultz excused herself to clear her desk and get her coat. The Second Secretary excused himself, hoping he'd never see the goddamn arrogant *SS-Standartenführer* again. But maybe *Fräulein* Schultz would soften him a bit. She was smiling brightly as she returned to the waiting room and to the waiting Carl Jacobson. The burly doorman goon clicked his heels, bowed, and smiled as he opened the front door.

"Goddamn arrogant SS bastard," the. goon thought, adding, "But good that such shits are on our side."

CHAPTER 21

As scheduled, Jeff Cabot met with his OSS pals at Operakällaren—literally, The Opera Cellar—the restaurant at the rear of the Royal Opera House. They chose the terrace, overlooking Kungsträdgården, a Royal park in the heart of the city. Across the park, almost opposite, they could see the bank.

Operakällaren, like every elegant restaurant in Stockholm, was well equipped by the Swedish secret police for keeping an eye on foreigners and foreign agents. Everyone knew that some tables were bugged. And everyone recognized the secret police watchers. So anyone with anything truly secret to talk about didn't talk about anything truly secret. It became a nuisance, but what the hell, the food was excellent.

The three Americans ordered the usual SOS, with O.P. Anderson, their favorite *akvavit*. Hank and Joe ordered broiled steaks. Sweden had discovered broiling during the war, as part of a national campaign to save fuel. It took far less heat to quickly broil steaks than to give meat the traditional hours-long Swedish oven roasting or stove-top simmering of stews. Some genius designed a stove-top broiler for home use. A housewife would place it right over the gas flames. Probably gave a coal-gas taste, but Swedes didn't know what good charcoal or hardwood broiling was anyhow. So they enjoyed the coal-gas. Restaurants installed large commercial size broilers.

Jeff Cabot ordered his favorite lunch dish—one of Operakällaren's classics—*pytt i panna*. It reminded Jeff of corned beef hash, also a classic at Durgin-Park in Boston, but hardly anything his elegant ultra-Yankee mother would ever serve at their Louisburg Square home or at their "cottage" on Cape Cod. Yeah, cottage: 25 rooms plus two smaller cottages for guests and three even smaller for staff. Jeff Cabot often wondered if his mother had ever eaten with the staff. Probably not.

He often thought of his home and his life in Boston when he was at Operakällaren. The restaurant's beautifully polished oak paneling, the oak furniture, the glistening crystal, the elderly waiters, all could have been transferred to Boston and plunked down in any one of several private clubs.

Big difference, however, was that the Operakällaren waiters probably earned more than the old waiters at the Boston clubs—since the clubs were run by tight-fisted old Yankees who were known to carefully count their grocery bills to see that they had not been charged one penny too much. Heaven help the shop if they were!

Another thing completely different from Boston clubs were the murals on the upper walls of the Operakällaren main dining room. They were done by Vicke Andrén, one of Sweden's most respected artists when the Opera House and restaurant were built. They showed wonderfully naked ladies frolicking in gardens *"al fresco"*, enjoying life to the fullest, just as guests in the restaurant should enjoy life, although probably not naked.

The King himself, Oscar II, a great gourmet—as was clearly evident from his tremendous girth—inaugurated the restaurant when it opened in 1895. The new Operakällaren replaced the one built in 1787 that was part of the original Royal Opera House, the one where the world-famous "Masked Ball" took place. That is, the original "Masked Ball, the one in which the King played a lead role by being fatally wounded by an assassin.

Oscar II wasn't superstitious about attending operas—although no Swedish King felt comfortable at any performance of "A Masked Ball", even though Guiseppi Verdi was forced to make his opera politically palpable so as not to give any revolutionaries any bright ideas about knocking off kings or lesser royalty.

So for the premier in 1859, Verdi and his lyricist Antonio Somma made Stockholm into Boston and the unfortunate fun-loving Swedish King Gustaf III into a Massachusetts Colonial Governor. No Massachusetts Governor, Colonial or elected, has ever been assassinated. Ever since the American Revolution, revolutionaries in the Bay State prefer packing ballot boxes as a friendlier simpler way to grab power.

Oscar II damn near pissed his super-sized royal pants when he saw the naked ladies. Shocked? He sputtered and harrumphed, his fat jowls shook and his face turned royal purple! Who would have known the King would be such a stuffed shirt, such a prude? Probably because he was such a man-about-town in his younger days. Nobody is ever as utterly boring as a reformed swinger.

The King demanded that the young ladies be clothed. However, a compromise was reached, and the insulted artist agreed to add a few branches and greenery to hide some of the more exposed parts of the lovely ladies' delicious bodies.

"In Boston, any artist would have known better to begin with," Jeff Cabot said when he heard the story. "Although there's a wonderful painting of a naked lady—we call her Mademoiselle Yvonne—in the main dining room at Locke-Ober Cafe. Everyone toasts to her, and she's toasting back. But, of course, it's men only in that dining room."

The Operakällaren *pytt i panna* was known as the best in Sweden, although each cook had his or her own recipe twists.

"It should be the best in Sweden, we've been making it long enough," the chef explained to Jeff Cabot the first time he tried it. Jeff Cabot had gone into the kitchen to ask for the recipe. He wanted to bring it back to Boston and the chef at his Union Club dining room. Locke-Ober had its own hash, and nothing ever changed at Locke-Ober since it was expanded to its present elegance in the late 1870s.

And Durgin-Park would throw him out if he suggested it. They had been serving Yankee food since 1826, and they didn't need any newfangled foreign Swede stuff, especially since *pytt i panna* depended on left-over meat and nobody dared leave left-overs at Durgin-Park. The waitresses saw to that. They were as tough on customers who didn't finish everything as any Irish mother would be who remembered the famine. And most of them were, or at least had close kin who remembered it.

Operakällaren did not use left-over meat, but trimmings and pieces of the best quality boiled beef, salt beef, veal or pork, plus the essential ingredient, *Falukorv*, the tasteless sausage that was the town of Falun's contribution to the gourmet world. Ed Kowalski, back at the internment camp, was trying to cure that failing by teaching Falun sausage makers how to make *kielbasa*, which the was the greatest favor anyone had done to Swedish cooking since a Frenchman opened restaurant Cattelin in Old Town.

Cattelin was the favorite gathering place of Continental émigrés. If a Nazi—a real one from the German Legation or a sympathizer from Sweden or anywhere—walked in, most customers walked out, taking with them, of course, any uneaten food in brown paper bags. And, of course, after quickly downing any snaps, with a toast that could be roughly translated as "Up yours, Nazi scum."

Jeff Cabot took down the Operakällaren chef's recipe as best he could. It wouldn't make the Fanny Farmer Cookbook, but it would have to do:

"Dice potatoes, twice as much as the meat. Fry them until brown outside, just right cooked inside. Add finely diced onions, about one quarter of the amount of meat. Dice sausage. Fry with diced meat, until meat is just a wee bit crunchy, but not dry. Serve topped with raw egg yoke, or a fried egg. Salt and pepper. Splash with Worcestershire sauce or ketchup or both. As a classic side dish: boiled beets, pickles."

Simple, but it was the greatest dish that Jeff Cabot had ever enjoyed, for lunch, or for a very late treat to top off a long evening of imbibing. Okay, so it was the greatest dish he ever had in Sweden.

"However," the chef said. "You can really make it with any meat and any sausage and in any proportions that you like. Very democratic dish. In America, you will probably cut up filet mignon and mix with hot dogs." He thought that was hilarious. Swedish humor.

Jeff Cabot had beer with his lunch. It went best with *pytt i panna*, although Swedish beer left much to be desired in Jeff Cabot's taste. He preferred Pickwick Ale, a New England favorite. Hank and Joe sipped their O.P. Anderson. Naturally, they didn't talk "business" while in the dining room. After paying the bill and leaving the regular huge tip—oh, how the waiters loved the Yanks, especially the spies—the three walked out and strolled over to the statue of King Charles XII, at the end of Kungsträdgården.

"They call him *Kalle Dussin*—Charlie Dozen," Hank explained. Hank was a bottomless well of Stockholm trivia, some of it true. "Charlie's pointing at Russia, he's still mad as hell. Got his ass beat there—like Napoleon and Hitler and every other brilliant warrior."

"I never could figure out why he's pointing, like giving directions," Joe said. "They should have made the statue with Charlie giving the Russians the middle-finger salute."

"Nah, that would have made the Russians only madder. He's pointing, saying, 'Holy shit! They're a'comin' from thata'way!'"

"Then they should have turned the statue 45 degrees, so he's pointing south, at Germany," Joe said.

"Are you nuts? That would have upset Hitler. Be like teasing a mad dog. The Swedes aren't stupid. Although now they can be brave and give Hitler the finger. But not the Russians. They're scared of them, as usual."

"Yeah, but not so scared they aren't figuring on big business with them after the war," said Joe. "That guy Myrdal—he's the expert who knows all about how America should treat Negroes—he heads post-war planning. He's working up a trade agreement. The whiz-kid thinks there's big money to be made with the Commies. He's certain America is in for a huge depression. Boy, is Sweden in trouble with business geniuses like him."

"Fuck 'em," said Hank, which was his usual succinct way of summarizing his conclusions.

Jeff Cabot was always fascinated with the deep geopolitical and world economy discussions of Hank and Joe. His professors at Harvard would not have been fascinated, or amused. They would be flabbergasted. But at least the OSS guys were fighting on the right side, even if their views of history and politics were rather down to earth, to put it politely. The three Americans strolled to the walkway alongside Strömmen, the main waterway running through Stockholm city.

It was too cold and too early for fishing. In the Spring and through December, you could fish for salmon there. Queen Christina, before she abdicated in 1654 and left for Rome, had ruled that fishing was free for all Stockholmers. If she hadn't converted to Catholicism, Swedish fishermen would have probably erected a statue to her. As it was, they'd have to remember her as Greta Garbo in a classic silent Swedish film. The Queen should only have been so beautiful.

Jeff Cabot told the OSS men of his new pastime at the bank: in the basement, digging into the 1800s files for material about his great grandfather's dealings with the Wallenbergs. He explained how this put him near the storage vaults and the safe storage shelving for boxes, suitcases and paintings—all wrapped in brown kraft paper and tied with cord and wax-sealed. He had seen the filing cabinet containing the Nazi accounts.

"And gentlemen, I have the perfect plan for borrowing the Nazi files," he said proudly. "And I won't need Patton's tanks."

"Thank the Lord," said Hank. "We asked him for a few, but got turned down."

"You should have mentioned my name," Jeff Cabot said. "His wife's from Boston, you know. I believe he is one of our clients. But not for insurance. Lousy risk."

"OK, how much will it cost?" Joe asked. "Who do we have to pay off?"

"Or do we drill? We might be able to drill a tunnel from the basement of the synagogue across the side street of the bank," Hank said. "We couldn't work on Saturdays, though. Sundays would be OK. Har, har, har."

"You know, you two could work up a comedy act," Jeff Cabot said. "I could book you at the Old Howard. Between a couple of strippers. How about Sally Keith and Dixie Evans?"

"Hey, is it true Sally Keith can twirl those tassels in opposite directions?" Joe asked.

"Sure is. Saw them many times," Jeff Cabot said proudly.

"What are you talking about?" Hank asked. It was the first time he didn't know something about everything. Every soldier, sailor, flier, hell, every man who ever walked the earth in Boston knew about the famous burlesque theater just off Scollay Square, the Old Howard, and its even more famous strippers.

"Sally Keith is world famous," Jeff Cabot explained. "She strips and reveals a tassel on each boob. Then she gets dancing and can make one boob's tassel spin one way and the other the other way. Like twin props, but spinning in opposite directions."

"Impossible! You saw this?"

"Sure. We'd cut high school classes to go to the Old Howard. We called it studying thermodynamics."

"Thermodynamics?"

"Yeah, we were thermal and Sally was dynamic. Har, har, har." It was Jeff Cabot's turn at the big guffaw.

"I'll be damned," Hank said. "You gotta take me there after the war. This I gotta see."

"If this war keeps on, Sally will be retired by time we get home," Joe said. "Her tassels will be in the Boston Museum of Fine Arts."

"Nah, the war'll end soon. The Captain here got a brilliant idea," Hank said. "OK, what's the plan? Dazzle the bankers with strippers? And while they're watching those spinnin' tassels, you steal the files?"

"Almost. You simply walk out with the files in two large sealed suitcases," Jeff Cabot said. "Piece of cake."

As they strolled across Riksbron, the bridge leading to the Parliament House, he explained his idea in detail.

"Every day or so, someone checks in a box or suitcase for safe storage in the vault area," he said. "And every day or so, someone else checks out something. Some of the boxes or suitcases are heavy as hell. Loaded with the family silver or gold bars or who knows what. Now, I work down there on a desk the security vault clerk has set up for me. He's a bank history buff. Helpful, friendly guy. Gets lonely all alone down there. He's in his 60s, so I help him haul the heavy stuff. He's glad to have an extra hand, doesn't have to wait for some lazy young guy to finally agree to get off his tail and come down from upstairs.

"So what we do is have someone, one of your guys, check in two very large suitcases. They gotta be wrapped in heavy paper, and sealed, with those wax seal things on the heavy cord around the cases. This is to guarantee they're not opened. However, you get someone to make them so I can open them up fast and easy, remove the papers inside, and replace the paper with the Nazi files."

"And we call for the suitcases in a week, and we walk out with the files," Hank said, picking up fast. "Sounds too easy. There gotta be a catch."

"The only catch I can think of is getting the files back," Jeff Cabot said. "If I don't get caught stealing the files, I'm batting 1000. That's perfect. That's enough. Trying to put the files back is doubling the risk."

"Who said anything about putting the files back?" Joe asked. "We replace the accounts with blank paper. Or telephone books. Or Life magazines. Or dirty French postcards. Anyhow, who cares? The bank sure as hell keeps duplicates."

"They don't, believe it or not," said Jeff Cabot. "I checked. I double-checked. I couldn't believe it myself. I assume the Nazi account holders have their own copies. Well hidden someplace."

"Well, screw the bank," said Hank. "That's their headache. They shouldn't have been playing footsie with the Nazis anyhow. Fuck 'em."

"We can do it, but I want to get the clerk out of there," Jeff Cabot said. "Poor bastard would be fired, humiliated, probably go to jail. The Swedes have no sense of humor, especially when it comes to stealing from a bank. Worse than murder. He's an old bachelor. We got to get him an official invitation, a Sabbatical or something to the States. He could work in our bank. Doing research on a history of the founding of the Wallenberg bank. Or something like that. He'd accept in a minute. But he gotta get out before they discover the files missing."

"They won't be missing. Just replaced with blank paper," Hank said. "Magic. All the printing simply vanished. Let the Krauts sue the bank. Har, har, har."

"And don't worry. We'll get your guy to Boston," Joe added. "That's the easy part."

"What's the hard part? My going to jail when they catch me stealing the files?" Jeff Cabot asked.

"No, they won't catch you if the place is as open as you say and you got the run of it," Hank said. "The hard part is making a suitcase that looks perfectly sealed but that you can open fast and easy. But we just happen to know some guys who are real craftsmen."

"You'll get your suitcases checked into the secure vault at the bank in a week," Joe said. "We'll show you how to open and close them fast. They'll be heavy as hell. We'll set it all up. Piece of cake."

Jeff Cabot certainly hoped so. But he started to wonder if it was such a brilliant idea after all. It sounded too easy.

CHAPTER 22

Carl Jacobson and Lili Schultz took the elevator to the top of Katarinahissen, and strolled into Gondolen Restaurant. The headwaiter immediately recognized them as Germans. Well, at least the tall blond blue-eyed guy in a black leather full length coat was easy to spot. The woman could have been a Swede, except she had a certain haughty air. He guessed they were with some German official office.

The headwaiter knew his Germans. He was a refugee from Czechoslovakia. Gondolen was owned by the Consumer Cooperative Federation, which had close ties to the Social Democratic Party and the trade unions. The Co-op had given a lot of jobs to anti-Nazi refugees.

Carl Jacobson spoke English to the headwaiter and politely asked for a quiet table. The headwaiter looked puzzled. He would have bet anything they were Germans. But who knows, times being what they were and Stockholm being full of strange people from all over.

Carl Jacobson and Lili Schultz were seated at a window looking west over the Old Town and the city. They ordered SOS. What the hell, when in Rome do as the Romans and when in Stockholm do as the Swedes. Naturally, they had to wait a short while to be served their *akvavit*. No booze before noon in Sweden. You could tell 12 noon exactly by the waiters rushing into a dining room with trays of shot glasses.

"You speak English well," Lili said.

"I try to practice. And one does get better service these days in Sweden when you speak English," Jacobson said. "A short while ago, it was just the opposite."

They talked, or rather Jacobson encouraged Lili to do most of the talking. He said his clerk was most anxious to hear of news from the hometown. She spoke of the old days, and of their families, and of how the town was so small it was not bombed.

She then went on about the British and American bombing of Berlin and Hamburg and other large cities.

"Terrible, frightful, horrid, inhumane," she said. "Our Luftwaffe only bombed military targets, never civilian. Never. Never."

Carl Jacobson didn't argue. Why mention Coventry? Or the devastation of working class districts of London? Or the Buzz Bombs? Plenty of time for education later.

"If I remember correctly, Marshal Göring said that if the Allies ever bombed Berlin, then you could call him Finkelstein," he said quietly. "I have been away from Germany for some time. Do many people call him Finkelstein?"

Lili's eyes opened wide. She was in total shock. She couldn't utter a word.

"Come, come, my dear," smiled Carl Jacobson. "I was only joking. We must be able to laugh a little to carry us through these dark days."

Lili relaxed. She smiled a wee smile. She said nothing but Carl Jacobson knew that the smile meant that a helluva lot of Krauts were calling Göring "Finkelstein"—but wisely, never out loud.

After that, the ice broke somewhat. The *akvavit* helped. Lili said she would write all the news to Carl Jacobson's clerk. Carl Jacobson said he would order that be it be sent in the regular pouch from the Legation to the internment camp, so there would be no delays. And he said he'd certainly arrange passes for his clerk to visit Stockholm and spend time with Lili. She was delighted.

They discussed Stockholm, and Springtime, which seemed so far away. Sweden was at its very best in the Spring. They talked of sports and the theater and movies, although Jacobson admitted his knowledge was limited when it came to the latter.

Lili told him of a young Swedish film and theater director—"a very good friend of Germany"—whose work she was convinced would become world famous.

"And he has not deserted us in these trying times," she said. "He is full of enthusiasm and is certain our brave armies under *Der Führer* will achieve final victory. He knows all modern film techniques and told us at one reception that the Russian films about what has happened in Poland and Russia—all those films about horrible camps—are definitely false. Pure theatre. Staged propaganda. He knows how to make such films. It's all make-believe. Terrible lies."

"Really?" asked Carl Jacobson, thinking how this dame sounds like she's reading from a Goebbels script. But come to think of it, the Krauts have heard that crap so long and so often they can't help but have it memorized. Most of them talk the same way.

So instead of saying what he though, which was, "Lady, you are full of, well, baloney," he said, "Fascinating. That director could be a valuable Swede to know."

"His family is even more valuable," Lili said. "They are respected leaders in the Swedish National Socialist Party. Oh, there are many others. Good friends, faithful supporters."

Carl Jacobson said he was impressed with her knowledge of important friends in Sweden.

"It's only that I was in charge of typing and organizing some lists," she said. "Boring work actually. But necessary. As you know, we plan for all eventualities—even the most unlikely. But I'm not doing that work any longer. Thank goodness. Typing and retyping names and addresses and details. It's out of the Legation's hands now."

"Actually, I've heard of a file. I think it's one of my assignments. Your old friend, my clerk, may have told me of it. I hate bookkeeping and records and papers, papers, papers,—as he well knows," Jacobson smiled. "Don't know what I'd do without him. The file I heard of, it lists friends and locations in Sweden that could be useful to assist some of our people to get—how do you express it?—established, yes, established, elsewhere. Just in case. To continue our cause, of course."

"That's precisely it," she said. "Supposed to be secret but everyone in the Legation knows about the *Sehr Guter Schwedischer Freund* file. We don't have it any longer. We transferred it all to the *Kultur* Section. The *Kultur* Attaché is responsible."

"That's it, the Very Good Swedish Friends file," Jacobson said. "And it's at the *Kultur* Attaché's office. That's the office on, on—what is the street? I never remember Swedish street names."

Lili laughed. "That one's easy. Kaptensgatan 6. They have streets named after every rank—except private and corporal. But then, I doubt if there is a Corporal Street in Berlin."

She put a hand over her mouth and widened her eyes, as if she had said a dirty word, which she almost had. The *akvavit* had done the trick. Evidently she was not used to hard liquor with lunch. Being an unmarried girl, she got no Swedish alcohol ration. And at Legation parties, she was extremely careful not to drink.

Carl Jacobson laughed and laughed.

"Kaptensgatan 6. Of course. It's been a long time since I was a captain. And a long time since *Der Führer* was a corporal. I wonder if we still have Paper-hanger's Street in Berlin? Maybe it has been renamed Schickelgruber Street."

Lili giggled. She couldn't remember anyone ever making jokes about *Der Führer's* old trade and his original family name.

"We have the Information Section and the Press Section in the same building as the *Kultur* Section," she said, getting back to the original subject, and worried that perhaps she should not laugh at such unpatriotic jokes, even if told by an SS officer. "But I guess you have nothing to do with them."

"Oh, sometimes they arrange for German reporters to visit our camp. But I don't think they write anything," Jacobson said. "We live very well. A story about us would be discouraging for our brave troops, especially those on the Russian front. Maybe give some of the weaker ones ideas—although it's not easy to get to Sweden."

"And how did you end up in Sweden?" Lili asked innocently.

"Very long, boring, story. In a transport plane, and no fighter cover by—what was the name?—Finkelstein, yes, Finkelstein's invincible Luftwaffe."

This time, Lili laughed and couldn't stop. It was undoubtedly a laugh that had been begging for release for years. The *akvavit* was great medicine.

They had drawn out the lunch for over two hours. Carl Jacobson paid the bill and left an extremely generous tip. He could be the big shot with the Legation money. They walked back to the Legation. Carl Jacobson said he hoped he could see her again. Lili said she hoped so. They shook hands at the door. The same burly goon opened it. Lili saw him and turned back to Jacobson. She made a face imitating the goon and smiled. Carl Jacobson understood.

"She's a Kraut, a bit of a Nazi, but curable, and she got great legs," he thought as he walked back to the Grand Hotel.

The next day he met with Hank and Joe in a safe house. He told them of his visit to the Legation and the lunch and the talk with Lili.

"So the damn list is with the *Kultur* Attaché," Hank said.

"You know any girls there I can take to lunch?" Jacobson asked. "Although Lili isn't half bad. For a Kraut Nazi."

"Wait a second, wait a second," said Joe. "I got it. We just demand a copy."

"Could work," said Hank. "We write out an order from whoever, saying a copy must be turned over to our SS Colonel. How could they refuse?"

"Easy," said Carl Jacobson. "Just say no. They gotta ask Berlin first."

"Look, you told us they were scared shitless at the Legation. They want nothing whatsoever to do with the SS. We know the *Kultur* Attaché. A fag. Goes to the theater and museums and tries to impress dumb Swedes that Germany is a *kulturnation*. A Nation of Culture. Yeah, sure."

"He'll piss his pants if he gets an order from the SS," Joe said. "I'd love to see it."

"You'd love to see it? So you go," said Jacobson.

Hank and Joe roared with laughter.

"I would, but they know us. We have lunch together. Like the other day at Riche. Your buddy Jeff Cabot was there. Well, we didn't really have lunch with the Krauts. Just across the room. Drove the Swedish secret police watcher nuts."

"What's Jeff up to?" Carl Jacobson asked.

"Oh, just screwing around the bank waiting for Spring Training."

"I can't wait either. Although I'll miss ordering the Krauts around."

"Well, you can give one last big order. At the *Kultur* Section, "Hank said. "We'll get the proper orders for you. Direct from your headquarters in Berlin. All perfectly kosher. Har, har, har."

"We'll even put on that little U-stamp—the official kosher mark you get on Maneschewitz wine," Joe added. "Signed by the chief rabbi of New York. Har, har, har."

"You guys ever think of trying out for show business?" Jacobson asked. "Broadway needs your talent."

"Where do you think they recruited us?" Hank asked, adding the inevitable, "Har, har, har."

"Actually, it was Hollywood," Joe corrected.

Jacobson believed it. Only Broadway hustlers or Hollywood producers could pull off some of the goofy things these guys dreamed up. When Hank and Joe lit up cigars, he could picture them strolling down Broadway after a lunch at Lindy's.

They promised Jacobson that they'd have the official requisition in a week.

Actually, it was ready in five days.

CHAPTER 23

Jeff Cabot spent evenings with Ulla at his small apartment and days with Ulla at his cavernous "research library", as they called the basement storage and safe deposit area of Stockholms Enskilda Bank. He got thoroughly interested in early correspondence between the bank—often by the Wallenberg owners themselves—and his family's bank in Boston—usually by his great grandfather and his grandfather and even his own father. Most was straightforward banking business: letters of credit, payment orders, deposits, transfers and letters of introduction, which were often the most important part of doing business. He even found personal notes of congratulations on marriages and births and letters of condolence on deaths. And even some Christmas cards. Ulla helped with translation when necessary.

He started to think that it all could be made into a short book. Privately printed in limited numbers for the Cabot and Wallenberg families and their very close associates and friends.

But at the same time, he was busy keeping a close eye on procedures of the safe storage facilities. After all, that was his main assignment and he'd have to get it done before Spring Training started in just a month or so.

He helped the chief clerk as much as possible. After getting to know the young American Air Corps officer and banker, the clerk opened up. Like the usual description of a Swede: a ketchup bottle. You gotta shake and shake and get the first spoonfuls out and finally you'll get it flowing nicely.

As agreed with Hank and Joe, Jeff Cabot brought up possibilities of a "Sabbatical Scholarship" in Boston to study bank history, or whatever the clerk would like. The clerk was clearly fascinated with the prospect. After all, the Wallenberg who founded Stockholms Enskilda Bank got its inspiration in Boston. He had hoped for such a study trip years ago, but the war halted all such dreams.

Jeff Cabot wanted the gentleman out of blame's way when the heist—no, it was never called that—when the "liberation" was made. The liberation of some bank papers in exchange for some blank papers.

The vault containing the filing cabinet that contained the *Särskilda Utländska Företagsdirektörskonton* was used quite regularly by clerks and tellers coming down for documents. The chief clerk always kept an eye on what was going on. However, as expected, the filing drawer of the *Särskilda Utländska Företagsdirektörskonton* was never touched. Evidently, the Nazi bigwigs had either run out of money to deposit or they had run out of time or they had simply run. Off to Switzerland or Spain, obviously for their health. They were counting on the honest Swedes to keep their money safe until needed.

Two weeks after their last meeting, Jeff Cabot got a phone call at his apartment. Naturally it interrupted a serious discussion with Ulla, a discussion of art and philosophy. Yeah, sure.

It was Hank. There was no need for secrecy. The Swedes and the Krauts knew who Hank and Joe were and they knew who Jeff Cabot was and they knew that they would meet regularly. They didn't know why, of course. Hank talked about having lunch the following week, and they discussed baseball. They figured the lines were tapped by someone. Hank razzed Jeff Cabot about the Red Sox's chances in the upcoming season, and said, "Yeah, if tomorrow Hell freezes over, that's when the Sox will win a Series."

That was the pre-arranged signal. The special suitcases designed for "liberating" the Nazi bank accounts would be delivered tomorrow.

"Yeah, and if Hell freezes over tomorrow, that's where the Yankees will be playing," Jeff said, acknowledging the signal. It was simple, but, like signs and signals in a baseball, it had to be simple. Get signals too complicated and nobody remembers what the hell they mean.

They chatted baseball inanities some more, totally boring any possible listeners on the line, and agreed to meet the following week. Then, it was time to continue the discussion with Ulla. It would now turn to literature. Yeah, sure.

The suitcases arrived at noon, when most staff were at lunch. Jeff Cabot didn't see who deposited the suitcases with the boss of the safety deposit department. An assistant, a pretty young thing in the main floor, called down to the vault for someone to carry them down. All the young fellows were at lunch. She said they were too heavy for her. Jeff Cabot volunteered to assist.

"Good Lord," he said as he lifted them. "What do they have in these? Gold bars?"

"Probably," said the pretty young thing, laughing.

Jeff Cabot knew better. The suitcases were packed with plain typing paper in standard Swedish files designed for the standard steel filing cabinets in the vault. He carried the suitcases to the elevator, and down to the storage room. By this time, he knew where the suitcases should be stored. Each was labeled with a registration number.

Hank and Joe had shown the suitcases to him a week earlier, when they met at a safe house. They taught him how they could be opened by pressing a button concealed under the wrapping paper at the top. This released one end, which could be slid open, almost like a Chinese puzzle box. The wrapping paper and the twine with wax seals were not disturbed. The files inside could be easily removed and new files put in. Jeff Cabot practiced for an hour: unlocking the end, opening the end, removing the files, replacing files, closing and locking the end. It all worked perfectly.

The trick now was to carry out the "liberation." This required getting the vault all to himself.

"No trouble at all," Hank had told him. "We kill two birds with one stone. We get your pal to come up to the Consulate to pick up his visa for his Sabbatical Stipendium or Scholarship or whatever the hell it is. Tell us the time when it's quiet in the storage area."

"What about Ulla?"

"Tell her to watch the front entry."

"She'll wonder what's up."

"You mean to tell me she doesn't know what's going on?" Hank asked.

"Not this stuff," Jeff Cabot said. "Sure, she used to get me some of the Kraut bank business papers, export, import stuff, but that junk wasn't all that secret. Damn stuff was lying around all over the place. Anyone could pick it up. Bank secrecy, my foot. But stealing bank accounts, even if they are Nazi, that's a horse of a different color. A color like jail and throw away the key."

"OK, send her along with your guy to the Consulate," Hank said. "She can help with any translation."

"Yeah, tell her some papers might be better typed out and they can do it right there," Joe added.

It sounded OK to Jeff Cabot. Maybe he could also finagle a visa and scholarship for Ulla, too. Of course, the family in Boston and all their Proper Bostonian pals would be shocked. At least he could bring home an English lady, from a fine family. But a Swede? Well, really! Although they do have Swedish Royalty. Jeff Cabot wondered if he could organize a title for Ulla. Every chinless wonder he met at the bank had some kind of title. Counts and No-Counts, he called them.

The Consulate visit was organized, the chief clerk was beside himself with excitement, and Ulla was delighted to go along. Jeff Cabot said he'd stay in the basement and continue working. He had just come across some fascinating documents dealing with Civil War transactions. John Ericsson, the Monitor designer, was mentioned.

The chief clerk had gotten the bank's blessing to take advantage of the scholarship and a trip to Boston. The bank executives were enthusiastic.

"Excellent way to start renewing the old bonds between the bank and their American contacts," they agreed. Scholarly historic research is highly appreciated in Boston, they added. It will smooth the way for the post-war business. Americans might be just a bit sensitive that Sweden chose strict neutrality over joining the Allies in the war.

"Yes, strict neutrality. That must be emphasized. And we were most delighted to be host to Mr. Jeff Cabot when he and his brave crew were Sweden's guests." The bankers had all the excuses and explanations ready. Just like other Swedish businessmen and politicians.

Jeff Cabot was brave all right. As long as the sign that the chief clerk placed on the door to the basement was respected. It read: "Closed. Please return at 1500 hours." There never were any urgent matters in the vaults, the clerk assured Jeff Cabot. He could work in peace and quiet. That gave Jeff Cabot three hours for the "liberation."

He got to work as soon as the clerk and Ulla closed the door behind them. He carried the suitcases from the storage shelf to the vault containing the files. Hank and Joe had given him the key to the filing cabinet, and surprise, surprise, it worked.

He opened the drawer and there they were: the accounts of Nazi big shots from A to Z. No, not Adolf himself, his file was not there. He evidently didn't trust the Swedes.

Jeff Cabot flipped through the file and came to a lot of names her never heard of, but also some names that he recognized. Hell, the world knew those names or pretty soon would: Martin Bormann, Wilhelm Frick, Karl Dönitz ("The admiral, sailing his submarine into the sunset," Jeff Cabot thought.), Walter Funk ("Hmmm, heard of him, the top banana banker."), Wilhelm Canaris, Hans Fritzsche, Rudolph Hess, Heinrich Himmler ("That SS bastard."), Hermann Göring ("Fat file for a fat Kraut. Got lots of dough in Sweden, he loves this country."), Joseph Goebbels ("Ahh, the little rat-face rat, hiding patriotic cash."), Ernst Kaltenbrunner, Eric Neurath, Raeder Halbach, Alfred Rosenberg, Horace Greely Hjalmar Schacht ("Hmmm, know that name. The Kraut banker named after a Boston guy. Low class social climber."), Fritz Saukel, Alfred Jodl, Albert Speer, Julius Streicher, Raeder Krupp von Bohlen und Halbach, Alfred Krupp ("Ah, yes, the cannon guys, pop and his kid."), Alexander Seyß-lnquart, Konstantin von Neurath, Gustav von Papen, Wernher von Braun ("Aha! the bastard scientist murderer dumping his V-bombs on London."), Joachim von Ribbentrop ("Don't shake hands with this crook diplomat, he'll stab you in the back at the same time."), Baldur von Schirach, and a bunch of other vons.

"The fancy rats leaving the sinking ship with their bank account life preservers," Jeff Cabot said to himself.

Jeff Cabot would have liked to read all the account details, especially the bottom lines of how much they were planning to pick up when they set up shop again. But he resisted the temptation. He was in the middle of stealing bank documents. Business came first.

He pushed the hidden buttons on the suitcases. The sides opened, as they should. He took out all the blank sheets of paper in the files and stacked it on the floor next to the filing cabinet. He filled the first suitcase with half the files from the filing cabinet. He snapped the suitcase shut. He replaced what he removed from the cabinet with the blank paper files. He repeated the job with the rest of the files. He snapped the second suitcase sides shut, double checked to see that the filing cabinet drawer was completely empty of the Nazi files and filled the file with the blank paper files.

He was about to close the drawer, when he stopped. He couldn't resist. He took out his pen, and on the top label of the first file wrote:

"KILROY WAS HERE"

He slammed the file drawer shut, locked it, and carried the two suitcases back to their place on the storage shelf. The "liberation" had taken exactly 20 minutes. He double-checked to make sure everything was exactly as it had been when the chief clerk and Ulla had left for the Consulate. The two suitcases would be picked up in a few days by the guy who left them. Jeff Cabot had no idea who the man was. He returned to his desk and to the old papers of his family bank's business with the Swedes.

And he suddenly had a brilliant idea. He saved it for his next meeting with Hank and Joe.

A week later, as scheduled, the suitcases were picked up. Jeff Cabot heard about what happened from Ulla who heard it through the bank grapevine. They all thought it was hilarious.

The man who picked up the suitcases insisted on carrying both of them, even though they were heavy as hell. He walked out the front door of the bank, and down the steps and slipped on ice on the sidewalk.

In falling, he accidentally pressed the button releasing the hidden side locks. One suitcase snapped open as it hit the ground. The accounts fell out. Luckily, there was no wind or the whole caper would have been blown, literally and figuratively. The driver of the car waiting for him jumped out to help. The bank doorman also ran down the steps to help. Luckily, he, too slipped and fell on his ass.

That made it doubly funny to the bank personnel. Swedes love it when someone slips on the ice. Break a leg, that's even funnier. Swedish humor.

The two OSS agents quickly gathered the papers and stuffed them in the suitcase. The doorman got up and apologized for the ice. The OSS guys carried the suitcases to the car, stuffed them in the back seat, and got in.

Of course, the car stalled.

A policeman walked over and asked if he could help. He never imagined, nor would he ever know, that he would be helping the greatest bank robbery in Swedish history. The driver, however, finally got the car started. He thanked the cop, who saluted. The other man thanked the doorman and handed him a couple of bills. The doorman refused the tip, until he saw that the bills amounted to half a month's pay. He couldn't insult the gentlemen by refusing, could he? The car drove off.

Luckily, Jeff Cabot didn't witness the scene, straight out of a Three Stooges film. He wouldn't know whether to laugh or run like hell.

Jeff Cabot met Hank and Joe at historic Den Gyldene Freden, in Old Town. The. OSS had booked the entire Zorn Room, the best room in the old restaurant. The restaurant was usually filled with so-called "intellectuals"—writers and film people and editors and artists and the usual hangers-on and phonies and moochers. The place had been a favorite of Anders Zorn, the great portrait painter of the turn of the century.

Jeff Cabot suddenly remembered that Zorn did a portrait of his grandmother. He made the rather plain—hell, admit it, she was horse-faced—old Yankee quite lovely, which was why Zorn was the most popular portrait painter of his time. He even managed to make President Taft look slim, which was a real achievement.

Hank and Joe had invited a few dozen people: diplomats from the Legation, some American correspondents, and a number of "American businessmen" and others with vague employment but who were all obviously working for the OSS. There were Norwegians and Brits. There were a couple of Swedes who had slightly mysterious titles. And there were some émigrés, who worked for God-knows-who. And, of course, a few executives of Stockholms Enskilda Bank.

The "official" reason for the party was the award of the Sabbatical Scholarship to the bank's chief clerk of archives. Naturally, Ulla was there, as were wives and girl friends of many of the men.

The real reason for the party, of course, was to celebrate the "liberation" of the Nazi bank accounts. But nobody knew this except Hank and Joe and Jeff Cabot. It was their own little secret, although it was obvious that others in the OSS knew about it. They would be knocking each other over getting to the front of the line when the awards for "meritorious service" were handed out. Jeff Cabot couldn't care less.

The evening was a happy one. Plenty of *akvavit* and wine and excellent food and more wine and *akvavit* and cognac, and the Swedes toasting to beat the band. They started singing drinking songs. Swedes could not simply drink without singing about it.

Someone sat down at the piano and the Americans responded with college songs to start with and then went on to mushy home-front stuff as the evening wore on. Jeff Cabot did a pretty good imitation of that young Sinatra kid the girls were going nuts over, with a rendition of *"I'll be seeing you..."* and Hank wasn't half bad—wasn't half-good either—with Vaughn Monroe's *"When the Lights Go on Again All Over the World."* There wasn't a dry eye in the room when one of the female American correspondents got to *"I'll walk alone..."* although Dinah Shore she wasn't.

The Americans brightened things by trying to teach the Swedish guests the lyrics to *"Mairzy Doats."* The bank clerk knew he was going to have a great time doing research in Boston.

Jeff Cabot figured it would take a while for the Swedes to understand why Mairzy Doats and Dozy Doats and Little Lamzy Divy, so he took Hank and Joe outside for a break.

"I got a brilliant idea," he told them.

"He's now an expert and is going to knock off the Bank of Sweden," Hank said.

"Naw, the Crown Jewels," Joe said. "Piece of cake."

"C'mon, you guys, be serious," Jeff Cabot said. "I've been thinking. Let's do another switcheroo, but this time we go into the files and leave records saying that all funds have been transferred to our bank in Boston. Your creative guys, the artists, could do the paperwork easy. They're brilliant. The bank wouldn't know how it happened."

Hank and Joe looked at each other.

"What actually do you plan to do with the accounts?" Jeff Cabot asked.

"Actually, we have no idea," Hank said. "Honest. We're shipping them to London. Out of our hands."

"But if the funds are transferred from the Stockholm bank to our bank, well, the Swedes would be delighted," Jeff Cabot said. "It would be off their hands. They could give the world that innocent Swedish look and say, 'Nazi money? Never heard of it. We have no Nazi money. Absolutely no idea what you're talking about.' Those blue eyes reek of honesty."

"You got it down pat," Joe said. "You could be on the Edgar Bergen show."

"Playing Edgar or Charlie McCarthy?" Hank laughed.

"Comedians. Comedians. Here I offer a chance for a perfect place to stash the money and wait for the bastards to turn up demanding it, and you guys fool around."

"Of course, your bank would sit on the money and the Krauts would never dare show up," Hank said. "And the Swedes would owe you guys something for taking it off their greedy hands. Well, since you did such a fine job, worth the Congressional Medal at least, which you'd get but since the job was secret, anyhow the best we can do is pass on the suggestion. But we can't guarantee anything."

"Well, that sounds better than nothing to me," Jeff Cabot said. "Let's drink on it."

Jeff Cabot was now making his ancestors proud in their heaven—a heaven of eternal money-counting. At last, this baseball-crazy pilot was thinking of how to make money. Something a true Boston merchant banker should do.

Jeff Cabot and Hank and Joe returned to the party. Someone was singing "Stardust." Jeff Cabot and Ulla got the dancing going. It turned out to be one unforgettable celebration party for one unforgettable liberation.

It was unforgettable all right, since only three people—and Kilroy—ever knew all there was to know about it.

CHAPTER 24

❁

"You evidently didn't have to send it to New York to get the Rabbi's blessing," Carl Jacobson said, as he looked over the official requisition form. There was no kosher-mark "U" on the order. Otherwise, it looked perfect, even though Jacobson had no idea whatsoever what the Directorate was that issued it. It ordered that a copy of the *Sehr Guter Schwedischer Freund* file—the Very Good Swedish Friends file—be turned over to the *SS-Standartenführer*, the officer in charge of the German internment camp.

"Tell me, how do you dream up this stuff?" he asked.

"Easy," Hank explained. "There are so damn many officials and offices in Germany, Hitler himself doesn't know who is doing what, as long as the last guy he talks to does what he says. After that, it's bureaucratic chaos. Everyone scared of someone else."

"Like Washington," Joe added. "Except worse."

"How about printing me up some extra Swedish liquor ration coupons. Now that would be really valuable," Jacobson said. "I could give them to my clerk and he'll be King of the Camp. Nobody would call him Ass-Kisser again. They'd be kissing his ass instead."

Hank reached into his briefcase, fished around and came out with a half-dozen Swedish liquor ration books.

"With our compliments," he said. "Made special for foreign visitors. Your guy is now King of the Camp."

Jacobson could only wonder at the gigantic forgery and counterfeiting organization the OSS had available—in Sweden or Switzerland or England or wherever. He studied the requisition closer. He was certainly no expert, but had seen enough German documents pass over his desk at the camp to recog-

nize a paper that was 100 percent official and that demanded immediate obe-
dience. This was the best make-you-piss-in-your-pants order he seen yet.

"Now, off you go to the *Kultur* Attaché," Hank said. "Watch the little pansy
squirm."

"But don't let him come on to you. He likes handsome Aryans," Joe said,
fluttering his eye-lashes.

"He's a pal of that faggot at the Foreign Ministry," Hank said. "I forget his
name. He's as bent as a hairpin, queer as a three dollar bill—hell, queer as a
three kronor bill. It's supposed to be a secret. Was a Nazi-lover for a while,
until after Stalingrad. Dropped the Nazis and switched to Socialists when he
saw which way the wind was blowing…"

"Blowing? Har, har, har." Joe couldn't let that one pass by.

"They call him the chameleon—turns colors to match the background,"
Hank went on. "They say he's so good at sucking up—literally, figuratively, or
whichever way—he's gonna have a brilliant career."

"He'd love a career playing Mata Hari," Joe added. "He goes nuts over the
gorgeous dresses. But Greta Garbo got the role."

Carl Jacobson was now sure these guys were recruited from Broadway.

"Oh, yeah, by the way," Hank said. "We got this extra large briefcase for you.
We think the list you're going to carry away is pretty big."

The next day, Carl Jacobson, armed with the requisition, walked from the
Grand Hotel and headed toward the offices of the German Legation's Cultural,
Information and Press Sections, at Kaptensgatan 6, a short street in Östermalm, the fancy residential district where a large number of Legations and
diplomatic offices were located.

The neutral position of Sweden was clearly seen in this upper-class neighborhood, particularly along Strandvägen, the city's elegant "parade street" that
ran along the waterfront, offering wonderful views of the busy inner harbor.
Built in the late 1800s, for new-rich bourgeoisie as well as old-money and titled
Stockholmers, the grandiose apartment buildings were designed to proudly
show off wealth, solidity and substance. The buildings housed legations, consulates, diplomatic and commercial offices, all kinds of innocent-sounding
fronts for spy organizations, as well as lavish apartments for diplomats and
highly-placed Swedes.

The American Legation was at Strandvägen 7, with its main entrance door
facing a small courtyard garden. On the opposite side of the courtyard, at
Strandvägen 7C, was the German Military Attaché's office, while the Italian

Legation was a few doors down, the British Legation was at Strandvägen 28, and the Japanese Legation at Strandvägen 57.

This, of course, made it most convenient for the warring nations' diplomats, spies, moles, informers, secret agents and security people to keep an eye on each other.

Turkey, an important neutral, also had its Legation on Strandvägen, at 5B, while Switzerland's was just a few blocks away, at Blasieholmstorg, around the corner from the German Legation.

Carl Jacobson walked down Strandvägen, turned up Artillerigatan to Kaptensgatan.

"I should have some artillery backing me up," he thought, as he translated Artillerigatan, Artillery Street. He walked past a large brick structure that housed the stables for the Royal carriages and the horses of the Royal Mounted Guard. The manure smell made the perfect background to the nearby offices of the German Culture, Information and Press Sections.

Carl Jacobson marched to the door, pressed the buzzer, and the door was opened by a Kraut goon who looked far from a cultural type. If he ever saw the inside of a museum he was in a museum guard uniform, and if he ever was at the opera, he was a spear carrier in Aida, or maybe he played an elephant in the big scene. Carl Jacobson handed him his official *SS-Standartenführer* identification, watched while the goon's mug immediately transformed from arrogance into respect. He actually clicked his heels and gave the *Heil* salute.

Carl Jacobson nodded at the salute and waved a hand. "I am here to see the *Kultur* Attaché." It was an order more than a request.

"Yes, sir, immediately," the goon said, showing Carl Jacobson to a waiting room, with the inevitable portrait of Hitler and with bookshelves and tables lined with far more propaganda than the waiting room at the Legation. Evidently, there wasn't much call for it these days. Carl Jacobson thumbed through a few magazines in Swedish and German. The latest issues of *Der Stürmer* was more vicious than ever.

Jacobson couldn't help but hum to himself:

> *When Der Führer says, "We ist der master race,"*
> *We HEIL! (phhht!) HEIL! (phhht!) Right in Der Führer's face.*

The *Kultur* Attaché pranced into the room and gave the swishiest *Heil* salute Carl Jacobson had ever seen. He smiled affectionately at the tall, blond, blue-eyed Nordic ideal in the beautifully-cut black leather coat, and asked if he could be of service. His eyes actually twinkled.

Carl Jacobson gave him his practiced SS stare and handed him his identification and official requisition. He didn't say a word. The Attaché's eyes opened wide and he gulped, and stammered, "Terribly sorry, but I transferred the list to the Information Section. According to orders, of course. I will accompany you there personally It's in the building."

He bowed and allowed Carl Jacobson to walk ahead of him. Carl Jacobson hesitated a moment while he picked up some copies of *Der Stürmer* and other magazines and propaganda. He figured he could bring it to the camp, put it in the officer's dining room, and have fun watching the reaction. At this point in the war, any Krauts with any brains knew they've been taken in for years by the Goebbels bullshit and didn't want any more reminders.

"Yes, help yourself," the Attaché smiled. "We have plenty. Not much demand these days, if you know what I mean." He smiled his slimy smile and winked. Carl Jacobson wondered if he'd blow his cover if he threw up.

"Definitely not the first thing to get blown around here," he thought, treating himself to a silent har, har, har.

They walked to the Information Section, next to the Press Section, which had once been a favorite hang-out of a long list of journalists, especially those from the pro-Nazi *Aftonbladet,* who were treated especially well. The liquor flowed like, well, like liquor being poured by Nazi fags greasing willing, thirsty journalists.

The Attaché introduced Carl Jacobson to the Information Section Director, who looked at the requisition and, relief showing in his red, pudgy face—a face that had seen too many bottles of German schnapps disappear, all in the line of duty—he said that the list had been transferred to the Press Attaché. As directed, of course.

The Attaché and the Information Director accompanied Carl Jacobson to the Press Attaché's office, and the routine was repeated. Carl Jacobson thought he was in some kind of Marx Brothers film. The Press Attaché looked relieved when he said the list had been transferred to the Radio Section, on Karlavägen.

"As ordered, of course," he added. "We can phone the Radio Section..."

"No, I'll go personally," Carl Jacobson said. Those were the first and only words he had spoken in the place.

Carl Jacobson figured, what the hell, he might as well check it out. He was having too good a time seeing what an official document accomplished when flashed in the face of one-time big-shot Nazis, now pissing in their pants. He walked the few blocks to Karlavägen 59, to the German Radio Section. This was a very important operation, since Hitler and Goebbels and their gang were masters of using the airwaves. The Kraut in charge took one look at the requisition, and said in a radio-announcer's voice, "Sorry, sir, but the list was transferred, as ordered, to the Military Attaché's office. I can phone...."

Carl Jacobson declined, recovered the requisition, and wondered what the hell he was walking into. The Military Attaché's office was Strandvägen 7C, around the corner from where he had started out at the *Kultur* section. Jacobson figured it wouldn't be too risky, since it was just across the courtyard from the American Legation. Yeah, sure, a lot of help he could get from the U.S. Marine Guards if he ran into trouble.

"Hi, fellows, ignore the Nazi ID and the black coat. I am really a nice Brooklyn Jewish boy, an Air Corps lieutenant...." Yeah, they'd fall over laughing.

The Military Attaché's office was easy to get into. The guard opened the door and bowed a welcome, hardly looking at Carl Jacobson's ID. Carl Jacobson figured they had been warned by the Radio guys. The Attaché himself, a full colonel, in a snazzy army uniform, gave the old *Heil* in a half-assed way. The formal *Heil Hitler* salute and salutation were getting less enthusiastic for every mile the Allies advanced. He looked at the requisition, and Carl Jacobson knew what he was going to say. It had been transferred "on orders." This time to the Naval Attaché's office.

"I can phone..." the Military Attaché offered.

"No, order a car," Carl Jacobson ordered. "You do have one, don't you?"

"Immediately." The Attaché scooted out of the office. Even though he held the same rank, and he was in his own office, he wanted to be rid of the SS bastard as soon as possible.

As he got into a huge Mercedes-Benz with diplomatic license plates, Carl Jacobson thought that he should have demanded a car earlier. Although it was a pleasant, sunny day, it was getting a bit cold.

"The guys on the corner should see me now," Carl Jacobson said to himself, sitting back and thinking of his pals in Brooklyn. "Riding around in a car just like Adolf. I should have a big cigar. Oh, how I wish there was someone around who could take my picture. The guys will never believe it."

They drove to the Naval Attaché's office, at Strandvägen 67, just a few blocks away. Carl Jacobson ordered the driver to wait. He had a feeling he was going to need the car all day.

Sure enough, the Naval Attaché's assistant—the Attaché himself was at an early lunch—told Carl Jacobson the files were transferred to the Luftwaffe

Attaché's office, "as ordered." He offered the usual phone call, but said the office was probably closed for the lunch hour. Carl Jacobson declined.

At this point, he figured he better close down for lunch, too. He was getting damn tired of playing "hot potato." And he was getting damn mad at the Krauts having him run all over Östermalm. Although now he could ride in style.

He walked out of building housing the Naval Attaché's office and was looking down the block to where his car and had been parked. He didn't notice the short man passing the door until he bumped into him.

"Sorry," Jacobson said, automatically, in English.

"*Gomen-nasai*," the short man said, automatically, in Japanese.

They looked at each other.

"Commander! What are you doing here?"

"Ahh, *Standartenführer*, what are you doing here?"

They shook hands and laughed like long lost brothers. The Commander explained he was at the Japanese Legation "making sure they send me our fair ration of whale meat when it arrives." The Japanese Legation was just a few doors down Strandvägen. He said he was going to lunch at the Japanese Naval Attaché's office, on Villagatan.

"That's a very exclusive street," the Commander explained. "The Russian Embassy is across the street. We can keep an eye on the Russians."

"And the Russians can keep an eye on you," Carl Jacobson said. "Swedes make it easy for everyone. Very efficient. Very neutral. Excellent hosts."

The Commander, naturally, thought that was hilarious. The commander invited Jacobson to join them for lunch. They'd have *sushi*. Carl Jacobson was tempted but he knew that a *sushi* lunch meant much *brännvin* and he had a lot of work to do that afternoon. He begged off, but offered to give the Commander a lift. The Commander was delighted.

They spoke of the weather, Hitler's promised secret weapon, the progress of getting the Commander's submarine released.

"I think they are saving it to give important German officials a cruise to Argentina," the Commander laughed at his own big joke. And they agreed to get together soon.

"We will show you how we are doing in training," the Commander said. "Maybe you will finally learn the rules of baseball."

"Too complicated for me," Carl Jacobson said, as the car pulled up before Villagatan 24, almost directly across the street from the huge Russian Embassy at number 17.

"Auf Wiedersehen," Carl Jacobson said, tossing off a salute.

"Sayonara," laughed the Commander, bowing.

Carl Jacobson got back in the car.

"What restaurant do you like?" he asked the driver, who, in all the driving around, had only repeated two phrases, "Yes, Sir," and "Here we are, sir."

"I am sorry, sir, but we non-commissioned officers rarely eat out," the driver replied.

"Well, what restaurant have you heard about?"

"Some of the officers like the Pagod. At the top of the skyscraper."

"Skyscraper? Do they think they're in New York already?"

"No, sir. The Swedes call Kungstornet a skyscraper. The claim it's the first one in Europe. Actually there are two towers, twin towers. Excellent view of the city from the Pagod."

"Let's go," Jacobson ordered. He wanted to tell his pals in Brooklyn he was in a skyscraper in Stockholm. They wouldn't believe him. He'd bet them he definitely was in one. He would win the bet. He would have to get a picture postcard to prove it.

They turned back down Strandvägen, up Birger Jarlsgatan, past the "Mushroom" bus stop shelter in Stureplan, and left up Kungsgatan. Jacobson had been in England and Sweden long enough to be accustomed to traffic on the left side. But the Swedes were special: the drivers sat on the left side of the seat, as if traffic were right-hand. Probably because most cars were American or German imports. But even the Volvos had left hand drive. Swedes. Go figure.

This made overtaking a bit of a thrill. Hell, it was often a hair-raising adventure. The driver would lean way over to the right to see around the car in front. Or he'd ask the passenger on the right if the coast was clear for passing. In city traffic it was OK, not much high speed passing, although it was a pain in the neck on streets like Kungsgatan with trolley cars in the middle. Maybe the Swedes kept the steering wheel on the left to add some excitement to their dull "Middle Way" lives of neutrality.

Looking up Kungsgatan, Carl Jacobson saw the "skyscrapers": two handsome office towers, about 15 stories, on either side of the busy shopping street.

"The Pagod Restaurant is at the top of the one on the left," the driver said.

"That's a skyscraper? Swedish-style illusions of grandeur," Carl Jacobson said.

"Park in front," he ordered, even though it was clearly a no-parking zone He knew the police wouldn't say a word to a driver of a car with diplomat plates.

At least they no longer came to attention and saluted when they saw it was a German diplomatic car, as they would have done before Stalingrad.

"Yes, sir," the driver said, a note of pleasure in following an order to break the law.

"Now let's go eat," Carl Jacobson said.

The driver was startled. No officer had ever invited him to lunch. Maybe the SS wasn't so bad after all. They took an elevator to the top floor and the restaurant, got a nice table looking east over the city and the waterways, and ordered the usual SOS. They had work to do, so they passed up *akvavit* and ordered pilsner. Carl Jacobson ordered broiled steak for both. The driver was in seventh heaven.

"Tell me about yourself, your career," Carl Jacobson said.

The driver explained he had been wounded on the Russian front, where he had been a tank driver. Carl Jacobson had noticed he limped quite badly.

"Never underestimate the Russians," he said. "They got tanks designed for Russian weather, Russian terrain. Damn tough soldiers. But, of course, *Der Führer* will stop them and the Allies. The secret weapon is being held in reserve. They have a surprise waiting for them."

"Of course," Carl Jacobson agreed.

The driver said he had been to Sweden during Summers when he was a kid—a relative was married to a Swede—and he had picked up Swedish pretty good. So while still in the hospital, he volunteered for assignment to the Stockholm Legation, and got a job as driver. Able-bodied men at the Legation had been called home. He proudly said that he sometimes picked up bits of information from Swedes who figured a German diplomat driver wouldn't know the language. Germans usually insisted on speaking German to the Swedes. After all, it was educated Swedes' second language, although many suddenly started to brush up on their school English after the Normandy landings.

"Every bit of information helps," the driver said.

"You are to be commended," Carl Jacobson said. "And I appreciate your assistance."

The steaks came, with boiled potatoes. They ordered a third round of pilsners, and they dug in. The driver relaxed and enjoyed the meal and the view and the good service. It was almost like the old days in Berlin. Although he didn't have lunch with any high-ranking SS officer there.

"You know," said Carl Jacobson in a most confidential tone, "I have orders to get the copy of a special list of people, but I get the feeling that the list doesn't exist or nobody wants to be caught with it. I am afraid we are going to do a lot of driving this afternoon."

"You don't mean the *Sehr Guter Schwedischer Freund* file, do you?" the driver said. "Ha! I've been moving that from office to office. Supposed to be secret. Ha! Secret! Everyone knows about it. Nobody seems to keep it long."

"Well, we go to the Luftwaffe Attaché office next. It was sent there from the Naval Attaché," Carl Jacobson said. "Wonder if they have an official photograph of *Reichmarshall* Herr Finkelstein on the wall?"

The driver tried to hold in his laugh. He damn near chocked. Tears came to his eyes. He finally roared. Nobody had ever said such a thing out loud. Even when drunk.

Carl Jacobson paid the bill, tipped very generously, and they took the elevator to the street and their car.

"Off to check on Finkelstein's boys," Carl Jacobson said, generating another huge laugh. The Luftwaffe Attaché's office was on Karlavägen, at number 99. A parkway, with trolley tracks, ran in the center of the street. Stacks of cut firewood were in the parkway.

Carl Jacobson presented his credentials to a Luftwaffe sergeant at the entrance desk. The sergeant called an officer, who explained the Air Attaché was in Berlin. He read the official requisition, and said, "Sorry, but this file was sent to the Merchant Marine office, as ordered. Shall I phone them for you?"

Carl Jacobson gave him his best SS glare, took back his documents, put them in his briefcase, and said, "No, thank you. I have a car waiting."

Then, nodding toward a large portrait of Göring, in full uniform obviously designed by a mad costume designer for a French operetta, he said, "And my regards to Herr Finkelstein."

Total silence. Stunned silence. Crushing silence. You could almost imagine the portrait itself changing color into violent purple. Göring's fat gut expanding like a balloon, exploding in rage and medals flying all over the place. Jacobson turned on his heel, forgot the *Heil* salute and got the hell out of there.

They drove back to Kungsgatan, to the Merchant Marine office in a building at number 37. It was only a few buildings from the "skyscraper" restaurant where they just had lunch. Carl Jacobson was not at all surprised when he was informed that the file had been sent, "as ordered" of course, to the *Wehrwirtschaft* office, at Nybrogatan 27, a block from where he had started the Odyssey. This was the office in charge of defense related business. Probably loaded with orders for Swedish steel and ball bearings, Carl Jacobson thought.

When he got there, he didn't see any such orders lying around, or any other papers, because, surprise, surprise, the list had been transferred "as ordered" to *Wehrmachtintendentur* office, at Birger Jarlsgatan 58.

Aha, thought Carl Jacobson, the military equipment purchasing office. "Here's where they buy the Bofors guns. Probably got a lot of special Swedish friends here."

He wasn't the least bit surprised to be told the list wasn't there, but had been sent to the official Transport Office, at Nybrogatan 21. This was just a few doors from the *Wehrwirtschaft* office that he visited 30 minutes earlier. Carl Jacobson was a patient man, and he loved seeing the Krauts almost piss in their pants when he stepped in with the official requisition.

The officer in charge of the Transportation Office said, "Yes, we had the list, but it was sent just yesterday to the Consul General. I can telephone...." But Carl Jacobson cut him off with a cold stare, and walked out.

The Consulate was at Birger Jarlsgatan 8, just off Nybroplan, and around the corner more or less from where Jacobson's search started early that morning, at the *Kultur* section. The Consulate, in a handsome modern brick building, was guarded by two Swedish policemen, who could recognize a high-ranking German officer, even one in civilian clothes, ten blocks away. They saluted as Carl Jacobson walked to the front door, which was opened almost automatically by the usual Kraut goon doorman.

"Where do they get these guys?" Carl Jacobson wondered. "They must turn them out in a sausage factory. They all look alike."

In the Consulate, he walked to a desk where a bored-looking Kraut glared at him for a moment before realizing he was not dealing with his usual clientele: German or Austrian émigrés who needed their passports stamped and other papers approved. Germans had stamps for everything. Carl Jacobson figured that if the Krauts could turn stamps into weapons, and bureaucrats who used the stamps into soldiers, they would have won the war years ago.

The waiting room off the hall was filled with men and women who could not be mistaken for anyone other than the émigré refugees they were. Poor bastards, Carl Jacobson thought, they escaped the Nazis and still have to get their papers stamped by insufferably arrogant Kraut bureaucrats.

The guy behind the desk stood at attention when he got over his shock at seeing what was obviously a German officer standing before him. He turned pale when Jacobson presented his SS identification. Out of the corner of his eye, Jacobson could see slight smiles on people in the waiting room. They loved seeing an overbearing Nazi squirming in front of another overbearing Nazi. It made their long wait a bit more bearable.

Carl Jacobson demanded to see the Consul General. Immediately! Surprise! He was not in Berlin. He would see Jacobson in his office, at once. Obviously, the Transport officer had phoned ahead. The guy at the desk bowed and showed Jacobson the way. The émigrés had a lovely German phrase, quite impolite, to describe such guys: guys who kissed up and kicked down.

Carl Jacobson presented his documents to the Consul General, a thin, neat, pale, elderly man, nervous, of course. Carl Jacobson wondered where this guy would send him to, although he figured he was running out of German offices. If they had any more offices in Stockholm, the city would be an official suburb of Berlin.

"We have the list here," the Consul said.

Carl Jacobson damn near said, in English, "You're shittin' me!" But he caught himself just in time. Instead he said nothing. Just stared at the Consul General. The orders were specific: hand over the *Sehr Guter Schwedischer Freund* file immediately.

The Consul General rose, walked to a filing cabinet, unlocked it using a key on his watch chain, removed a thick file, neatly tied with twine, and sealed in wax, and covered with ominous Swastika stamps declaring "Top Secret" and "Strictly Confidential" and "Authorized Eyes Only". It looked as if you dared touch it without permission from *Der Führer* himself, you would be shot immediately. Or worse.

The Consul General handled it delicately, as if it were loaded. Carl Jacobson had a receipt all made out. He signed it, dated it, and handed it to the Consul General, who handed him the package. He looked quite relieved to be rid of the damn thing. Carl Jacobson stuffed the file in his briefcase, gave a quick *Heil* salute, and walked out, singing, almost loud enough to be heard as he passed the obligatory official photo of Hitler:

> *When Der Führer says, "We ist der master race,"*
> *We HEIL! (phhht!) HEIL! (phhht!) Right in Der Führer's face*

And suddenly it hit him. Each boss of every Nazi ministry, office, agency, division, unit, the Navy, Army, Luftwaffe, the SS, each and every top Kraut was fighting to get the list so he and his pals could save their own necks—or asses, whichever was most important. Thus, there was one order countering the previous order. Each big-shot Nazi topping the next.

Jacobson caught the package at the top of the heap, when it was at a trusted diplomatic office of one of Hitler's most important sleaze-balls, Foreign Minister Joachim von Ribbentrop. Obviously, from his joy at getting rid of the list, the Consul General hated his boss, as did every other old career diplomat. Let Hitler's boot-licker von Ribbentrop try to get the list from his pals at the SS. Carl Jacobson was certain the Consul General was laughing like hell. But to himself, of course. The war still wasn't over.

Carl Jacobson had the driver drive him back to the Grand Hotel. He gave the driver a package of liquor ration coupons. What the hell. Be a sport. He had plenty more to give Finkelstein at the camp. The driver couldn't believe his eyes. He couldn't stop saluting and saying thanks.

In his room, Carl Jacobson first phoned Lili Schultz at the Legation, and she quickly agreed to join him for dinner at Berns Salonger, the best night club in town.

"Maybe I can convert her to humanity," he said to himself. "I'll be doing a *Mitzvah*." His Mama would be happy. A *Mitzvah* was a good deed, a blessing.

He then went to the Grand Bar, carrying his briefcase. He put it under his table, just as Hank and Joe had instructed. It wasn't at all unusual for businessmen to carry their briefcases with them into the bar. A man he had never seen before, also carrying a briefcase, joined him. They ordered drinks and talked of the weather. They finished their drinks, shook hands, and left. Naturally, the briefcases had been switched, just as Hank and Joe said would happen. The oldest spy trick in the book.

Carl Jacobson figured he had spent a most productive day. Now, he would spend a most productive evening. At least he hoped it would be productive.

"Mama, it's for the war effort," he silently explained to his mother. He knew she didn't approve even if she knew nothing about it. Going out with a *shiksa* was one thing. But a German Nazi Kraut *shiksa*, oy! Forget the *Mitzvah* baloney. You can't fool Mama.

When he went out to meet Lili, he left the briefcase on his bed. Hank and Joe told him that the Swedish secret police would open it when he was out. They would be delighted at the contents: latest copies of *Der Stürmer*. They can have fun trying to figure it out.

And when they escape to neutral Sweden, let the Nazi big shots try to find their favorite Swedish pals. Good luck, *shmucks*!! Without the *Sehr Guter Schwedischer Freund* list and the blackmail documentation it contained, no Swede Nazi-lover would ever volunteer to come within an inch of a fugitive German, no less help him hide until the heat died down. Indeed, no old Nazi-loving Swede would ever have existed. Swedish chameleons: the fastest color switchers in Europe.

Von Ribbentrop and his Foreign Ministry goons—the last guys who thought they had secured the list for themselves—will go nuts trying to find their old Swedish champagne sipping buddies.

"Fuck 'em," Carl Jacobson said, quoting Hank's philosophy.

CHAPTER 25

Major Karlsson didn't believe it.

"They played strictly to the rules, when they played my team," he said.

"Then they play different in Japan," Carl Jacobson said. "Of course, I didn't give a damn about their killing each other. It looked like the Three Stooges playing the Marx Brothers. But if those monkeys try that stuff with us, it's going to be war."

Jeff Cabot reminded Carl Jacobson it was war. The three were meeting in a private dining room of The Jeff Cabot Bank, as Stockholms Enskilda Bank was generally referred to by the crew. It didn't seem much like war. Spring was finally in the air. The park across the street from the bank was filled with girls sunning on the benches. All benches faced south, like one big bus. The girls had their faces turned to the sun. In a few weeks they would be beautifully tanned. Swedish blondes tan fast.

Major Karlsson, Jeff Cabot and Carl Jacobson had met to make final arrangements for Spring Training. The crew would be taken off their "essential assignments" and transferred to a base in Skåne, the southernmost Swedish province, where Spring arrives a month ahead of its finally reaching Stockholm. Their official orders would have them maintaining B-17s and waiting for flights back to Britain. Major Karlsson had made certain they'd wait a long time, long enough for the Series with Sharks.

Major Karlsson had quietly informed his friends at the American Legation about the planned games. What American could resist seeing the Japs beat to a pulp on the diamond? The Series got backing from the highest officials. Naturally, plans were made for a pool.

Things moved pretty fast after that. The crew, or rather, the team, was shipped to Skåne. There were plenty of tearful farewells, although several girls decided to follow along.

"Just like playing in the minors," said B.J. Jones. "Nothing like having a woman traveling with you."

Jones had been fully cleared of all paternity claims. He eventually convinced the Swedish authorities that he was in Britain when the other Jones airmen were in Sweden. If indeed there were other airmen who were actually named Jones. Of course, three girls who had babies later that year insisted B.J. Jones was the father, but by that time our man was back home playing ball in Alabama.

Carl Jacobson's departure from his assignment was perhaps the simplest. He just never returned to the German camp after a trip to Stockholm on "official business". If any of the Germans wondered about it, they never asked. They figured that the lucky bastard was on his way to Brazil, although they hoped the SS bastard was on his way to the Russian front, if you could call it the Russian front any longer. Carl Jacobson's girl-friends shed many tears, for at least a day or two, until they found new officers.

Jeff Cabot gave up his job at the bank. In addition to his great haul of the Nazi bank accounts, he had provided the OSS with excellent information about Swedish transactions with Germany. Only he and Hank and Joe knew exactly how he got the documents, although it wasn't hard for the OSS document experts to figure out. Jeff Cabot didn't know Swedish or German, and wouldn't know a receipt for a shipload of iron ore from a payment for a ton of gold.

But his assigned assistant, the tall, blonde, buxom secretary to the international banking manager sure did.

"Ulla, my love, I'll never forget you," he told her over cognac on their last date, at the Opera Källaren. "You have brightened these many dark days."

"Bullshit," replied Ulla, a lovely, down-to-earth creature, who was working on a scheme to accompany the records and vault clerk to Boston on his stipendium. He certainly would need an assistant for his research into the Cabot family bank and the early days there of the founder of Stockholms Enskilda Bank. She thought she'd surprise Jeff Cabot in the not too distant future.

Ed Kowalski turned over his *kielbasa* business to his chief assistant, a Polish Cavalry captain. They promised to have a reunion in Warsaw, or, better, in Pittsburgh.

Pete Fielding surprised everyone by actually turning up in Stockholm, not only on time but at the right place.

"How the hell did you ever find Stockholm?" asked Ed Kowalski.

"I used my own maps, obviously," replied Pete Fielding.

"You're the only one who can read them," Ed Kowalski said. "I heard we are going to drop them over German air bases, just to confuse the enemy."

Actually, Pete Fielding's maps were not half bad. He had linked up with Mickey O'Mallery, who included maps of the American and British internment camp towns, featuring directions to the Welcome Wagon sponsor shops.

Mickey O'Mallery gave his Welcome Wagon business to his two blonde assistants. They could run it on their own. But they said it wouldn't be half as much fun without their New York boss. They, too, cried, for one whole day, until they took in a British airman as a partner. He was a cockney, and the girls said that if Mickey O'Mallery and the Brit had ever teamed up, they would soon be richer than the Wallenbergs.

Joe Bacciagalupo was given a farewell party by his students at the Falun High School. His students sang just about every popular American song they could think of, from *"Autumn Leaves"* to *"Mairzy Doats"*. As a final lesson, Joe Batch had rewritten the Boston classic *"Southie is my Home Town"* into a local version, *"Falun is my Home Town"*, which the kids learned by heart and sang with more gusto than the original had ever been sung in South Boston.

"I ain't teaching no Irish ballad to my students," Joe Batch explained. "You see, Southie, that's Irish. Falun, that's cultured."

His students didn't quite follow, since they thought all Americans were American, except of course, their relatives in America, who were Swedes.

Yeah, they were Swedes like Napoleon Anderson. His departure was one of the saddest. He had become a leading figure on the island of Möja, and with his guiding hand and insistence on slow, multiple charcoal filtering, and use of the purest deep-well water they could find, the local *brännvin* had attracted widespread acclaim. The boys had printed up a special label for this absolutely best product: "Napoleon's Prime Reserve". It featured a portrait of Napoleon Bonaparte.

"It will sell better that way than if you put my handsome face on it," Napoleon Anderson said. He knew his Swedish kin-folk.

Of course, marketing and advertising was not much of a problem in selling the product. The problem was getting it past the police and to the bootleggers in Stockholm. But the Möja moonshiners had been in the business for years, and knew the Stockholm archipelago and its thousands of islands far better than any cops or customs agents ever would. The Möja shippers also had the fastest boats in Sweden. Private enterprise is what made the world go round, no matter what the Socialist politicians preached.

Two of the girls from the island accompanied Napoleon Anderson to Spring Training. Unlike most of the people on the island, they insisted they were not related to him.

"It wouldn't be moral to be with a cousin," they said. But it was perfectly proper to share him between them.

"That's different," they explained. Napoleon Anderson loved Swedish logic.

Joshua Bennett gave up his preaching tour, much to the disappointment of thousands of followers in revival halls all over Sweden. Joshua Bennett had done extremely well. Old ladies forced generous contributions on him. Young ladies forced generous contributions on him. He finally understood why his family was really in the preaching business.

"Lord, I thank Thee, spreading Your Word is a far, far more worthy task than working for a living," he said.

If he didn't make it in the Big Leagues when he got home, he could always get a preacher's degree at the Bible College of Missouri.

"I figure I can work up sermons wrapped around baseball," he told the team, as they rode the train south to training camp. "The Saints playing the Devils. I can preach a seven-game World Series for a seven-day revival meeting. I can see it now: Joshua Bennett Brings you the World Series of the Lord in Heaven."

Mickey O'Mallery liked the idea. "I'll manage you," he said. "You'll need a good manager."

"You're Catholic, that won't go over so good in the Bible Belt," Joshua Bennett reminded him.

"Guess that also counts me out," Napoleon Anderson said. "I don't think your Bible Thumpers would appreciate my own special colorful Baptist denomination."

"Counts me out, too," Carl Jacobson said, "even though our guy is the guy you guys are rootin' for."

Joshua Bennett figured he could use one of his Swedish assistants. Maybe two. They knew the preaching business. And they would certainly be more spiritual than any of these mugs on the team. But of course, that's only if he didn't make the Big Leagues.

Major Karlsson had to break the sad news to the Mexican Consul General that Gus Sanchez would have to leave. It almost broke the Consul's heart. But

Gus Sanchez had been kind enough to leave his own chili recipe with the Consul's Swedish secretary and very close friend, Señorita Eva. But having a recipe is one thing. Making chili is another. It's an art. The Consul did not mind that Gus Sanchez spent many a long evening teaching Eva the secret.

"She is coming along very nice," Gus Sanchez explained. "Little slow, but you know how Swedes are."

The Consul was not disappointed after Gus Sanchez left. The Mexican ball player had taught Señorita Eva more things than simply how to make great chili.

CHAPTER 26

❀

The team was housed at an air base, one of the several in south Sweden designated for emergency landings of Allied aircraft. Even before the team arrived, Major Karlsson had a diamond laid out on part of the field, had a backstop put up, and even some bleachers built. His team was highly impressed. Yes, they considered themselves the Major's team, a Major League team, more or less.

"We should have called ourselves Karlsson's Raiders," Pete Fielding said.

"The hell with that," said Mickey O'Mallery. "Carlson's Raiders, they're in the Burma jungles, up to their ass in swamps and crazy Japs."

"I still say we got the best name going: the Falun Angels," said Carl Jacobson. "Wait until the Japs try to pronounce that."

Carl Jacobson had made several more courtesy visits to the Japanese camp, enjoyed the *sushi*, and enjoyed listening to the Japanese plan great sea battles once they sailed their submarine home and their shipyards could turn out greatly-improved copies of it. Especially with navigational systems that weren't backward.

Carl Jacobson had invited the Commander to his camp, and the Commander did make a visit. He brought a box of beautifully wrapped whale steaks, packed in ice, two bottles of precious *sake* he got from the Legation, and a framed portrait of Emperor Hirohito.

"Ahhhh, Hirohito-san," said Carl Jacobson who had learned to use the polite *"san"* title. "Beautiful portrait. What does the Japanese script say?"

"It says, 'Honored *Shmucku* Emperor Hirohito.'"

"Shmucku?"

"Yes. We gave him same honorable title as honorable Hitler. *Shmucku.*"

Carl Jacobson was proud of his introducing a valuable new word into the Japanese vocabulary. If the German officers at the reception understood any of this, they didn't blink an eye. Not being too familiar with English to begin with, the Commander's accent was totally confusing.

Carl Jacobson could not offer a baseball game, but he had his men play some soccer for entertainment after lunch.

"Very nice sport," said the Commander. "But not as exciting as *besubaru-ju-jitsu*."

Now, at the Skåne air base, Carl Jacobson thought of those games as he and the others looked over their equipment. He would have preferred ice hockey or football gear to the stuff B.J. Jones had manufactured, and the uniforms that Major Karlsson had tailored at MEA, the fancy shop in Stockholm catering especially to officers. Indeed, the shop's original name meant "Military Outfitting Inc." The Falun Angels was probably the only baseball team in the world with tailor-made, hand-sewn uniforms.

B.J. Jones's gloves were excellent, and his bats as good as Louisville Sluggers. The special Johansson model with the finger-fit handle was politely rejected. It just didn't feel right.

But B.J. Jones's partner, Johan Johansson, wasn't discouraged. When B.J. Jones departed, Johansson was busy at work trying to design a machine that could automatically sew baseballs. B.J. Jones had told him that a baseball manufacturer in the U.S. had a standing offer of $50,000 for anyone inventing such an automatic machine, which would eliminate thousands of jobs held by women hand-stitchers. Luckily, the team had a plentiful supply of balls, brought over on courier planes. They didn't have to wait for Johan Johansson's invention.

The *Jumpin' Jimminy* crew—or rather, the Falun Angels—was officially assigned to the care and maintenance of a half-dozen B-17s. The planes were on the other side of the field, nicely lined up. The crew never went near them. Swedish mechanics had them patched up where it was necessary, and had put the engines into excellent working order. It was like they had their eyes on those planes. The Yanks had so damn many B-17s in Europe by now, that maybe when the war ended they would simply tell the Swedes, "You want the ones in Sweden? You fix 'em, you can have 'em."

What the Swedes would do with the Forts was anyone's guess.

"They want to use them to start an airline," said Jeff Cabot. "I heard it at the bank."

"They'll probably use them to haul Nazis to Latin America," said Carl Jacobson. "Charge a fortune for one-way tickets."

"Don't be so damn cynical," said Jeff Cabot.

"Cynical? I know what's up. Wasn't I a German Army Colonel? They army runs on its Colonels."

"Naw, it runs on its corporals," said Joe Bacciagalupo, even though he was a sergeant.

"Not the German army," said Carl Jacobson. "We Colonels run it."

"And right now, you aren't running it so well," said Joe Bacciagalupo.

"That's because a corporal is the supreme number one commander, the *shmuck*," replied Carl Jacobson.

Conversations among the crew were long and intensive, but never got anyplace. But then, what could one expect from GIs, no less ball players.

The weather was beautiful. The war in Europe appeared to be coming to an end as the Allies pushed into Germany. The crew of the *Jumpin' Jimminy* figured that their contribution to victory in the air war over Europe was not absolutely necessary at this point. They agreed that new B-17 crews should be given every chance to become heroes.

"It's like coming up from the minors," said Joe Bacciagalupo. "These guys have been training in the states. They've shown their talent. Now they can move up to the majors. They're young and eager. We can step aside, like coaches, and give them a break. They deserve it."

"It's not that we aren't doing our part," Joshua Bennett pointed out. "After all, we got the Japs to beat. Right here on the field of glory in Sweden. Hallelujah!"

The philosophizing was totally unnecessary. The crew had started Spring Training, and it may sound corny, but they were like young colts let out to pasture in the Spring. Since they had no real manager—Major Karlsson was their unofficial General Manager—they gave Jeff Cabot the honors. He organized the general physical conditioning, the warm up calisthenics, jogging, fielding batted balls, pitching, batting.

Each of the players had a special talent, and shared their skills as good teammates should. Of course, all suggestions were readily and thankfully accepted.

"You ought to keep that right arm and shoulder down a bit when you swing," said Joe Bacciagalupo to Ed Kowalski. As catcher, Joe Batch was in an excellent position to see where batters were weak.

"Screw you," said Kowalski. "I had a better batting average in high school than you'll ever have."

"Just trying to help."

"Help better if you watched the runner on first instead of my swings."

"Hey, c'mon. I had the least stolen bases in the league the last year before I got drafted."

"Yeah, you were drafted in the army, not the Red Sox."

Yes, it was just as the guys remembered the game. Put a guy in a ball park, give him a glove, watch him field, watch him hit. You could immediately tell a real ball player. But you could never tell him much.

The practice sessions started to attract spectators. First to come were other American Air Corps internees assigned to work on the Forts and Liberators at the field and at nearby fields. A few Canadians showed up, from British camps.

Then Swedes started to stop by. They had heard of baseball. Few had ever seen it played. The Swedes had their own version of the game, "*Brännboll*", literally translated as "burn ball". They demonstrated it for the guys. A team of six or eight or whatever you wanted would be in the field. There are two bases, and home. The batter himself throws the ball up and then hits it as it falls, a fungo thing. If he hits a fly and it's caught, he's "burned", or out. If not, he runs to first, then second and home. He's out if the ball is thrown home before he gets there.

"They had to keep the rules simple so the squareheads could understand the game," Napoleon Anderson said.

"Hey, I thought you were a Swede," said Joe Batch.

"That's how I know," Napoleon Anderson said.

CHAPTER 27

By the end of March, the team was in pretty good shape. They had shed about 200 pounds, combined, which they had acquired during their rigorous Winter duties, contributing to strengthening Swedish-American relations and to the Allied war effort. They were working well as a team again, probably even better than they had been in England. They were not distracted with the petty nuisance of flying bombing raids over Germany.

Back when he got the idea, and when the *Jumpin' Jimminy* crew agreed to a Series, Major Karlsson had approached the Japanese very carefully and extremely diplomatically. He made a formal appointment to visit the Commander, put on his best uniform, and brought along several cases of cigarettes and brandy. They chatted for a long time, had lunch, and started on the brandy. The conversation turned to baseball.

"You recall, Commander, how your excellent team beat my miserable team so badly, that you suggested we not play again until I have a team that can really play the game."

"Ahhh, yes," the Commander smiled. "We did not want your Swedish *Meatbarus* to lose more face."

"Well, I have put together a completely new team, and we want to arrange a Series."

The Commander's face lit up. He smiled, looking exactly like a Japanese officer in a Hollywood movie, in a scene where the Japanese officer is about to pull off an especially treacherous trick.

"Where did you find a new team, may I ask?"

"An American team. From the American camp."

The smile disappeared. It was replaced by the face of a Japanese officer in a Hollywood movie who was totally surprised by a brilliant and courageous American counter-attack.

"It is perfectly correct and legal," Major Karlsson continued. "There is absolutely nothing prohibiting this in the Geneva Convention. Obviously, the neutral host nation cannot force internees to participate."

"You mean, we pray *besubaru* against Americans?" Excited, he lost the L sound.

"It would be entirely up to you. The Americans have already agreed. They look forward to it. They are confident they can beat your team even without ever having seen you play, and even after I told them how badly you beat my boys."

The Commander was silent a long time.

"Of course, if you are afraid you would lose, well, we can simply call it off," Major Karlsson said. "Naturally, I would not be able to prevent the Americans from claiming you were afraid of playing them."

"Afraid!! We are not afraid!! We are Imperial Japanese Navy. We are Yokosuka Sharks. We can beat any *miserabaru* American team. We *pray baru*!!"

He had lost the Ls completely.

It was far easier than Major Karlsson figured it would be. He had been prepared for tedious bureaucratic wrangling involving the Japanese Legation, the Japanese Admiralty, Tokyo, even Hirohito himself.

He had prepared a schedule for a Series of games, to be played on Gärdet, a field in Stockholm where he had seen the exhibition games of the 1912 Olympics. The more they discussed plans, the more enthusiastic the Commander became. The Commander's Ls had returned. The Commander was now cool and calculating.

"Well invite entire Japanese colony," he said. "Legation staff. Businessmen. Swedish friends. German friends. We can have Gadelius sponsor us. We need new uniforms, special for the Swedish World Series."

He was referring to the Gadelius family, owners of a Swedish trading company that had been active in Japan since the late 1800s.

And he had inadvertently and unconsciously created an official name to the Series: "The Swedish World Series."

Major Karlsson had a ready answer to the Commander's question about umpires. He had scouted around the various Embassies, Legations, Consulates and trade missions in Stockholm, and discovered far more baseball enthusiasts than he had dreamed existed. So many, that he could easily field an umpiring staff completely from neutral nations.

A Swiss attaché, the son of a career diplomat, had actually played ball when he was in high school in Washington. A Portuguese Legation driver and handyman played ball when he lived in New Bedford, Massachusetts, working on an uncle's fishing boat. A Turkish journalist, who everyone knew worked for one or more of the various spy organizations, learned baseball well enough to pass as an American during an earlier assignment in New York. He readily volunteered. Several Swedes who had returned home after spending years in the United States, were available. One had actually played for a semi-pro team in Minnesota in the 1920s. A Swedish professor had studied oriental art in Japan had played baseball on a Japanese college team.

Karlsson emphasized that the umpires would maintain strict neutrality. The Commander was most impressed.

"It be very good Series. A real World Series, not just American," he said. "The Swedish World Series."

Major Karlsson had actually figured on having far more games than just the seven in a World Series. The Commander solved that for him.

"We'll play the Series and then play a full season. We'll play as long as the Americans can accept being beaten," he volunteered. "We'll play as many games as you want."

He readily agreed to the Major's schedule for the Series. Two games each week-end, starting in early April. And after the Series, a new Season would open, continuing through the Spring and Summer.

"Excellent," the Commander said. "We have nothing else to do anyhow. Just as happy to beat Americans here in Sweden as in the Pacific." He thought that was hilarious.

Major Karlsson was diplomatic enough not to mention Iwo Jima, which had just been invaded by the U.S. Marines.

"Then it's agreed," he said. The first true World Series will be played in Sweden."

The two raised their glasses.

"*Skål!*" said Karlsson.

"*Kampai!*" said the Commander. "Play ball!"

CHAPTER 28

As opening day drew near, a wave of excitement swept through Stockholm. It wasn't because of the push of the Allies into Germany and that victory and the end of the war in Europe was in sight. It was the unbelievable, totally unprecedented, historic wartime event that was about the take place in Sweden: athletic teams consisting of military from nations at war would meet on the field of honor, competing as amateurs and gentlemen, with no gain other than love of sport itself.

"We'll whip their Royal Jap ass," said Joe Bacciagalupo, a true sportsman.

"*Tora, Tora, Tora,*" the Japanese manager would shout during practice, repeating the Pearl Harbor attack command.

Major Karlsson met the Falun Angels after one of their final Spring Training practice sessions. They played an exhibition game against a team brought down from Västerås, the industrial city that had volunteered a team to play exhibitions against the Americans at the 1912 Olympics.

They had played only five innings before it was called on account of darkness. The Angels thought it would never get dark: they stopped counting runs after they reached 23. The Swedes scored one run, when Pete Fielding, in right field, couldn't find the ball that went sailing past him. He had been studying a blonde sunning herself nearby, when a batter actually got a hit.

"Who's makin' book?" Joe Bacciagalupo asked as they dressed after showers. He knew betting was organized on the Series with the Japs.

"The director of long-term forecasting at the Finance Ministry," Major Karlsson replied.

"What're the odds?"

"Right now, it's four to one."

"What? Is that all?"

"Against you."

There were loud screams among the Angels.

"Who the hell is betting against us?"

"Just about everyone, except the Americans and the Mexicans," Major Karlsson replied.

"We invented the game," Joe Bacciagalupo protested. "The Japs can't play. They're not good enough for the World Series even. They never played in them. They never even won a pennant."

"What's going on?" Jeff Cabot asked.

"Well, its just that everyone knows how badly the Sharks beat my boys," said Major Karlsson. "And word has leaked out how the Japanese have, how do you explain it? Well they have a special way of playing. A very determined way. A very rough way."

"Now, how did anyone learn that?" Carl Jacobson asked innocently.

"*Non te hagas el Sueco,*" Gus Sanchez scolded.

"How do we get in touch with that bookie?" Joe Bacciagalupo said. "We're going to have some money to put on the Angels."

"But we'll wait for the odds to get better," said Jeff Cabot.

"Yeah, against us," said Joe Bacciagalupo.

They did. It was well-known by this time in Stockholm that the Yokosuka Sharks were the toughest, roughest, dirtiest, sneakiest, cheatingest, rule-breakingest bunch of *ju-jitsu* artists that ever put on a baseball uniform. Or any other kind of sporting uniform, other than that for *ju-jitsu*. If *ju-jitsu* even had a uniform for that sport. If indeed it was a sport.

Americans were softies. They had too much money, too much food, too much beer, too many women, too pampered a life. Just how could these softies be winning the war? Well, it's only because they were so rich, they could make more airplanes and tanks and guns.

The opinion-makers in Stockholm had an opinion for everything. They knew all about war, especially since they had not fought one since 1815. There is no expert like a Swedish expert. Of course, they are modest about their superior knowledge and expertise. So modest that they don't have a good word for someone who knows it all. They use the German: *Besserwisser.*

Therefore, the Swedish experts, the guys who wouldn't know a baseball game from a head of cabbage, were putting their money wisely on the Sharks. They had also bet on Hitler winning the war, but it wasn't polite to remind them of such slight forecasting errors. And especially not publicly.

The staff of the German Legation was among the heaviest bettors in town. The Germans had tons of money from bank accounts the Nazis had plundered. They wanted it invested someplace that would pay off and not be easily traced. They knew the end of the Third Reich was near and wanted nest-eggs that the Allies would not be able to seize.

So they bet through their Swedish friends. The number of these friends was being reduced at a fast rate, as the Allies advanced. More and more Swedes who had openly and proudly supported Hitler and the Nazis for years, were now insisting that they were anti-Nazi all along. They had only appreciated German *kultur.*

"Oh, I may have thought Hitler did some good for unemployment in the 1930s," said one up-and-coming theater director and film-maker. "And, of course, I'm certain that those news films of liberated concentration camps are just American propaganda. I know what you can do with trick films and make-up and studio sets. But I never actually joined the Nazi Party. I am totally non-political."

"*Non te hagas el Sueco,*" Gus Sanchez would have said had he heard the innocent gentleman. Carl Jacobson had been told by Lili Schultz about that guy.

The Germans at the Legation had little choice but to trust their Swedish friends to place bets and hold the winnings for them, for the day they could recover it. Of course, no Swede would want to be publicly revealed as a true and trustworthy Nazi supporter if they didn't turn over the money. Not that a cultured German diplomat would ever stoop to blackmail. Oh, never!

Meanwhile, in the American Legation, betting was heavy on the Angels. The Americans had heard reports of the Japs' combining *ju-jitsu* with baseball, and figured that even a half-blind umpire would throw out anyone pulling any rough stuff. They were convinced the Angels could handle themselves.

Several of the Legation staff had served in Tokyo, and considered themselves experts on Japanese baseball.

"They're not half bad," said one attaché, who had actually spent several decades in Japan, working for an English-language newspaper. "But they're not half good either. They're fast runners, good fielders. But they don't have power. No heft. No weight. They can't maintain pitching speed. They can't put much on the ball. Their batting is weak. Again, no power. Any Jap with good shoulders and arms is a wrestler."

"I saw the Tokyo Giants play for the Jap pennant in 1940," said another attaché. "If the Yokosuka Sharks are anywhere as good as they were, the Angels are in for a tough time. Those guys were one damn determined bunch."

"Aw, c'mon," replied the former newspaperman. "I saw them in those play-offs. The Bronx Girls High softball team could beat 'em."

"The Bronx Girls' High softball team could beat the St. Louis Browns," a Cardinals fan piped in.

"And that's just who did beat the Browns," a Red Sox fan continued.

Baseball in Stockholm was as exciting as the war in Europe, as the first Swedish World Series—the original, truly world World Series—approached.

CHAPTER 29

Opening Day was April 14, a Saturday.

In the weeks preceding, Major Karlsson had met with neutral representatives of each team to agree on the game schedule. There would be a seven-game Series, with two games played each week-end of April. The deciding game, if needed, would be played May 5. Of course, a game or games would be pushed up to the next day or week-end in case it was called because of snow, which was more likely than rain this time of year.

Major Karlsson was busy readying the ball park, which the representatives agreed to be named Stockholm Field. It was a slightly more neutral name than Meiji Stadium West or Yankee Stadium East. Meiji Stadium was built in Tokyo for the 1940 Olympic Games, which were called off on account of war. But now, war or not, there would be games in Sweden.

The two teams had arrived in Stockholm a couple of days before Opening Day. They were put up at The Grand Hotel, courtesy of Major Karlsson's connections. The Americans were at lunch on Thursday, April 12, when they heard the news that President Roosevelt died at Warm Springs, Georgia.

They didn't say much. They couldn't. The catch in their throats wasn't anything any grown man, any soldier, wanted to reveal. Even Jeff Cabot, who would have given up baseball before he'd vote anything but Republican, was saddened.

"What do you say?" he asked. "Shall we postpone the first games?"

"And let the Japs laugh at us?" shot back Carl Jacobson. "Are you kidding?"

"Roosevelt loved baseball. Hell, he played it before he got crippled," Fielding said.

"He was a better President than ball player," said Joe Bacciagalupo. "I knew an old guy in the West End who used to play ball for a bar-room team and they'd play college guys for beers. He said Roosevelt used to play for Harvard. Said he couldn't hit."

"He'd want us to play," said Joshua Bennett, dropping into his best preacher mode. "He's up there, looking down and saying, 'Win the war and win that Series.'"

The guys said nothing for a long while.

"We'll play," Jeff Cabot finally said.

They finished their lunch silently. The Japanese team had been seated at the far opposite end of the large dining room. They, too, were somber. They had been warned that just one smile, one smirk, one comment—even if the Americans wouldn't understand it—would touch off a riot. They were eager to play ball and were smart enough not to spoil what looked like a wonderful World Series. A World Series at which they would humiliate the Yanks. They ate in silence.

The two teams were on different floors and at opposite ends of the hotel. But they couldn't help but run into each other in the lobby and restaurant. They had been carefully instructed not to have anything to do with each other, especially after Roosevelt's death.

"Save it for the game," Major Karlsson said. "Any incidents may jeopardize the Series."

"Yeah, it might kill the pool," Joe Bacciagalupo added.

"Or get our asses sent back to England," said Mickey O'Mallery.

"Yeah, and we'd miss all these Stockholm dames," said B.J. Jones. "We gotta cement Swedish-American relations."

"If you do any more cementing, they'll put up a statue to you," said Joshua Bennett.

"Hey, I was cleared of those paternity suits," said B.J. Jones. "Well, all of them filed so far."

The Japanese did not have similar pre-game pep talks. They discussed strategy. They simply wanted to beat the Americans, get their submarine back, and rejoin the war. They didn't say so, since it would be highly unpatriotic and dishonorable, but they would certainly miss the fresh whale meat.

They had taken their *sushi* master with them to the hotel. Major Karlsson had made arrangements for him to work out of a corner of the kitchen. The hotel could get the absolutely freshest, finest fish in Sweden. Through the Japanese Legation in Norway, they got fresh whale meat.

The Sharks were eager to play ball. They would eat up the Angels.

Opening Day. Bright. Sunshine. Cool. Major Karlsson had dreamed of having King Gustav V throw out the first ball. After all, he officiated at the 1912 Olympics in Stockholm. He put out feelers, but the 86-year-old old King was being kept out of the limelight as much as possible these days. He had pro-German sympathies, and at his age, you never knew what he might say.

Major Karlsson asked the Prime Minister, Per Albin Hansson, for whom he had done some delicate favors at the hotel. Per Albin liked to bowl. Maybe he'd be the first person ever to throw out the Opening Day ball with an underhand pitch. But Per Albin declined. What would happen if the Japanese won the Series? He had enough trouble with Winston Churchill, who always complained that the Swedes were more help to Hitler than to the Allies. Franklin D. Roosevelt might not like Per Albin playing ball with Japanese. Per Albin would have had an even tougher time with Harry Truman. Like Roosevelt, he thought the Swedes played too damn much ball with the Axis.

The teams arrived at the ball park in separate buses. The ball park, in Gärdet, was set up beautifully. Gärdet was a large open field, originally used in the 1700s as a military training ground. It was in walking distance from the center of the city.

The game would start at 2 p.m. There was a fair-sized crowd. The bleachers were filled early. Just about the entire American colony of Stockholm was on the first base line bleachers. The small Japanese colony of Stockholm, along with only a hand-full of the very large German colony, were on the third base line bleachers.

"Where are all the other Germans?" the Japanese Minister asked a low-level German attaché, who was the highest-level official German attending.

"We are extremely busy these days. We have so much work to do. Most of our people must work week-ends."

He didn't say that the reason the Germans were not there was that any German with any brains was trying to distance himself, or herself, from anything to do with official Germany. The few Germans from the Legation or the Consulate wouldn't have been at Opening Day either, except they had direct orders from Foreign Minister Ribbentrop. They thought it would be humiliating if the Japanese could demonstrate they could beat the Americans in Sweden, while the Germans were facing a catastrophe at home. But, orders were orders. So they were at Stockholm Field.

The ballpark wasn't half bad at all, considering there were no experts in Stockholm in laying out and preparing such a field. Major Karlsson got the donation of carpenters from a construction company that he often hired to work on internee camps. They built the backstop, and foul ball nets, and set up bleachers.

Major Karlsson recruited gardeners from Drottningholm Palace, which the Swedes like to say was a miniature Versailles. They had made the bumpy field level, trimmed the grass, penned in the royal sheep that grazed there, put in gravel baselines, built the pitcher's mound and prepared a very neat home plate and on-deck area. Major Karlsson and his workers used rule-book drawings and photos of American ball parks as their guide.

"This place is more beautiful than Fenway Park," said Joe Bacciagalupo.

"Anything is more beautiful than Fenway Park," said Mickey O'Mallery, a true Yankee fan.

"Wait a minute," said Jeff Cabot. "I heard that."

"You tell 'em, skipper," said Joe Batch. "You're in command."

"I'll tell you this," said Jeff Cabot. "We have one fine ball park here, and we're going to beat the hell out of those Japs."

The Sharks were having a very similar conversation at their dugout, which wasn't dug out, of course, but consisted of sheltered benches. The Sharks were very carefully confirming distances. In place of real outfield fences, Major Karlsson had erected poles with boards running between them, at a top height of about 15 feet.

Copying dimensions of Fenway Park, the only dimensions he could readily find, Major Karlsson had home run distance at left field exactly 315 feet, center field 420 feet, and right field 302 feet. Being a neutral diplomat, he explained to the Japanese that he had simply taken an average of the major league American and Japanese ball parks.

The Japanese certainly would have objected if they knew they were playing in sort of a Fenway Park replica. It was historically justified, too, since the first ball game in Stockholm was played in 1912, and that's the year Fenway Park was built. What the Japanese didn't know didn't hurt them, Major Karlsson, the pragmatist, reasoned.

CHAPTER 30

The Captains of the two teams and the umpires met at home plate. The Japanese captain, the pitcher, bowed formally. Jeff Cabot touched the peak of his cap in a half-assed salute. The umpires shook hands all around. The crowd was silent.

Because there was no home team in this Series, they had agreed to flip a coin to see who would bat first. The coin was a Swiss franc. Nothing more acceptable world-wide than that. The plate umpire, the Swiss attaché, would flip. Nobody more neutral than a Swiss diplomat.

The Sharks won the flip. The Japanese pitcher smiled victoriously.

Jeff Cabot smiled back. "Well, we get last raps," he said, and didn't add what he was thinking, in the true spirit of international sportsmanship: "And we'll rap it right down your yellow buck-tooth face."

A roar went up from the American fans as the Angels took the field. They looked pretty nifty, in new uniforms sewn up by the tailors at MEA, which had been one of the most profitable clients of Mickey O'Mallery's Welcome Wagon. He had expanded his sponsors far outside of Falun, and into the fine shops of Stockholm.

He had arranged sponsorship by a maker of *Falukorv*, the famous sausage. But the crew flatly refused to wear it. No matter what design Mickey O'Mallery had come up with for the sausage insignia on the uniform, it looked like a pecker, limp or otherwise.

Napoleon Anderson came to the rescue. He got his moonshining relatives to sponsor the team. In return for picking up "team expenses", each shirt carried a patch in the shape of a bottle, with simply the word "Möja" on it. The advertisement was as subtle as triple shot of "Napoleon's Prime Reserve".

The Yokosuka Sharks also had brand new uniforms. They carried the name of their sponsor, Gadelius, the Swedish-Japanese trading company. The uniforms were striped, reminiscent of the Yankees, which made the players look taller. They needed it: they were at least a head shorter than the Americans. Jeff Cabot said that if they were any shorter the strike zone would be measured in millimeters.

Each team's uniforms had small national flags sewn on the left shoulder. Not that they would be any real need for identification. You couldn't mistake a Yank for Japanese or vice versa. But Major Karlsson thought it would add a nice international touch. Like at Olympic Games.

Major Karlsson wanted the Opening Day game to start with a band playing the national anthems of the two teams. But here he ran into what seemed like an insurmountable problem: which anthem should be played first? He finally hit upon the obvious answer: out of courtesy, the anthem of the "visiting team" would be played first. And the "visiting team" would technically be determined by the outcome of the flip of the coin. The Japanese anthem would be played first.

The band was made up of students at Stockholm Royal Institute of Technology, which was located not far from the field, just a way down the broad boulevard, Valhallavägen. The band loved to dress up in screwball uniforms, not two of which were alike. All wore chests-full of medals purchased at flea markets. They were a colorful lot, and sometimes were even quite sober when they performed. They weren't too bad on this occasion, although Major Karlsson had wished they had practiced the Japanese national anthem, *"Kimigayo"*, once or twice before trying to play it.

The Japanese stood proudly at attention, hats off. The Americans stood, but hardly at attention. Half of them chewed gum, and not even in time with the music. But you had to give credit to the other half of the team, with wads of chewing tobacco making their cheeks bulge. They didn't spit. They would have, had they known the words of the Japanese anthem: *"May the reign of the Emperor continue for a thousand years…"*

When the band then played the Star Spangled Banner, which they did far better and much closer to key than when they played the Japanese anthem, the Angels snapped to attention, whipped off their hats and placed then smartly over their hearts. They stopped the gum chewing. The wads of tobacco kept still. Nobody was going to say the Falun Angels didn't have class.

The plate umpire went to what had been set up as the VIP box in the bleachers, and handed a ball to a tall, portly, distinguished gentleman, with a beautiful handlebar moustache and wearing a top hat, striped pants and tails. He was the Turkish Minister. The teams had accepted him, as representative of a neutral nation, to throw in the first ball.

Major Karlsson had failed to get a Swedish dignitary to throw in the ball, and all other neutrals were contributing umpires. The Turkish Minister was delighted to help out. He was intrigued with the idea of throwing the first ball. He hadn't thrown anything since tossing bombs with Kemal Ataturk.

"With this, I officially declare open the First Swedish World Series—the truly world World Series," he said, throwing the ball out toward first and barely missing the head of the umpire.

The crowd cheered. The umpire walked to the plate, brushed it, took his position behind the catcher, looked over the field, and shouted, "Play ball!"

The first Swedish World Series and the truly world World Series was underway.

CHAPTER 31

The first batter was a fielder whom Carl Jacobson recognized as a particularly fast base-runner, who was damn clever in giving a chop with the back of his hand to the guy covering first base as he rounded the bag. Or when he took off from first. Or when he was just standing on first and the first baseman wasn't looking.

Carl Jacobson had briefed the team at great length at what he had seen of the Sharks' baseball-*ju jitsu*. But Major Karlsson insisted the Japanese would play straight and honest ball.

"Now we'll see if the Major's right," Carl Jacobson thought, as he watched Jeff Cabot wind up.

A fast ball, straight down the middle, just as the catcher, Joe Bacciagalupo, ordered. The batter swung and missed. He evidently was completely surprised at the speed. The Japanese pitchers didn't have half the heat on the ball.

"Forget your glasses? You blind?" Joe Batch said, as the ump called, "Strike one."

Joe Bacciagalupo knew it was a time-honored baseball ritual for the catcher to rag the batter. He only wished he knew some Japanese. They had asked the OSS guys at the Legation for some choice insults, but evidently the request didn't have very high priority. They were still waiting for a reply from Washington. A committee at the Pentagon was undoubtedly studying the strange request.

Joe Batch would have to do his best in English, even if he did know excellent and colorful expressions in at least 10 languages. He used them with great enthusiasm playing sandlot ball.

The West End of Boston where Joe Batch grew up was one of the most polyglot neighborhoods in the entire United States. There were Italians, Jews, Greeks, Poles, Irish, Albanians, Lebanese, Ukrainians, Portuguese, Russians, Latvians, Negroes, and even a few Chinese. Yeah, and at least one Swedish family, the Olsons.

Conspicuous by their absence were WASPs. Some kids grew up thinking English was a language only for kids and the Irish school-teachers. All adults, mostly immigrants, spoke something else. How they spoke to each other was a mystery. Maybe that's why they all seemed to get along.

Trained in this wonderful community language school, some of Joe Bacciagalupo's pals who got drafted wound up at Yale, studying Japanese so they could serve as interpreters. Napoleon Anderson, with his linguistic talents, would have been a professor at Harvard by now if he had grown up in the West End.

Joe Batch wondered if he should try the Chinese phrases he learned from Wong the laundryman. But maybe they were wishes of health, wealth and long life. That would hardly do to rag a batter.

Joe Batch signaled for another fast-ball. It was a low. That's OK, Jeff is only warming up. Then an outside curve, which the batter swung on and missed.

"Keep fannin', you ugly monkey, we need the breeze," Joe Batch said.

The batter looked at him and smiled. Joe smiled back.

Joe Batch signaled to brush him back from the plate. They guy was crowding. Jeff Cabot threw an inside fast-ball, and to his great surprise, the batter didn't jump back. He only sucked in his gut. It was a fraction of an inch too little. The ball just touched his uniform.

"Take your base," called the ump.

The batter gave Joe a look of scorn mixed with triumph, tossed the bat down and trotted to first.

Carl Jacobson, playing first, met him at the bag.

"Watch those hands of yours, one chop and I bust 'em," he said.

The Jap's eyed widened. He said something in Japanese to his first base coach. The coach looked at Carl Jacobson and his mouth fell wide open. He called across the field to the Commander, the Sharks' general manager. He wore a nifty uniform that sported three stripes on the sleeve. No question of his rank.

The Commander looked at Jacobson. It was the first time he had really looked carefully at him or at any of the Angels. All Americans looked alike, especially in uniform. At least until then.

Carl Jacobson was smiling at the Commander. It was the biggest, broadest, widest smile anyone had ever seen. He took off his cap and tipped it gallantly to the Commander.

The Commander was stunned. Here was the German camp's ranking officer. They had eaten together, got drunk together. They exchanged gifts. He had to put up that portrait of Adolph Hitler, *Shmuck*, the ugly maniac, whenever a German visited. And here is the German colonel playing baseball! What in the name of the Great Buddha at Kamakura is going on?

"Nice to see you again," Jacobson shouted across the diamond. "Maybe we can have *sushi* after the game. Loser buys."

The Commander uttered a string of what were undoubtedly classic Japanese curses. The German had either deserted, or was never a German to begin with. An American? Posing as a German? Right in the German camp? Impossible.

"Play ball!" the ump shouted.

The next batter popped out. Carl Jacobson kept a close watch on the runner at first. The first sneaky move with that back-hand chop, and he'd need a complete new set of buck teeth. But the runner played exactly as a runner should play. Jeff Cabot tried to pick him off as he took a long lead, but he was too fast back to base.

The third batter went down swinging. And so did the fourth. It was clear that they hadn't had much practice against real fast pitching.

The Angels' first time up was led off by Pete Fielding. He may not have been able to find his way home without a map, but he could hit. He actually smiled as he swung at the first pitch, coming in nice an slow, just where he liked them. He missed it a mile, as it made a cockeyed curve the likes of which he had never seen.

"He's spittin' on the ball, the sneaky bastard," he protested to the ump.

"That's what they all say," the ump said. He may have been a Swiss, but he sure knew his umpiring.

Pete Fielding swung and missed at the next ball, another curve. And went down watching the third pitch, a perfect strike. The pitcher had unleashed his sidewinder submarine ball. It caught Pete Fielding totally amazed. He could only watch the ball, his mouth wide open, as it zoomed up from almost the pitcher's mount dirt smoothly into the strike zone.

Carl Jacobson had warned the team again and again about the pitcher with the total change-up, going from overhand to sidearm without losing a bit of control. But they all figured he was seeing things. Nobody could pitch that way. Now they knew better.

"This guy is the cheatingest pitcher I've ever seen," Pete Fielding said to B.J. Jones, the second batter.

"Yeah, we'll get you a map the next time at bat," Jones said, spitting a stream of tobacco juice over his shoulder.

Jones took two balls, then hit a long one to left field, an easy out. Third up was Napoleon Anderson. His appearance on the field had caused considerable conversation, among the fans on both sides It was doubtful if the Sharks had ever seen a Negro, except in Tarzan movies, and now they were supposed to play against one. Japanese racism made Mississippi look like the land of true brotherhood. The Sharks had done a lot of muttering, but couldn't refuse to play.

"Well, ah'll be damned, if it ain't a nigra we got playin' for us," said a new-comer to the American Legation, an attaché of some type, from Georgia.

He hadn't heard about the black airman from Chicago, who had spent the Winter visiting his relatives on an island in the Stockholm archipelago. Or how he had become a local hero, what with having greatly improved the quality and quantity of the island's most famous product, moonshine.

"Hey, boy, you do right and hit that ball," the Georgian shouted. "Use yo' haid, and not as a bat."

Jeff Cabot got up from the bench and strolled over to the man.

"If I hear one more comment out of you, I'll climb up there and knock your teeth right down your red-neck throat," Jeff Cabot said to the man, smiling. "That's a Yankee promise."

"And ah'll help him," said B.J. Jones, in pure Alabamian, which was the only thing he could speak anyway. "And that's a Rebel promise."

The man paled visibly, and didn't open his mouth again. He couldn't figure it out. This wasn't real.

Napoleon hit a grounder neatly between first and second and made it easily to first. The next batter whacked a line drive into right field, enabling Napoleon to move to third. But the team retired when the fifth batter popped out, trying to get a real piece of wood on one of the pitcher's cockeyed screw balls, delivered sidearm, despite the first two batters' warnings.

Live and learn.

CHAPTER 32

The game continued, with the score remaining 0-0. It was quite obvious that both teams were rusty. The Angels had only two real pitchers, Jeff Cabot and Gus Sanchez, although they figured that if absolutely necessary, Mickey O'Mallery could pull some relief duty, and Gus Sanchez or Jeff Cabot could rest out in center. The Sharks didn't seem to have enough muscle to hit anything in deep center anyhow.

Major Karlsson had a half dozen of his Swedish ball players suited up, to sit on the Angels' bench, just to make the team look larger and stronger, and maybe the boys might even be needed in an emergency. They could also maybe learn a thing or two. The Japanese had not objected to this reserve. They figured that Swedish *meatbaru* ball players were so bad that they would be more hindrance than help.

The Sharks pitcher was tiring, as the fifth inning ended. Still no runs. You would have thought that he'd be relieved. The Sharks had plenty of players: the entire 50-man crew of the submarine was on the team. Even the *sushi* chef.

"If he breaks a finger catching a fast-ball, the Commander will have him shot," Carl Jacobson commented.

The guys didn't doubt Carl Jacobson's wonderful stories of his days as senior officer of the German camp, and of his visits to the Japanese camp. But they never believed he actually ate raw fish and rice and liked the damn stuff.

"You never ate raw fish, because it ain't kosher," said Joshua Bennett, the expert on all things religious.

"How about lox?" Jacobson said. "That's raw."

"No it ain't, it's smoked and that's what cooks it," chimed in Napoleon Anderson, who was the established authority on everything Swedish and especially smoked and pickled fish, from his thorough education at Swanson's Fish Market. "Even gravlax is cooked. Well, it's marinated. Now that's good eating."

"Yeah, I had gravlax at the Grand restaurant," Carl Jacobson agreed, "and it wasn't half bad, even if they didn't have bagels. But you want something that's absolutely deeelicious, you gotta try *sushi*. I think I'll move to Hawaii after the war. Got a lot of Japanese there. Must have some terrific *sushi*."

"Nah, if they did, the Japs would've invaded it long ago," said Pete Fielding, the authority on grand strategy. "They figured there were better fish-heads and rice in the Philippines."

Curiously enough, the Angels seemed to talk far more of food than of girls. When the subject of ladies arose, they would become perfect gentlemen, clean-cutters, the boys next door, Jack Armstrongs, the square-jawed, upright young men mothers dreamed about for their daughters. Actually, the Angels were none of these. They simply didn't want to spoil their own good fortunes. Each of them had steadies, and several had several steadies.

It was a beautiful way to spend a war, and you don't talk of good fortune, lest you jinx it.

It's like mentioning a pitcher's got a no-hitter going. So they talked food instead. And baseball. Especially in the breaks between innings.

"I don't know what position the *sushi* chef plays," commented Carl Jacobson. "I just hope it's not catcher. He might ruin his fingers."

"He's not pitching, either," said Jeff Cabot. "Why don't they pull that guy? He's so tired he's killing himself. We'll knock him out of the park next time up."

"They never pull a pitcher," Major Karlsson said. "He'd lose face. He'll stay in nine innings. Of course, the pitcher also loses face if they lose the game."

"They're nuts with that face stuff," said the deeply insightful Joe Bacciagalupo.

"I asked one of the Gadelius brothers about it," explained Major Karlsson. "That family has had a trading business in Japan for over 50 years. The boys were born there, grew up there, speak Japanese. Closest thing to Swedish-Japanese we have. And you know what he told me. He said: 'Don't ask me. The longer I know the Japanese the less I know the Japanese.'"

The first batter in the top of the sixth got a neat line drive when Jeff Cabot tried to change pace to a slow-ball. It put the man on first. The second batter got a nice hit to short center. The third batter put down the first bunt of the game, a nice bouncer just inside the first base line.

The man on second had a long lead, and took off. And here he evidently forgot what game he was playing. He slid into third, with spikes high. Joshua Bennett was concentrating on the bunt, being fielded by Jeff Cabot. He didn't fully see the runner, and the slide came too fast. The base-runner slammed one high foot right into Joshua Bennett's *cajones*. There was a loud intake of breath from the Angels and their fans. At least from the male fans.

Bennett went down, clutching where it hurt most. Jeff Cabot had thrown the ball to third and it went over the base and far into foul territory. The runner stood up and figured he could make it home easily. Joe Batch had thrown down his mask and stood squarely on the third baseline, blocking the plate. The runner was coming right at him. Before Jacobson could shout a warning, it was all over. The runner had put his head down and was charging ahead like a bull, screaming something in Japanese that everyone later agreed sounded like "*Banzai!*"

Joe didn't move. There was a tremendous crash. They both went down in a heap. Only Joe got up. He hadn't forgotten his days playing hockey and the cross-checking he had seen so often at Boston Bruins games. It was a natural reaction. Timing was perfect. He had used the edge of his heavy chest protector just as he would a stick, catching the base-runner across the neck.

"Dumb bastard, ran right into it," he said.

The base-runner was out cold. But what was most amazing was that the Sharks were jumping up and down and cheering and applauding wildly.

The Commander, surprisingly fast, got to the base-runner with a bucket of water. He dumped it on him. The base-runner woke up, and staggered to his feet, groggy. The Commander said something to him, smiled, bowed, and then gave him a quick chop to the side of the head. The base-runner went down again. Two teammates carried him off.

The Commander bowed, first to Joshua Bennett, who had limped off to the bench, then to Joe Bacciagalupo, then to Jeff Cabot, then to the ump.

"Very sorry," he said. "It will not be repeated. Play ball!"

It wasn't repeated. The Angels never saw the offending base-runner again. They speculated on whether the Commander had had him shot.

"Lots of face lost there," Major Karlsson said.

"Yeah, if my timing was just a bit better, he would have lost his face completely," Joe Batch said.

The Sharks couldn't drive anyone home in the sixth. The Angels came to bat, just waiting to face that very tired pitcher. Ed Kowalski was first up. He took two balls, and then Stockholm April weather hit. What was a beautiful sunny day suddenly turned into a snowstorm. The teams retreated to their buses and the fans ran for their cars and nearby shelters.

The umpire called time out. But it kept snowing. After an hour, the game was called. The score was 0-0.

"I wonder if that's the first time in baseball history that a World Series game's been called on account of snow?" Pete Fielding asked, as the bus returned them to the Grand Hotel.

"Of course it is," said Joe Bacciagalupo. "They play the Series in the Autumn, and it never snows then, not even in Boston."

"Well if they played the Series in the middle of Winter, no game in Boston would never be called on account of snow because Boston teams never play in a Series," Mickey O'Mallery laughed.

"That's only because the Sox have been cursed by the Bambino," Joe Batch replied. "Once the curse is lifted, you'll see. Just wait."

"I'll wait and so will my grandchildren."

"Not to change the subject of this fascinating conversation, which I think I may have heard at least six thousand times before, but I think we didn't do half bad today, considering everything," said Jeff Cabot.

"Yeah, considering we played lousy," said Napoleon Anderson. "I even heard the Swedish kids making a few comments."

"We're rusty, that's all," said Jeff Cabot. "We only had a few weeks Spring Training, and never had a decent team to play against."

"But these Japs are lousy, too," said Kowalski. "We should have killed 'em."

"I'd like to," said Joshua Bennett, who seemed to have recovered from the spiking, with just a pair of aching *cajones*. "Good thing that guy didn't draw blood."

"He's probably drawn a lot by now. His own," said Carl Jacobson. "The Commander isn't a guy to screw around with. Believe me. He's serious about winning the Series."

"So are we," said Jeff Cabot.

It sure looked like a most interesting World Series ahead.

CHAPTER 33

The teams had hoped to be able to play the second game on Sunday, the day after the Spring snow-storm, but the field was too muddy, and in places still had some snow. The umpires and managers agreed to postpone the game to the following week-end. This meant the whole Series would be pushed up a week.

The two teams didn't waste the Sunday, however, nor their trip to the field. Automatically, without even discussing the matter, they divided the field in two and started to work out. Every now and then a batter would hit the ball to the wrong side of the field. A player from the other team would retrieve it and throw it back.

"What the hell, they need the practice," Ed Kowalski said.

"And if we didn't throw 'em back, they'd steal ours," said Mickey O'Mallery, always thinking of business.

"Only when our backs are turned," said Joshua Bennett, who was not quite his usual Christian charitable self, and who had good reason not to be. Two good reasons, actually, although he had pretty much recovered.

"Don't worry about that guy," said Carl Jacobson, "You don't see him, do you?"

"They all look alike to me," said Napoleon Anderson.

Over on the Japanese side, the conversation was much the same.

"Are you absolutely certain, Honorable Commander, that the first baseman is the German camp commander, an SS colonel?" asked a Japanese Legation official who was watching the practice session.

"Absolutely."

"After all, they all look alike," the diplomat said. "I once had trouble telling the difference between the German Minister and the Italian Minister. Then the Italians surrendered, and it was no longer a problem. The Soviet Ambassador is easy to tell. She's got big boobs."

The diplomat and the Commander laughed loud and long at that one. The Commander got serious again.

"The Yank playing first base smiled at me, and tipped his cap and shouted something about having *sushi*," he said. "Maybe I should talk to him."

"You can't talk to him without authority from Tokyo," the diplomat said, horrified at the thought of an officer of the Imperial Japanese Navy having a friendly conversation with an American soldier.

"But maybe he is actually a German, posing as an American," the Commander said.

"Then you should not blow his cover," the diplomat said.

"I guess not, but it is certainly very puzzling."

"Well, you know how sly and sneaky these Westerners can be."

"But they play pretty good baseball."

"You Sharks are much better," the diplomat said. "You'll win the Series. I have plenty of money riding on you. If you lose, the Japanese Emperor loses much face. It would be too much a shame for Japan to bear."

The Commander knew full well what the diplomat meant. But if he wasn't allowed to lead his crew in *hara-kiri* after their submarine shamefully went on the Swedish rocks, he certainly wouldn't be expected to do so just because they lost a few ball games. After all, he thought, our Japanese athletes who didn't do well at the last Olympics—in Berlin in 1936, the Olympics that *Shmucku* Hitler made into a showcase for the Nazis—they didn't seem to lose all that much face. They were heroes, just for competing.

A foul ball came speeding their way and was grabbed bare-handed by the Commander, although he was tempted to let it bounce off the officious diplomat's bureaucratic head. Especially since he wasn't the man at the Legation who arranged the steady supply of their *sushi* makings.

"Excellent catch, Commander," the diplomat said.

"But it was a bad hit, foul," he replied.

"Don't worry, the Sharks will win," the diplomat said, bowing and smiling a farewell. "You simply have to win. You must win."

The Commander returned to the practice session. He shook his head in wonderment. Tokyo was being bombed horribly, Iwo Jima had been lost, most of the Imperial Navy was on the bottom of the Pacific, the Americans had invaded Okinawa only two weeks before, and this over-stuffed diplomat is threatening me about winning the Swedish World Series.

"Madness," he thought. "Pure madness."

CHAPTER 34

The teams spent the following week at their camps, seriously practicing. The Americans had brought Major Karlsson's Swedish players with them, and were trying to make real players of them, even if it was a monumental task. The guys were big, damn big, and strong, and enthusiastic. But it seemed it took a while for them to think out things, to figure out what to do next. But they were needed as reserves. While the Japanese had an entire 50-man submarine crew on the team, the Falun Angels consisted of the ten-man crew of the *Jumpin' Jimminy*. And a few reserve meatballs.

So they practiced all week, and took the train to Stockholm on Friday, to be ready for the second game, April 21, which would be the new first game of the Series since the first game was called on account of snow.

The field was now in great shape. Dry. Well trimmed. There were almost twice as many fans out today, since word had gotten around, and because it was a beautiful day, and no place better than getting the sun than in Gärdet park, or now, Stockholm Field.

The Angels almost felt sorry for the Sharks, since they had only a few rooters, all Japanese, sitting behind their bench. It was like the Yankees playing the Red Sox at Fenway Park. But the war in Europe was coming to a victorious end for the Allies, and all former German sympathizers in Sweden had suddenly vanished. Poof! Like magic! Swedes long ago learned that it's best to be on the winning side, even if it's only on the winning sidelines.

The Angels batted first. The Sharks pitcher was the same guy who had pitched all innings of the first game. The Angels got going nicely, scoring a run but leaving two men on. The Sharks evened it up. And so it went through nine innings. A pitching duel, it wasn't. The fans loved it.

Gus Sanchez relieved Jeff Cabot in the seventh. The Sharks stuck to their original pitcher, who was giving it his all in an amazing performance. But in the top of the ninth, with the score tied 8-8 and with two on base, Mickey O'Mallery connected for a homer. The next batter fanned for the third out.

The Sharks were not in an enviable position. They were three runs behind. Gus Sanchez, fresh and eager, made short work of the first three batters.

The Angels won the first game 11-8.

"One down and three to go," said Jeff Cabot.

"Don't get over-confident," said Major Karlsson.

He was perfectly right, as usual. The Sharks came back the next day and humiliated the Angels something awful. The Americans started playing cocky and by time they got down to business, after a bunch of errors, the Sharks were ahead by 5-0.

The Angels couldn't seem to do anything right and the Sharks couldn't do anything wrong. They had a new pitcher for this game, and he, too, went all the way. The Angels didn't make it especially difficult for him. When the last Angel struck out in the bottom of the ninth, the Sharks did not hoot and holler and shout and cheer. They simply stood there, smiled those god-awful smiles of theirs, and bowed politely, first to the umpires and then to the score-keepers, and, can you beat that, to the Angels!

The teams returned to their camps, and when they were not practicing, they spent most time around their radios, listening to the war news. Berlin was getting pounded by the Russians, and book was being made on if and when Hitler would surrender. Rumors were rife in Sweden that the Germans would make a last stand in Norway. This could very well bring Sweden into the war at last, since a large force of Norwegian "police" had been trained and equipped in Swedish camps.

"They'll probably want us to ferry the Norwegians in," said Joe Bacciagalupo. "That's why they keep putting the Forts back in good shape."

"Or, to bomb the Krauts," said Mickey O'Mallery.

"Yeah, more milk runs," said B.J. Jones. "I wonder what the dames look like in Norway."

"Just like us Swedes," said Napoleon Anderson, the authority.

The Japanese team was not especially worried about the fate of Berlin or Hitler or the risk of a German last-ditch hold-out in Norway. They worried, privately, about Japan, and with very good reason. But they had a unique ability of hiding all their inner concerns or doubts or fears. They put everything they had into a display of enthusiasm for the Swedish World Series.

The third game of the Series, on Saturday, April 28, went to the Angels, who had been shocked into serious play by the 5-0 defeat the Sunday before. The Angels played errorless ball, got two homers and walked off the field feeling pretty good with a 6-1 win.

They didn't do as well the next day. The Sharks brought in an entirely new pitcher whom Carl Jacobson didn't recognize at all. He wasn't the fastest pitcher they had seen, but he had amazing control, and the smarmiest smile that any batter had ever seen. Maybe it was that smile that put the Angels off pace. When it was over, the Angels got the smiling, bowing treatment again, which only added to their embarrassment of losing 5-2.

The following week, at their camps, the teams spent more time around the radios than practicing. Hitler committed suicide on April 30, and victory in Europe was obviously only a matter of hours or days.

"If *Shmucku* Hitler knew about the World Series, maybe he would have waited to see us win," the Japanese Commander said to his officers.

They were not amused, but smiled anyhow.

The fifth game was played May 5. There were more fans at Stockholm Field than ever, with dozens of American and British and even Russian flags being waved from the packed bleachers. There were several thousand sitting and standing on the grass along the outfield foul lines. It was a beautiful day.

Peace was near. At least in Europe.

The Angels couldn't help but be caught up in the enthusiasm, and played better than they had so far. A Shark batter, with two out and bases loaded, popped-up for the final out in the bottom of the ninth. The Angels won the game 7-0.

But the Angels didn't cheer and whistle and pound backs as they usually did when they won, especially a shut-out. Instead, they smiled and tipped their caps to the umps, then to the score-keepers, and finally to the Sharks. The Sharks bowed in return.

The sixth game, to be played Sunday, May 6, was a fiasco for the Angels. Again, it was the over-confidence that Major Karlsson had warned them about. The Japanese were far better psychologists and actors than anyone could imagine. When they took the field, they exuded gloom and defeat. When the game was over, they smiled, bowed in the usual ceremony, and walked off the field, having evened up the Series by beating the Angels 6-2.

The Sharks returned to their camp after the game, to practice for the final game the following Saturday, May 12. And to get instructions, if any, from Tokyo.

The Angels said the hell with going back to camp; we're staying in Stockholm. The Third Reich had collapsed and on Monday, May 7, the surrender of all German forces, was announced. There would be no suicidal hold-out in Norway.

VE Day was proclaimed May 8. Stockholm went wild. You would have thought Sweden won the war. But the team didn't get into political discussions. The Stockholm girls were more beautiful and more enthusiastic this day, and in the days to come, than they had ever been. And American fliers were more popular than they had ever been. The Angels celebrated. And celebrated. And celebrated.

Until one evening, Joshua Bennett, always a thinking man, raised the question of the war continuing against Japan.

"The way the Japs fought on Iwo and Okinawa, they won't give up," he said. "They'll fight forever."

"I heard they're going to ship millions of troops from Europe to the Far East," said Mickey O'Mallery, who always heard things.

"Yeah, and bomber crews, too," said Jeff Cabot, who had even better sources.

This put a damper on the celebration. But only for about four minutes, when B.J. Jones came in with a dozen blondes from Stockholm University.

"They are studying history, and want to interview us," Jones said.

The celebration was resumed.

The Angels had no practice that week, at least no baseball practice. It was a rather sorry team that took the field for the decisive game, May 12. Not only had they been celebrating VE Day for a week—assisted by dozens of enthusiastic, sports-minded, sports-bodied Swedish girls—but they had just heard that Jeff Cabot's report had some truth behind it. Bomber crews would be transferred to the Far East.

The final game had attracted an even bigger crowd. There were thousands of Angels fans, waving flags of every Allied nation, but mainly the Stars and Stripes. The players got lumps in their throats as the band played the Star Spangled Banner and then the Japanese anthem.

The Angels actually felt sorry for the Sharks. Poor guys had just two fans that anyone could determine. Two guys from the Legation. And they were wearing sour mugs that only a Japanese mother could love.

Jeff Cabot started for the Angels. He was in pretty fair shape, considering the most exercise his right arm had gotten during the entire past week was when he was raising a glass. Joe Bacciagalupo, catching, immediately realized this final game wasn't going to be easy.

The Sharks went down. And the Angels did, too. The original Shark pitcher was pitching. The Angels knew him, but it didn't do much good. One, two three, down.

And then the Sharks went down. And back and forth. A few hits by both, a few errors, mainly by the Angels, walks, easy outs, no scores. Inning and after inning. The score was 0-0 into the ninth. The Angels got a man on, but couldn't do anything. The Sharks, facing Gus Sanchez, who relieved Jeff Cabot in the sixth, also got a man on, but couldn't do anything.

The game went into extra innings. Finally, in the 12th, the Angels scored a man. The Sharks tied it up. By the 15th inning, both sides were dragging something awful. The Sharks still had their original pitcher, still putting everything he had on each ball.

"The guy's brilliant," said Ed Kowalski. "I've never seen anything like it."

"The guy's loco," said Gus Sanchez, who had pitched 10 innings himself. "He kill himself."

The game went on for another inning and was called, 1-1, on account of darkness.

CHAPTER 35

It was an unprecedented situation. The umpires and score-keepers and managers and captains and players and bookmakers searched the rule books and baseball history. They couldn't find a rule or precedent covering a decisive seventh game's being called on account of darkness. They all agreed there was just one thing to do: continue playing.

So the teams took to the field the next day, Sunday, May 13. It was an absolutely beautiful day. Bright sun. Warm. Girls in shorts. Just as many fans were at the field as there were yesterday. Flags by the hundreds.

The hot dog sellers were doing better business than ever. Naturally, Ed Kowalski had gotten a few of the men well-supplied with *kielbasa*, which could get a premium price. Mickey O'Mallery kicked himself that he hadn't organized popcorn production. Napoleon Anderson had his cousins bring in a good supply of the island's finest. Joe Bacciagalupo and Jeff Cabot had the pools nicely organized through the bank.

"Play ball," called the ump, and a roar went up.

There had been long discussion on whether to call the opening inning the 1st inning of the 8th game or the 17th inning of the 7th game. It was finally settled by agreeing to a compromise recommendation of Major Karlsson, always the pragmatic Swede.

"We'll play the continuation of the 7th game, but only for nine innings," he said. "Whoever wins the game, wins the Series. And if it's a tie, we play again next week-end."

Jeff Cabot was the Angels' starting pitcher. He took it slowly. First three batters went down. Naturally, a new pitcher was on the mound for the Sharks.

"That pitcher from yesterday pitched his last game ever," said Joe Bacciagalupo.

"His arm six inches longer today," said Gus Sanchez.

The Angels went down, leaving two men on. The Sharks did the same. And it went like that, inning after inning, inning after inning.

The fans who knew baseball agreed later that it was one of the finest games they had ever seen. The weather was one of those absolutely perfect days you can get in mid-May in Stockholm. The green of the budding leaves was a bright, light green the likes of which you don't see anywhere else. The grass was at its softest, cleanest, freshest. The girls were tan as only Swedish girls get tan in early Spring.

The game ended with score tied, 2-2.

The teams spent the next week at their camps. The Americans were concerned about orders. Most American and British internees were anxious to be flown back to England, and to home, but there was a shortage of transport planes in the victory chaos.

The *Jumpin' Jimminy* crew wasn't the least bit anxious to leave. They could beat the Japs right here in Sweden. They didn't ask about orders to England and didn't hear anything. It was almost as if they had been forgotten. They wondered if Major Karlsson hadn't arranged it.

He had.

He organized a new meeting of the umpires and score-keepers and managers, and this time had a new proposal. The first Swedish World Series will end in an official draw. And an entire new Season would open, with games every week-end through the Summer and into the fall, with the second truly world World Series, the Swedish World Series, held to coincide with the U.S. World Series.

Nobody objected. Who in their right minds would turn down an entire Summer of baseball?

Thus, the 1945 Official Swedish Baseball Season opened on Saturday, May 19, with the Falun Angels playing the Yokosuka Sharks.

The Season never ended.

They played through the Spring and into Summer. The game on August 5, a Sunday, was won by the Sharks, in a shutout, 6-0.

The following day, Hiroshima was bombed.

The next game, Saturday, Aug. 11, was played with little enthusiasm. The Sunday game was called on account of rain. That day, Nagasaki was bombed.

On August 15, Japan surrendered.

The Sharks beat the Angels 10-2 on the following Saturday. In what had become a tradition, the winners bowed to the umps, then to the score-keepers, then to their opponents.

The Angels came back next day and won 8-1. They tipped their caps to the umps, to the score-keepers and to the Sharks.

In the years to come, Major Karlsson would recount how the Angels and the Sharks played into early October, with their own Swedish World Series coinciding with the World Series in America. Major Karlsson would tell how the Angels-Sharks Series did not end as neatly as the World Series in the States, where the Detroit Tigers beat the Chicago Cubs in the seventh game.

"They're still playing that first truly world World Series, the Swedish World Series" Major Karlsson would say. "Just go out to Stockholm Field. You'll see. You'll see."

Epilogue

It was one of the longest days in June. An elderly man emerged from the Japanese Embassy in Stockholm. A few blocks away, an elderly man walked out of the American Embassy. The two elderly men turned north, and strolled to nearby Gärdet, the large grassy field that was once a military exercise ground, then a sheep grazing ground, and which was now slowly being encroached upon by various embassy buildings and the ever-expanding Swedish radio and TV complex.

The man who emerged from the Japanese embassy was, not surprisingly, Japanese. He wore a baseball cap, with the word *"Yokosuka Sharks"* embroidered on it.

The man from the American Embassy was, as could be expected, American. He wore a baseball cap with the words *"Falun Angels"* embroidered on it.

They strolled slowly across the field, stopping now and then, obviously trying to get oriented. Then they seemed to find what they were looking for and walked to a slight rise in the field.

When the two men were within a few feet of each other, they stopped and faced each other. The elderly Japanese bowed. The elderly American tipped his cap.

# # #

0-595-31248-9

Printed in the United States
23875LVS00005B/285